LAST of the INDEPENDENTS

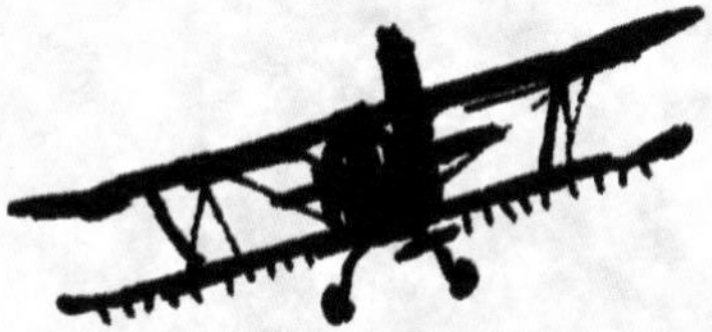

MATT FRACTION - KIERON DWYER

Other Image books by Kieron Dwyer

LCD: LOWEST COMIC DENOMINATOR

UNPRESIDENTED

SEA OF RED (with Rick Remender & Salgood Sam)

XXXOMBIES (with Rick Remender)

CRAWLSPACE (with Rick Remender)

kierondwyer.com

Other Image books by Matt Fraction

ADVENTUREMAN! (with Terry & Rachel Dodson)

CASANOVA (with Gabriel Bá, Fábio Moon & Michael Chabon)

THE FIVE FISTS OF SCIENCE (with Steven Sanders)

NOVEMBER (with Elsa Charretier, Kurt Ankeny & Matt Hollingsworth)

ODY-C (with Christian Ward)

SATELLITE SAM (with Howard Chaykin & Ken Bruzenak)

SEX CRIMINALS (with Chip Zdarsky)

mattfraction.com

www.lastoftheindependents.store

IMAGE COMICS, INC. • Robert Kirkman: Chief Operating Officer • Erik Larsen: Chief Financial Officer • Todd McFarlane: President • Marc Silvestri: Chief Executive Officer • Jim Valentino: Vice President • Eric Stephenson: Publisher / Chief Creative Officer • Jeff Boison: Director of Sales & Publishing Planning • Jeff Stang: Director of Direct Market Sales • Kat Salazar: Director of PR & Marketing • Drew Gill: Cover Editor • Heather Doornink: Production Director • Nicole Lapalme: Controller • IMAGECOMICS.COM

INTRODUCTION - PATTON OSWALT

Charley Varrick is one of my favorite films from the golden age of 1970s Hollywood movies. Right up there with *The Taking of Pelham One Two Three* and *The Bad News Bears*.

All of those movies, of course, star Walter Matthau. All movies should star Walter Matthau, but this isn't heaven.

Walter Matthau was the absolute king of small stakes. A little league baseball pennant. A single subway car full of passengers, most of whom don't even seem too anxious to be alive in the first place.

The film *Charley Varrick*, with which **THE LAST OF THE INDEPENDENTS** shares some crucial DNA and a sort-of title (it was the working title of the film before it was changed to *Charley Varrick* or, for the European release, *Kill Charley Varrick!*) is a pure kick. Matthau is a small-time criminal looking for a quiet, small-time score that he can live quietly on in some small-time trailer park. But the shithole bank he hits is a drop for the mob. And pretty soon the whole world is after him and his squirrely partner, who are in possession of nearly a million dollars of laundered mafia loot.

Pretty simple plot. Pretty *overdone* plot, huh? We've seen this story, and variations thereof, long before *Charley Varrick* and certainly long after. I remember one evening in the late 90s, emerging from the Sunset 5 in Los Angeles after seeing yet another gritty, post-*Reservoir Dogs* snark-noir, and my friend said to the night sky, "The only indie movie plots we have left are Hitman On His Last Job, How Do We Hide This Dead Body, and Oh My God We Ripped Off The Mob."

What Matt Fraction and Kieron Dwyer do with this simple framework, however, is something as glittery and wicked as a switchblade on a desert highway. Yes, there's a heist that nets way more loot than expected. Yes, it's the mob's money. Yes, they're pissed.

But the zigs, zags, and zephyr-shimmers they put into a story you think you see coming until the twists creep up on you? All of them are fantastic, fun and fuckin' awesome. And the layout! Widescreen, like you're reading the storyboards for the movie you just watched on Sunday afternoon with your dad.

Enjoy **THE LAST OF THE INDEPENDENTS**. And then go mow the lawn before dinner.

Patton Oswalt
March 2020, Los Angeles

MATT'S DEDICATION:

FOR DADS THAT TAKE THEIR KIDS OUT OF SCHOOL TO CATCH MOVIES INSTEAD OF MATH CLASS.

KIERON'S DEDICATION:

FOR JIM ROCKFORD. AT THE TONE, LEAVE YOUR NAME AND MESSAGE, HE'LL GET BACK TO YOU.

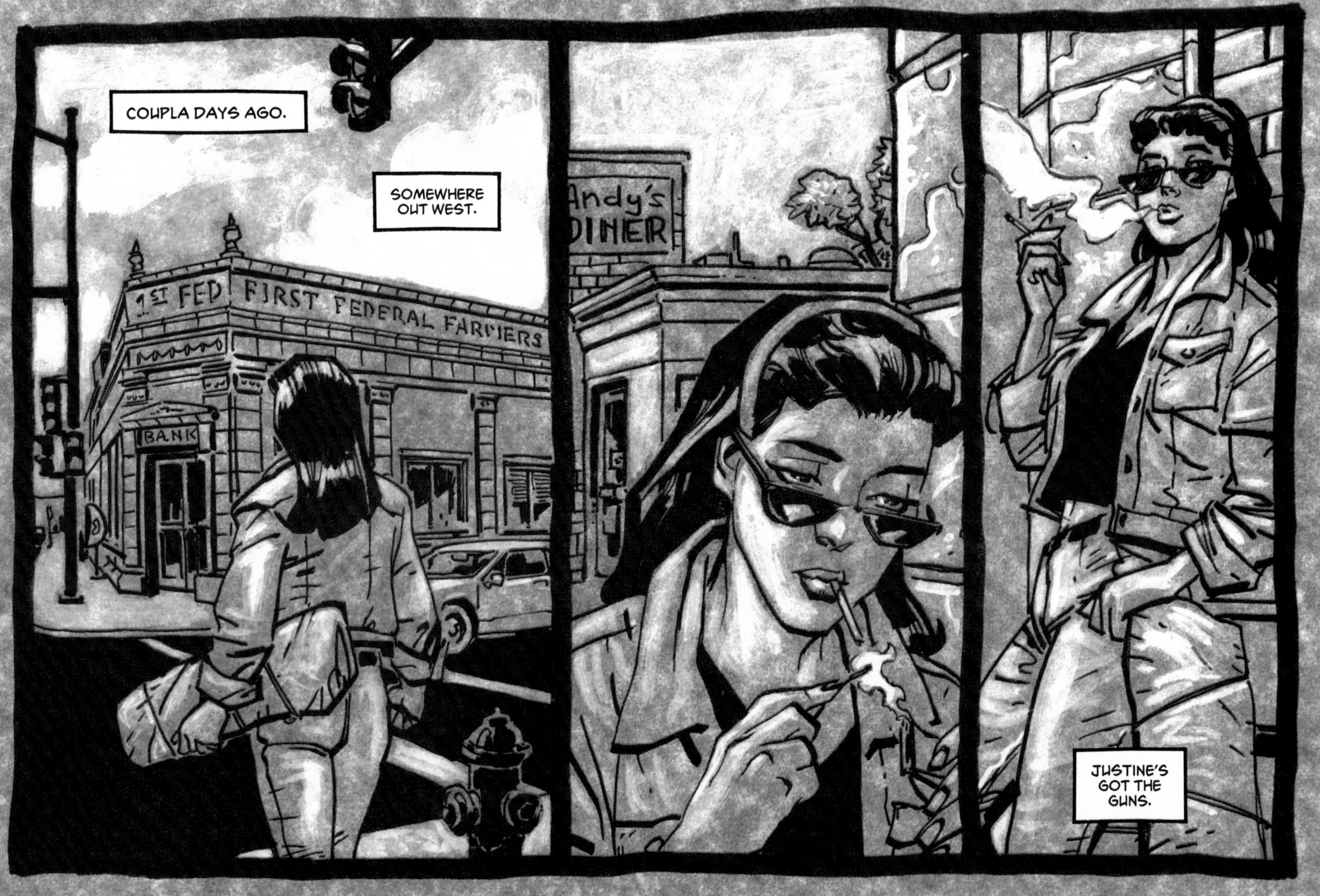
COUPLA DAYS AGO.
SOMEWHERE OUT WEST.
1ST FED FIRST FEDERAL FARMERS
BANK
Andy's DINER
JUSTINE'S GOT THE GUNS.

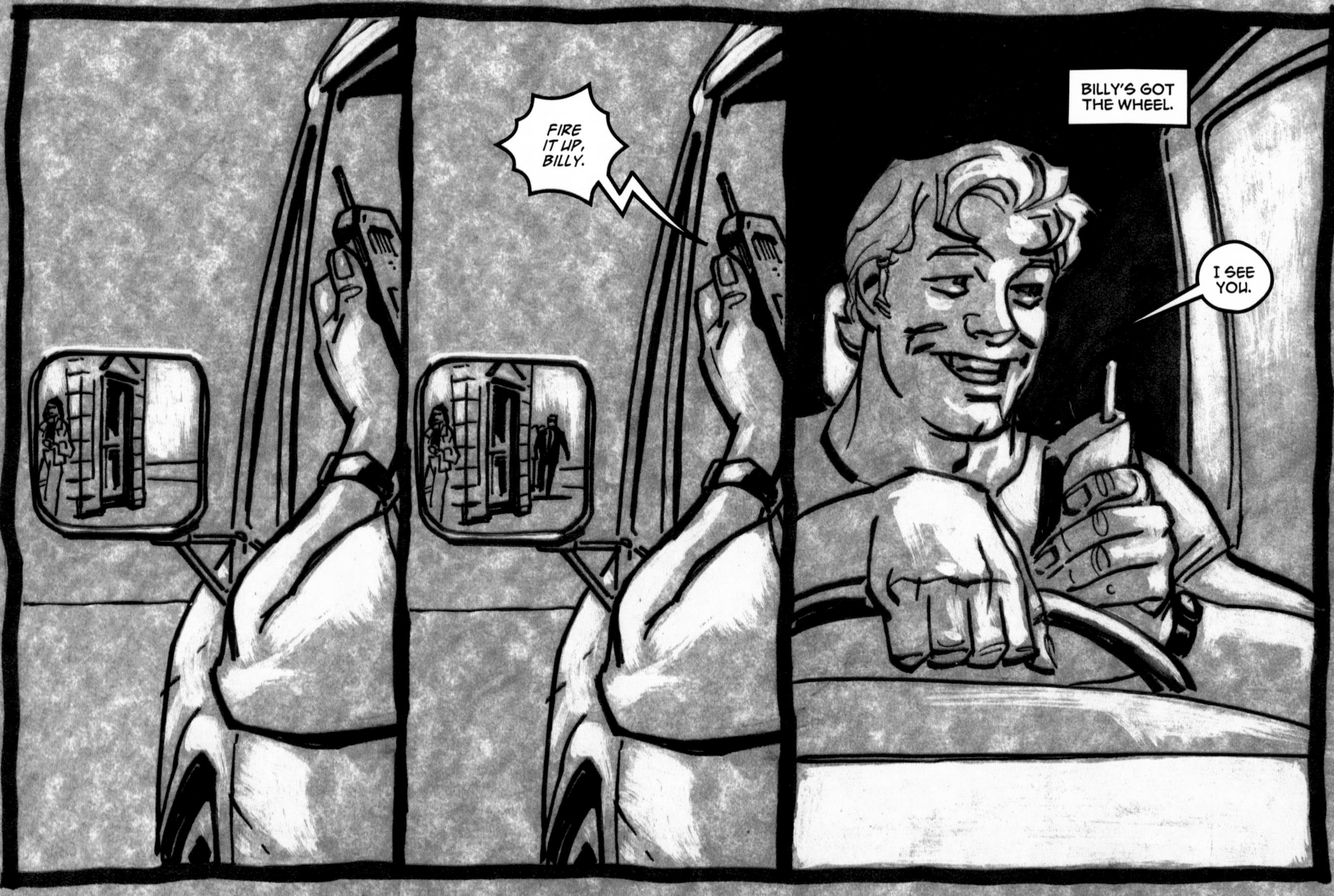
FIRE IT UP, BILLY.
BILLY'S GOT THE WHEEL.
I SEE YOU.

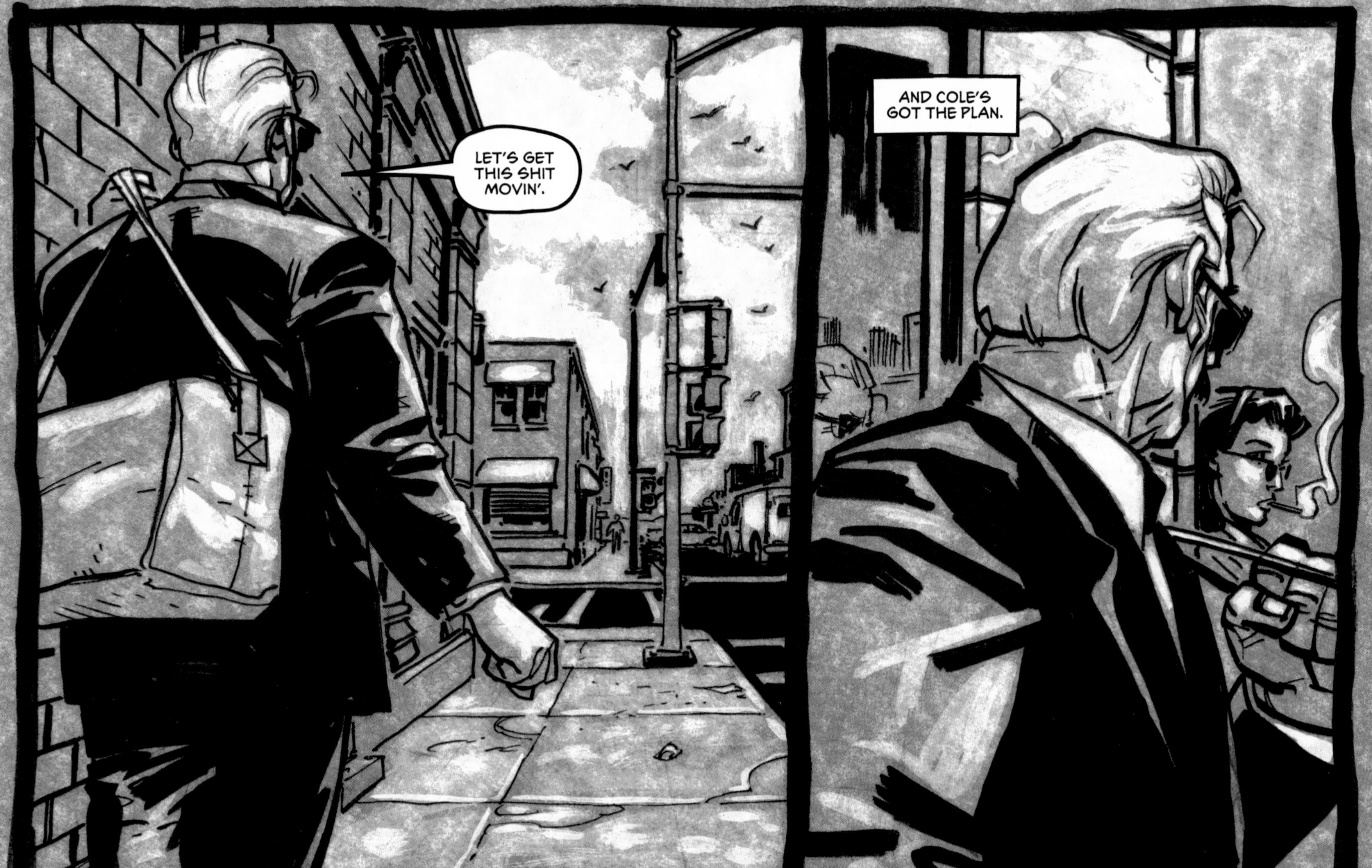
LET'S GET THIS SHIT MOVIN'.
AND COLE'S GOT THE PLAN.

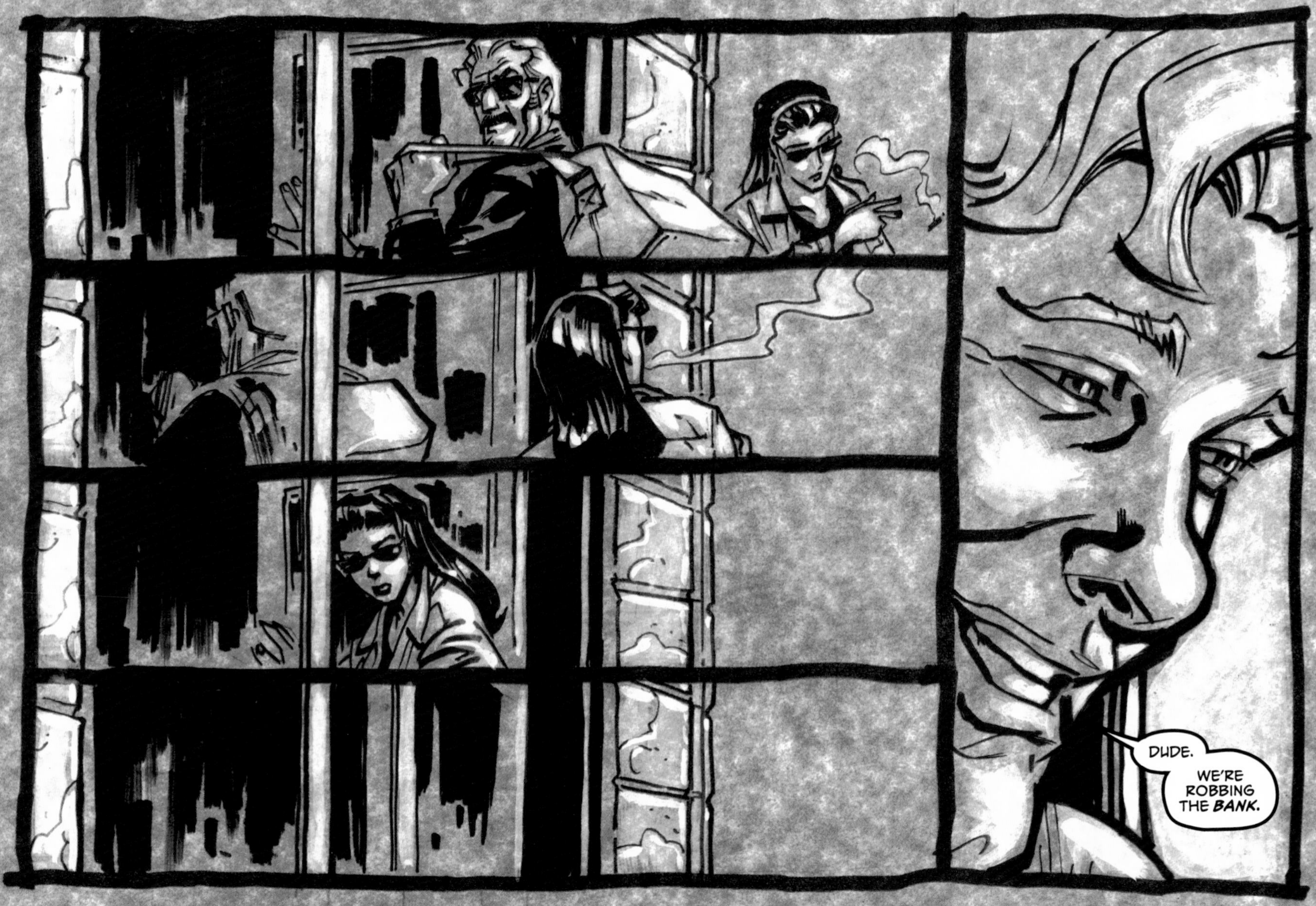
DUDE.
WE'RE ROBBING THE **BANK.**

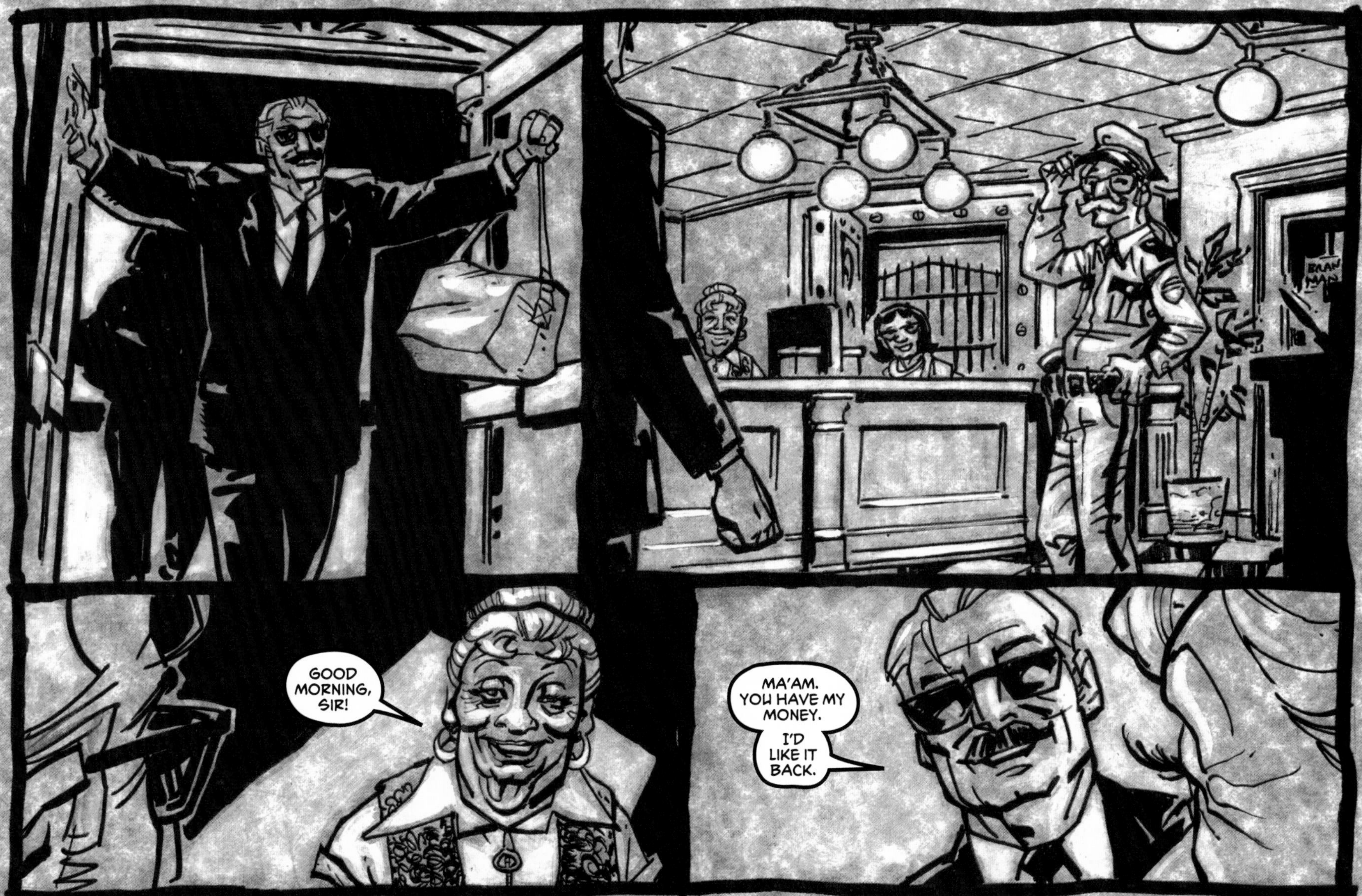
GOOD MORNING, SIR!
MA'AM. YOU HAVE MY MONEY.
I'D LIKE IT BACK.

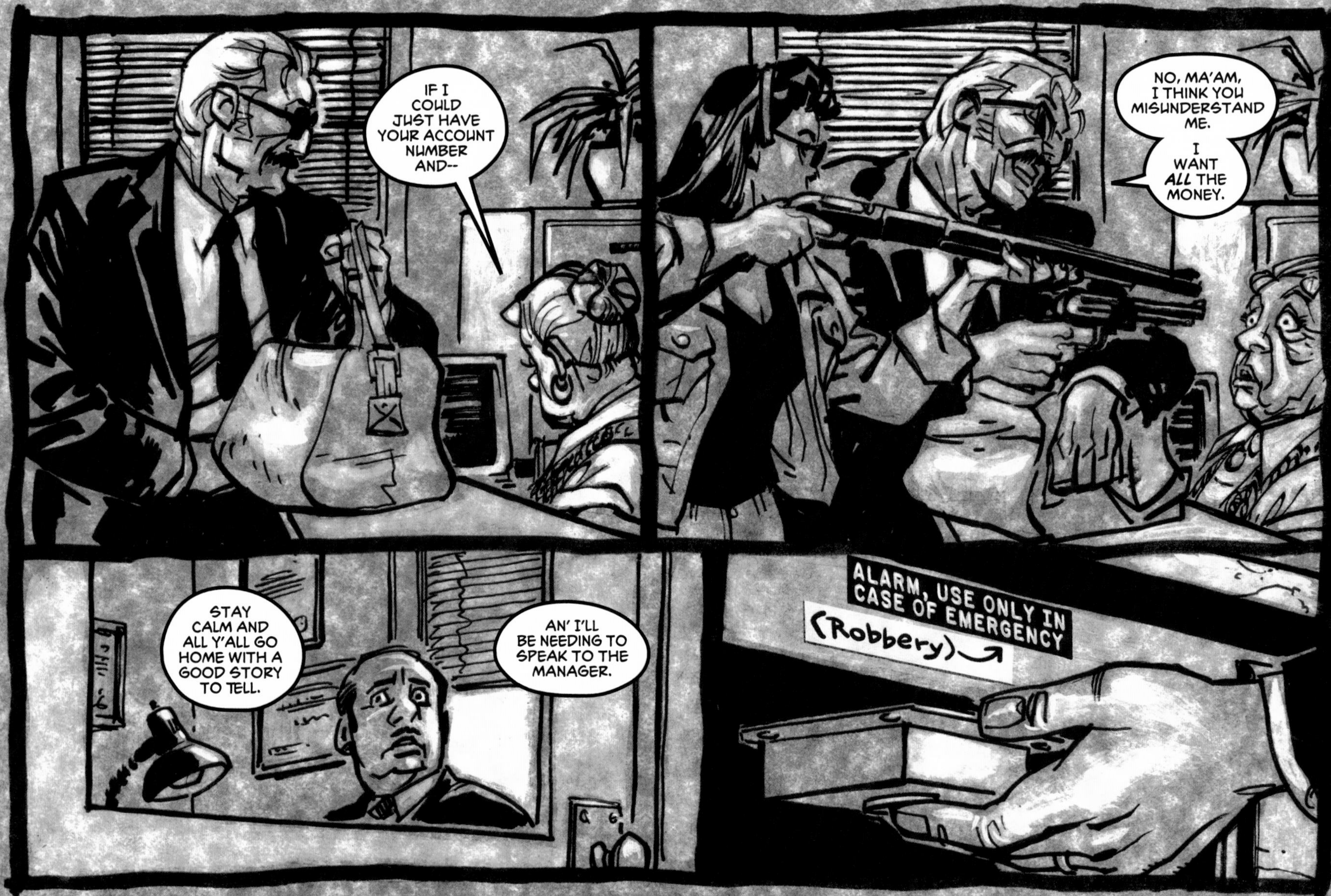
IF I COULD JUST HAVE YOUR ACCOUNT NUMBER AND--
NO, MA'AM, I THINK YOU MISUNDERSTAND ME.
I WANT ALL THE MONEY.
STAY CALM AND ALL Y'ALL GO HOME WITH A GOOD STORY TO TELL.
AN' I'LL BE NEEDING TO SPEAK TO THE MANAGER.
ALARM, USE ONLY IN CASE OF EMERGENCY
(Robbery)

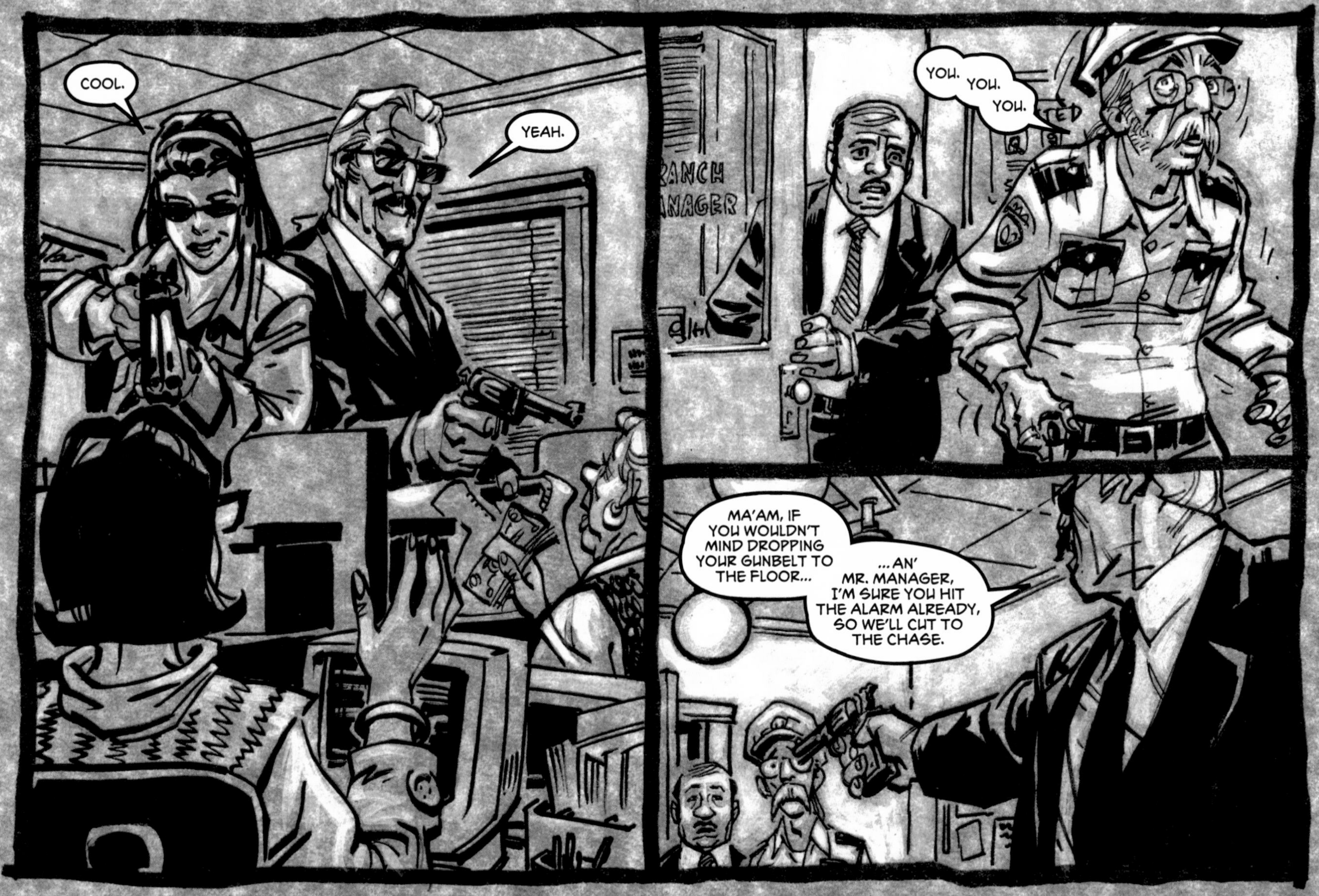
COOL.
YEAH.
BRANCH MANAGER
YOU. YOU. YOU.
MA'AM, IF YOU WOULDN'T MIND DROPPING YOUR GUNBELT TO THE FLOOR...
...AN' MR. MANAGER, I'M SURE YOU HIT THE ALARM ALREADY, SO WE'LL CUT TO THE CHASE.

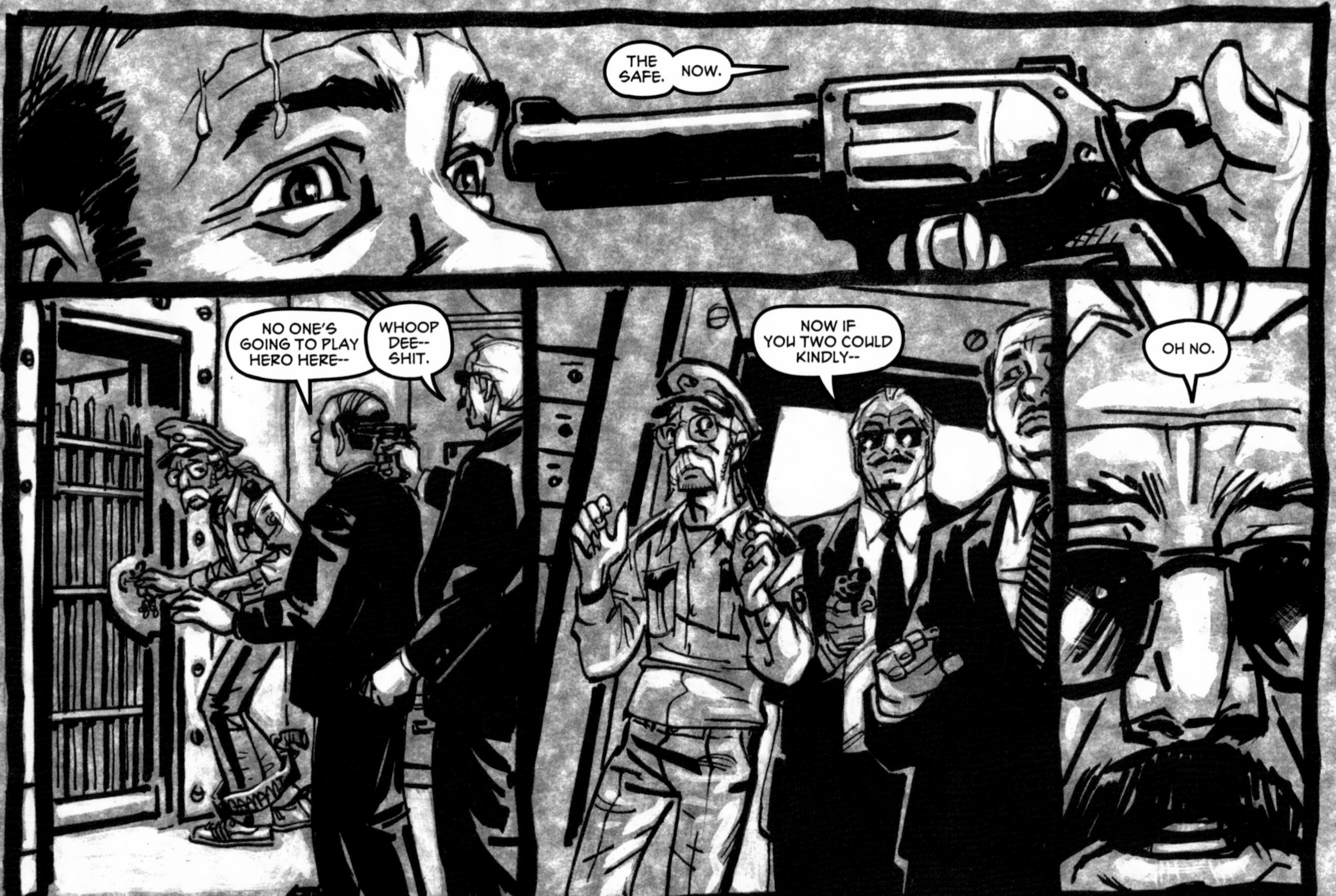
THE SAFE.
NOW.
NO ONE'S GOING TO PLAY HERO HERE--
WHOOP DEE-- SHIT.
NOW IF YOU TWO COULD KINDLY--
OH NO.

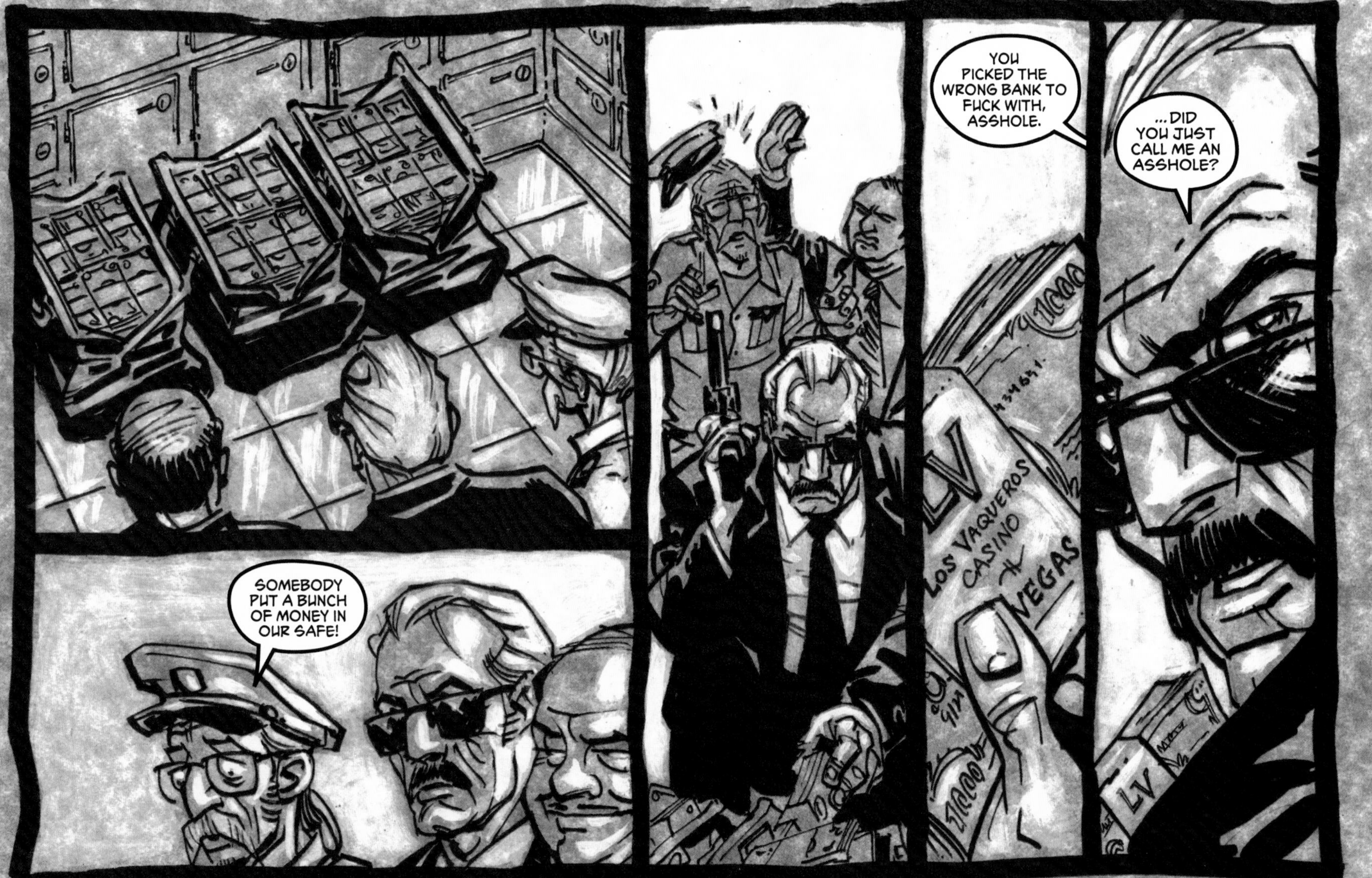
SOMEBODY PUT A BUNCH OF MONEY IN OUR SAFE!
YOU PICKED THE WRONG BANK TO FUCK WITH, ASSHOLE.
...DID YOU JUST CALL ME AN ASSHOLE?
LOS VAQUEROS CASINO
VEGAS

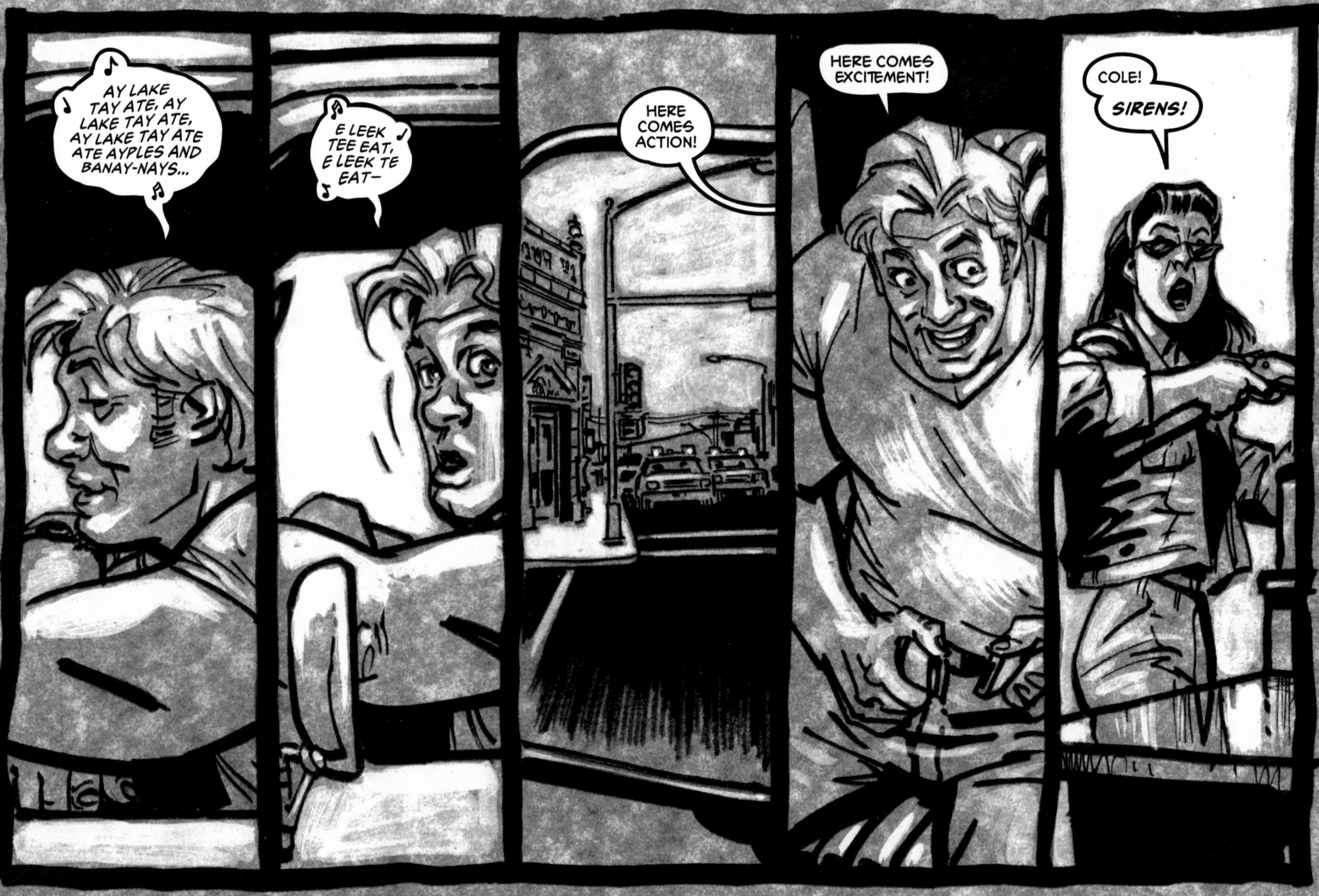
AY LAKE TAY ATE, AY LAKE TAY ATE, AY LAKE TAY ATE ATE AYPLES AND BANAY-NAYS...
E LEEK TEE EAT, E LEEK TE EAT–
HERE COMES ACTION!
HERE COMES EXCITEMENT!
COLE!
SIRENS!

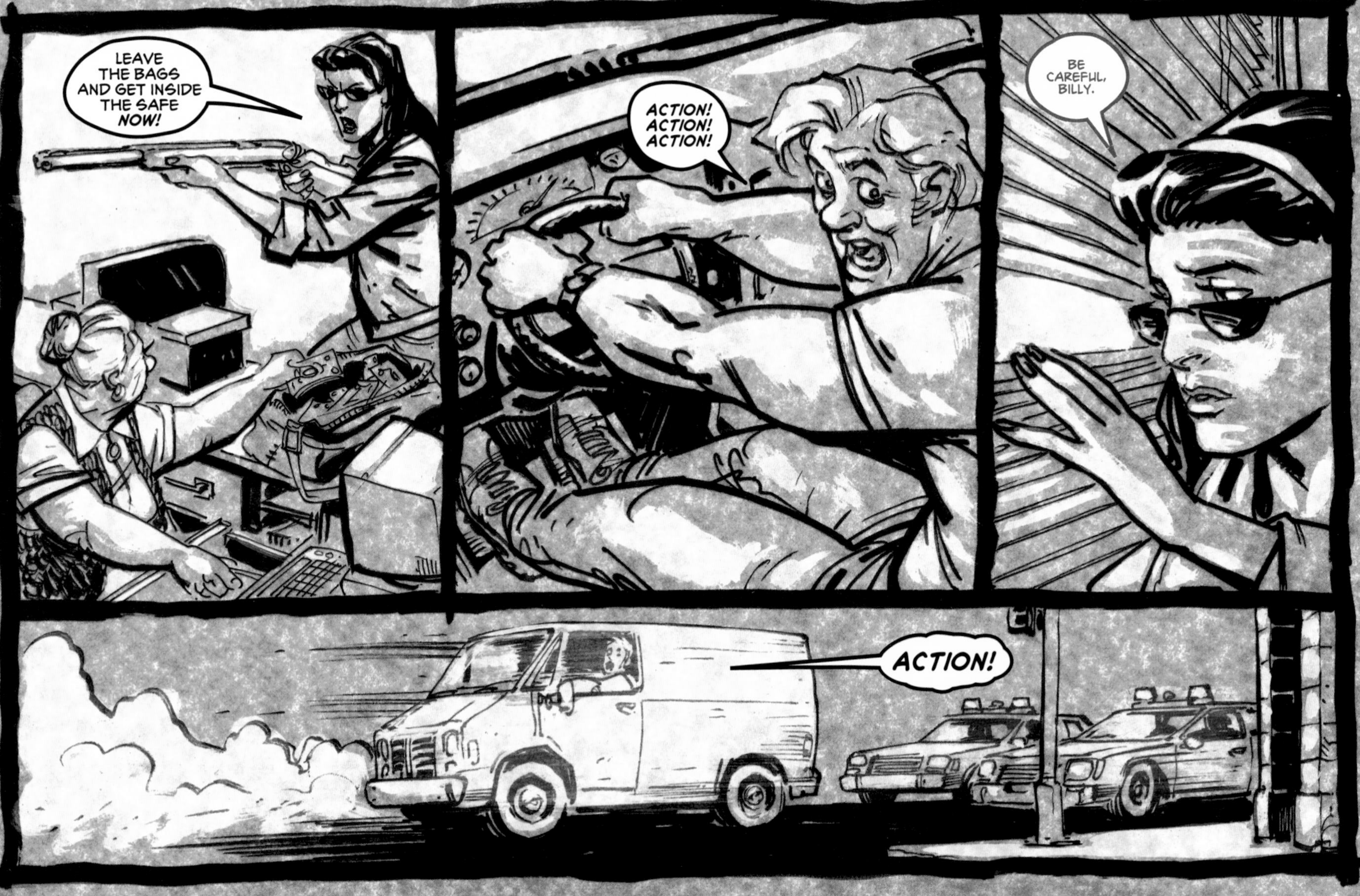
LEAVE THE BAGS AND GET INSIDE THE SAFE NOW!
ACTION! ACTION! ACTION!
BE CAREFUL, BILLY.
ACTION!

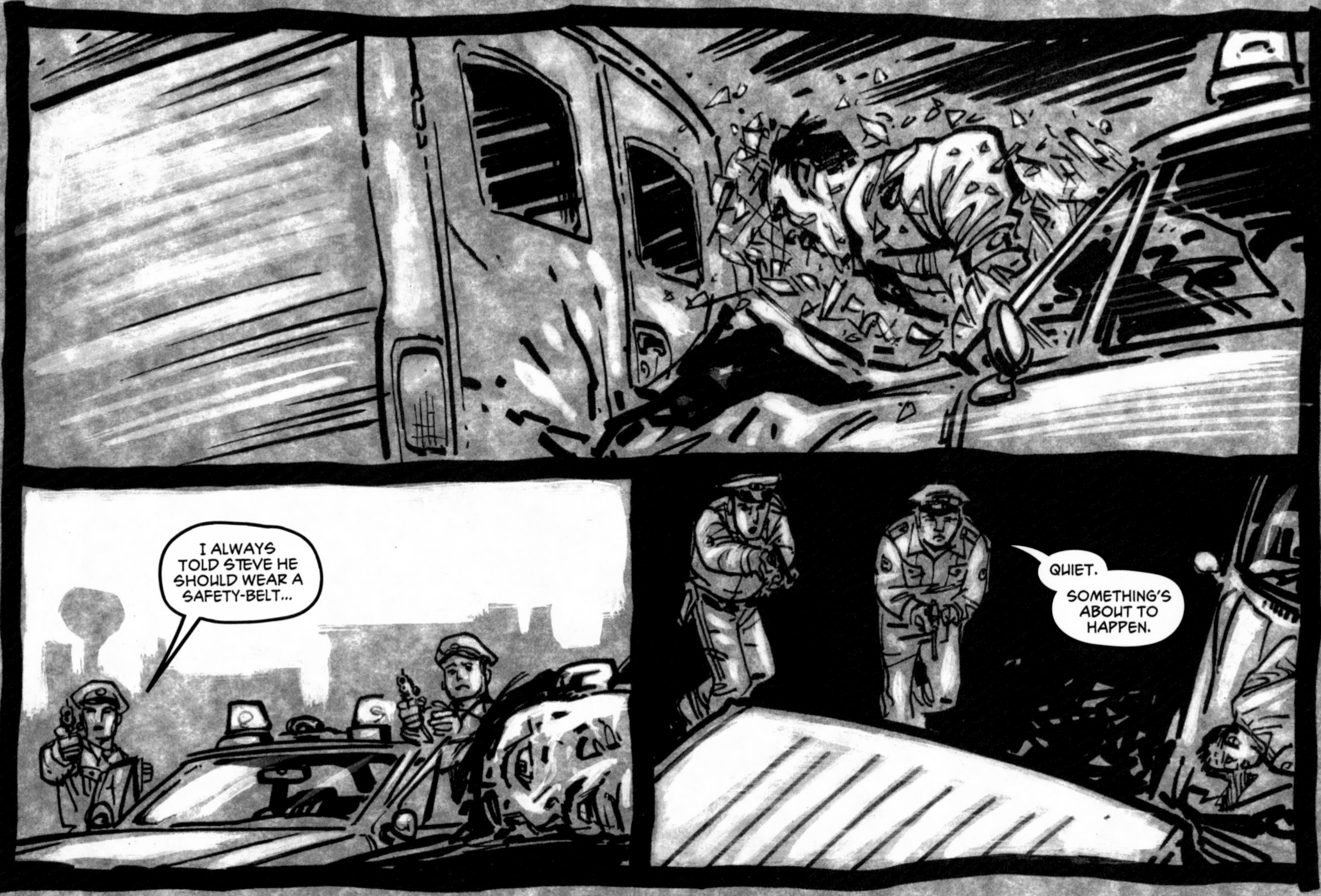
I ALWAYS TOLD STEVE HE SHOULD WEAR A SAFETY-BELT...
QUIET.
SOMETHING'S ABOUT TO HAPPEN.

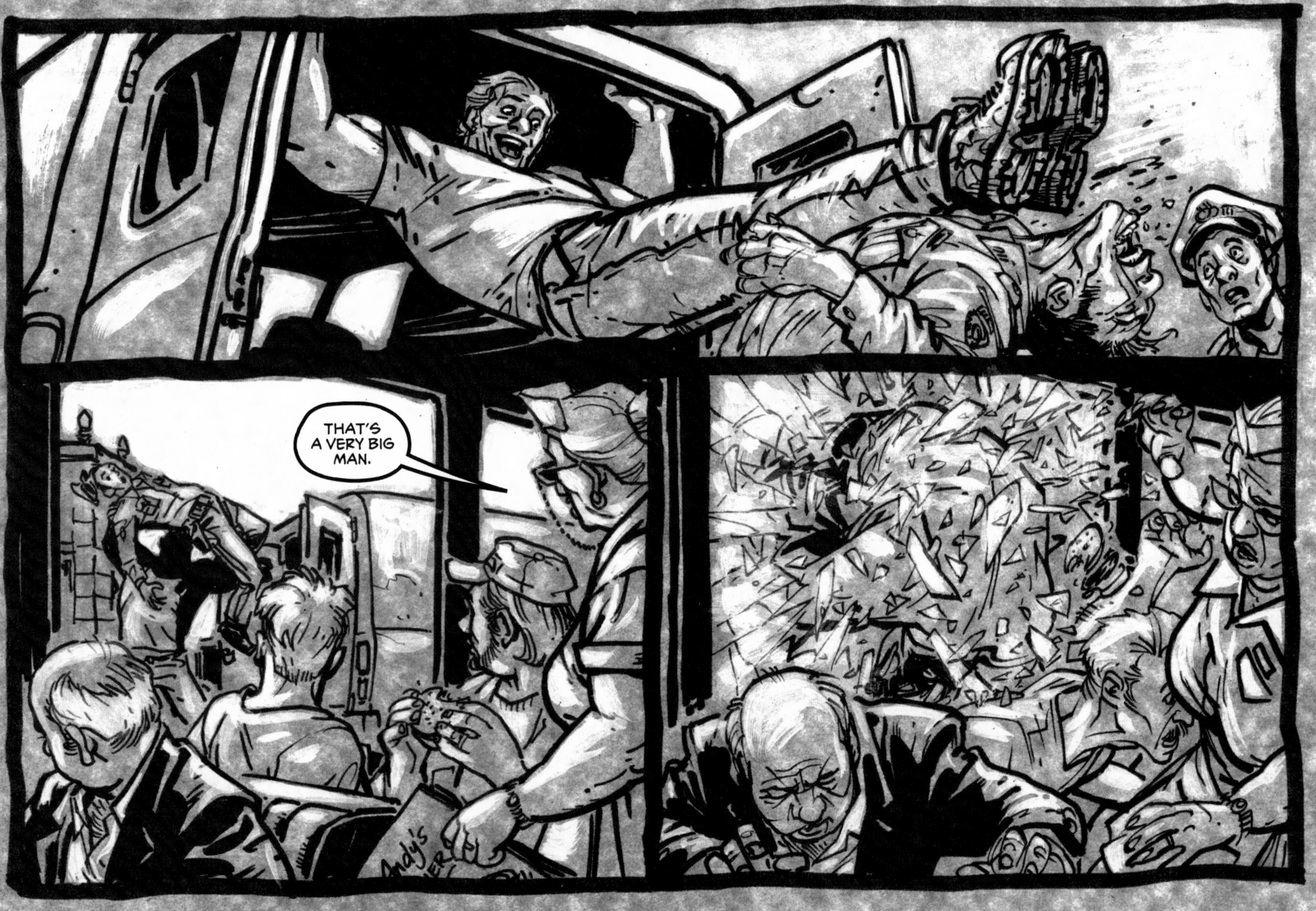
THAT'S A VERY BIG MAN.
Andy's

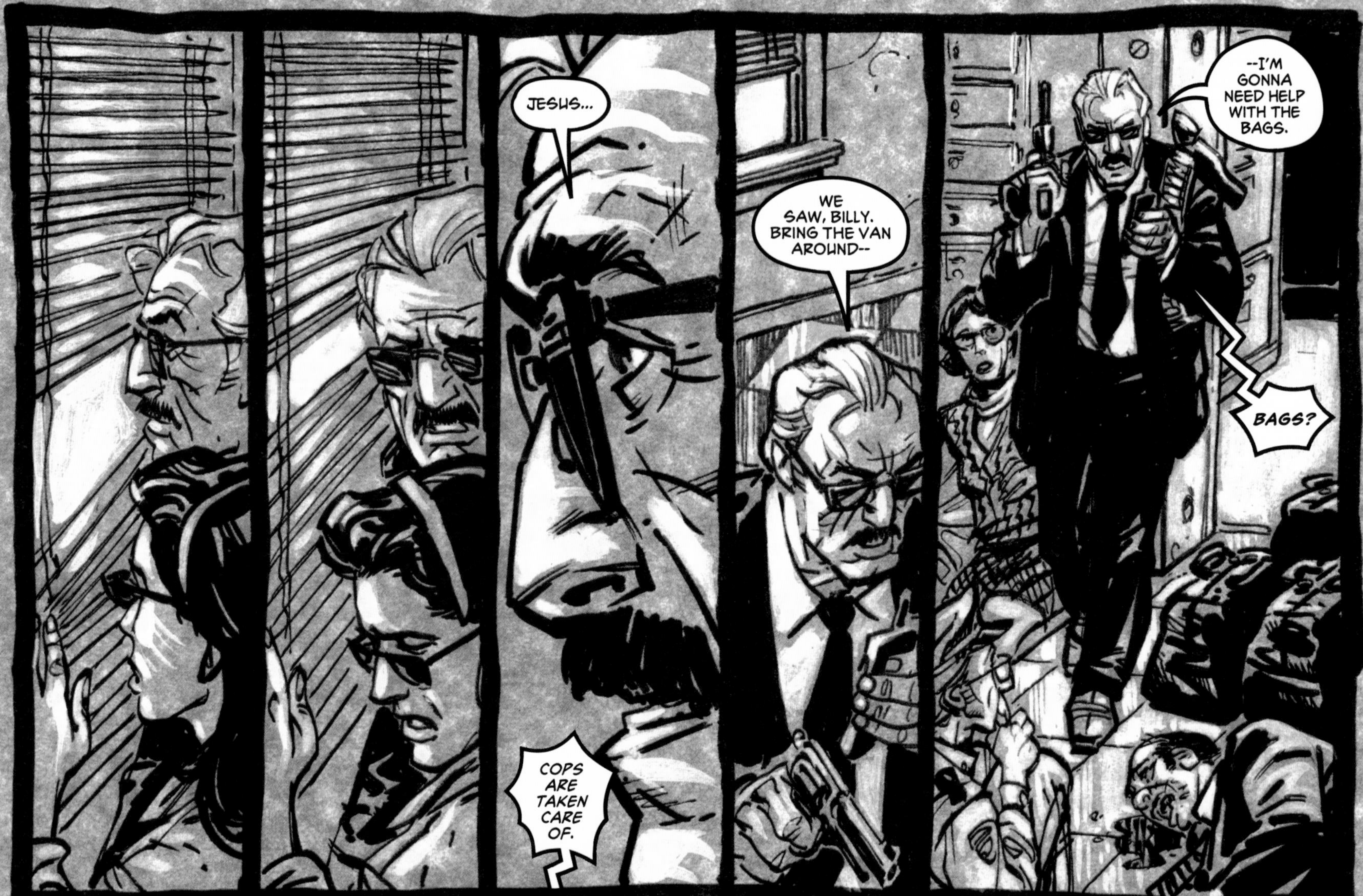
JESUS...
COPS ARE TAKEN CARE OF.
WE SAW, BILLY. BRING THE VAN AROUND--
--I'M GONNA NEED HELP WITH THE BAGS.
BAGS?

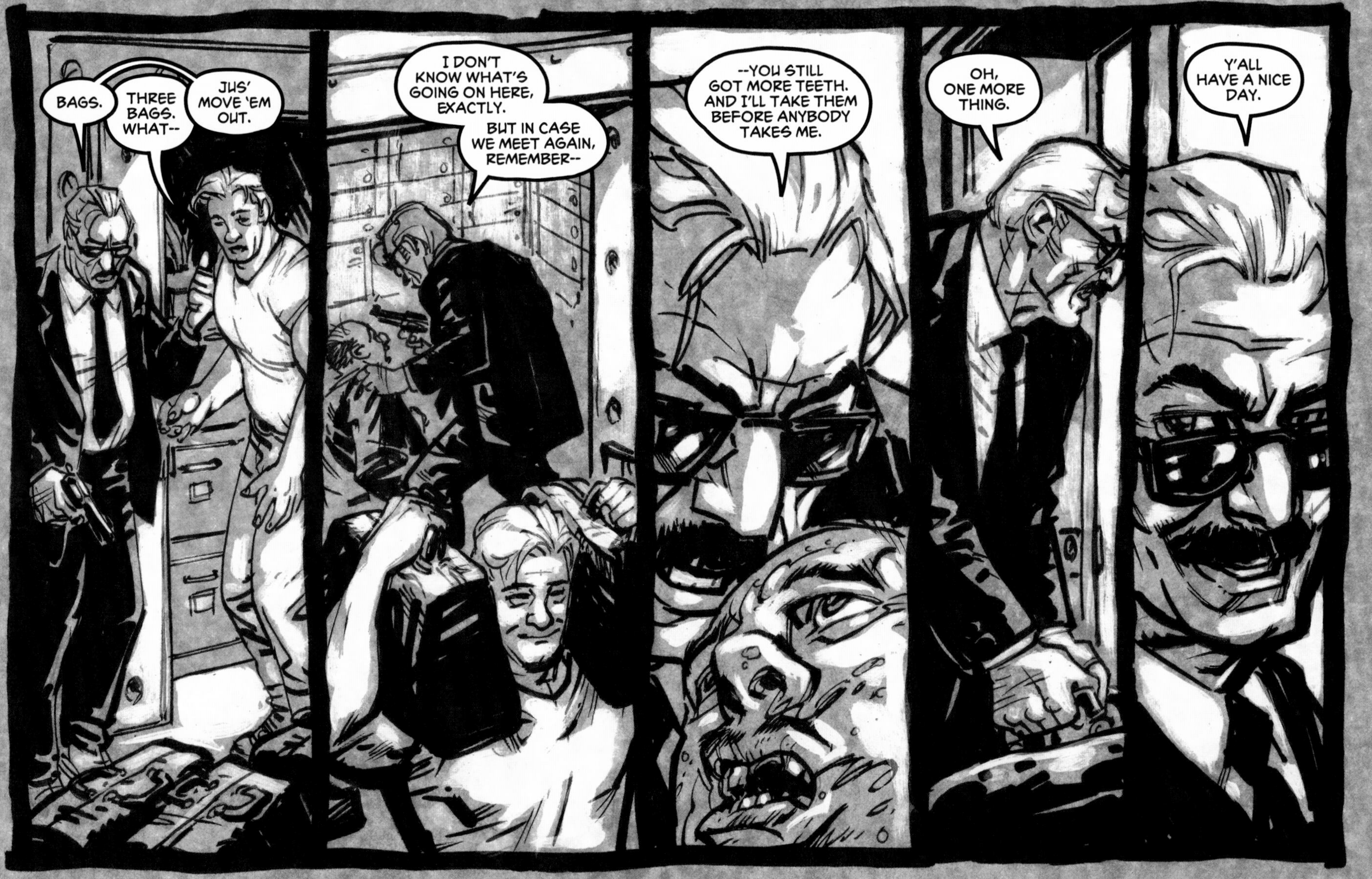
BAGS.
THREE BAGS. WHAT--
JUS' MOVE 'EM OUT.
I DON'T KNOW WHAT'S GOING ON HERE, EXACTLY.
BUT IN CASE WE MEET AGAIN, REMEMBER--
--YOU STILL GOT MORE TEETH. AND I'LL TAKE THEM BEFORE ANYBODY TAKES ME.
OH, ONE MORE THING.
Y'ALL HAVE A NICE DAY.

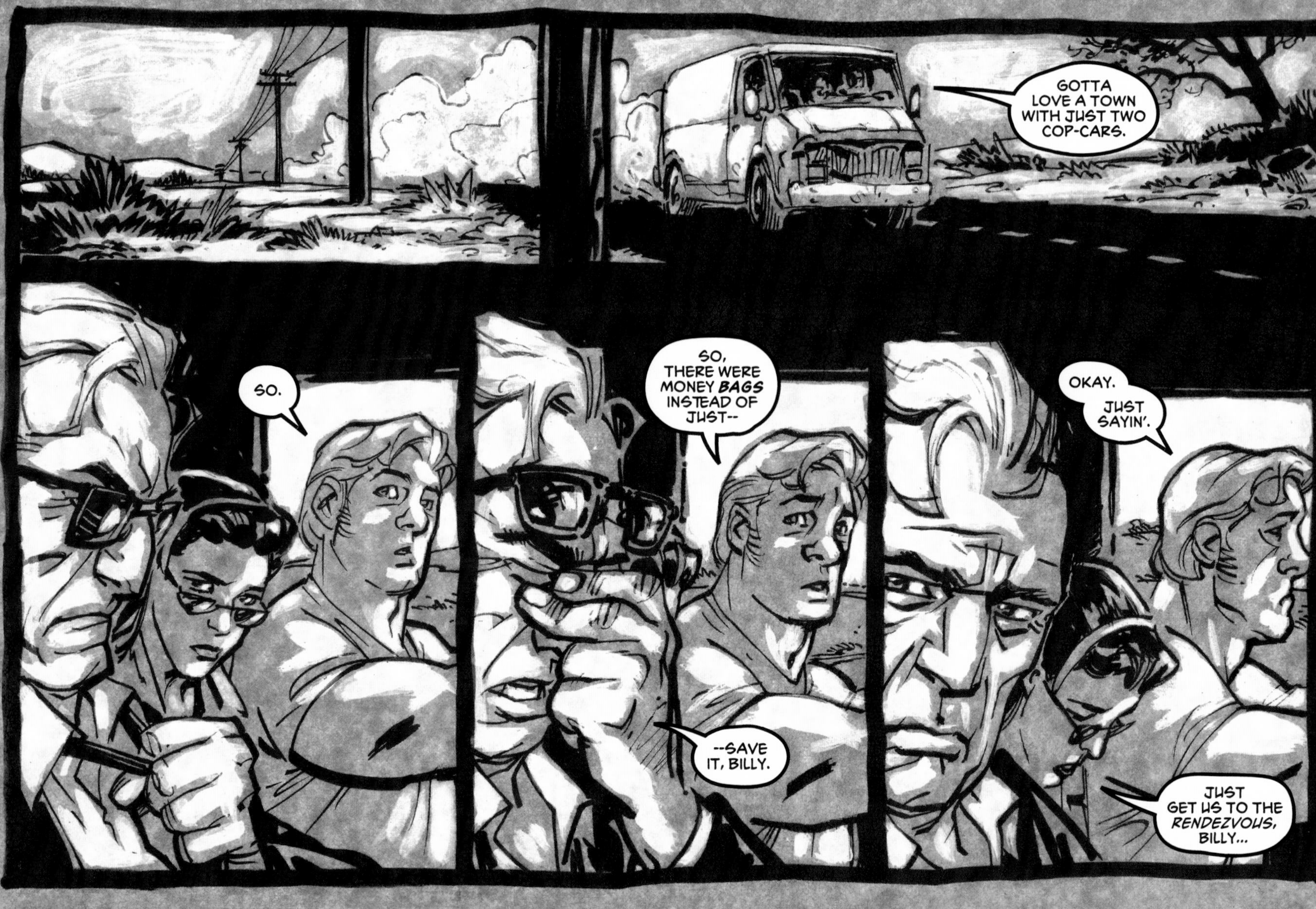
GOTTA LOVE A TOWN WITH JUST TWO COP-CARS.
SO.
SO, THERE WERE MONEY BAGS INSTEAD OF JUST--
--SAVE IT, BILLY.
OKAY.
JUST SAYIN'.
JUST GET US TO THE RENDEZVOUS, BILLY...

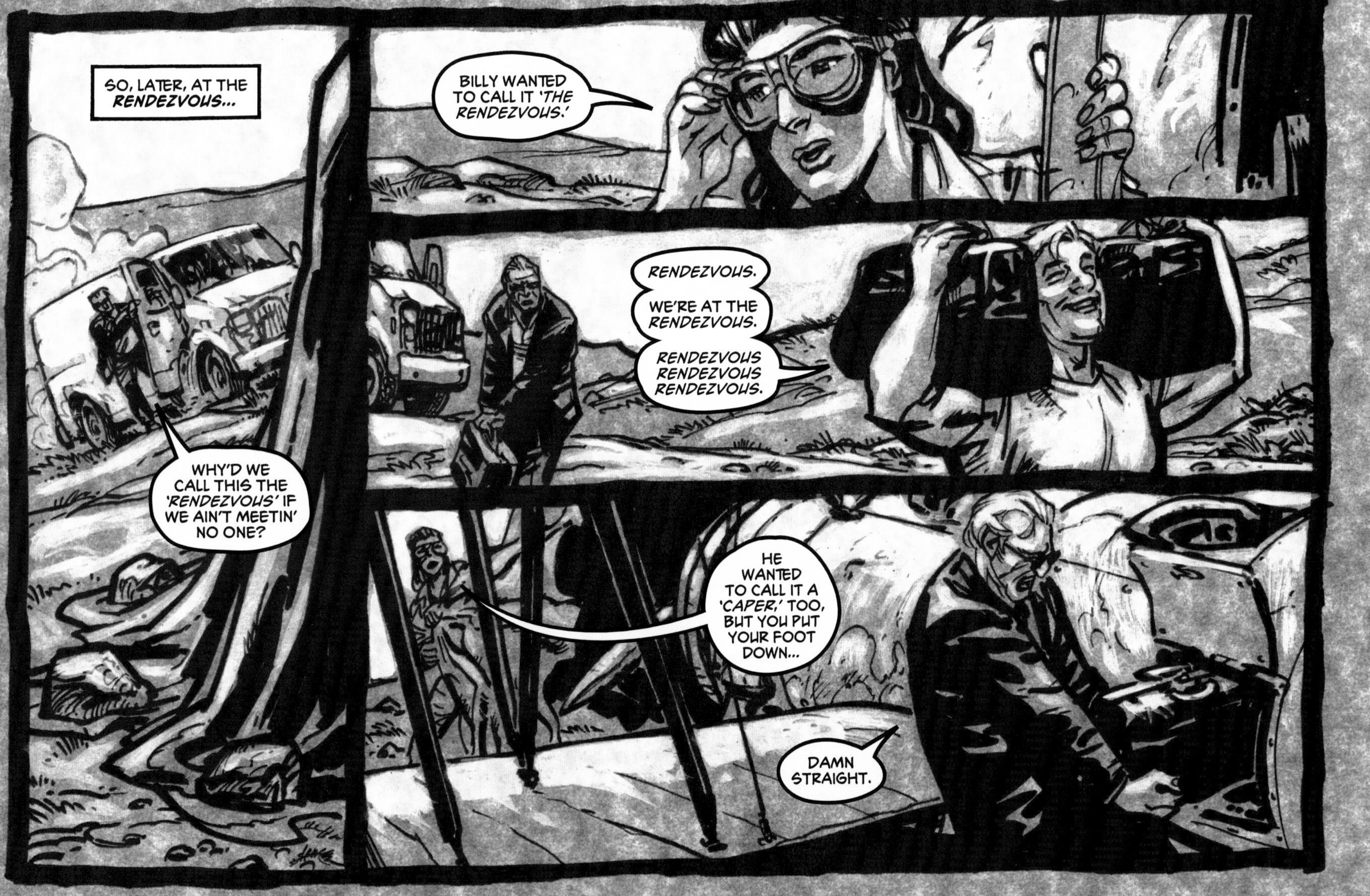
SO, LATER, AT THE *RENDEZVOUS*...
WHY'D WE CALL THIS THE *'RENDEZVOUS'* IF WE AIN'T MEETIN' NO ONE?
BILLY WANTED TO CALL IT *'THE RENDEZVOUS.'*
RENDEZVOUS.
WE'RE AT THE *RENDEZVOUS.*
RENDEZVOUS RENDEZVOUS RENDEZVOUS.
HE WANTED TO CALL IT A *'CAPER,'* TOO, BUT YOU PUT YOUR FOOT DOWN...
DAMN STRAIGHT.

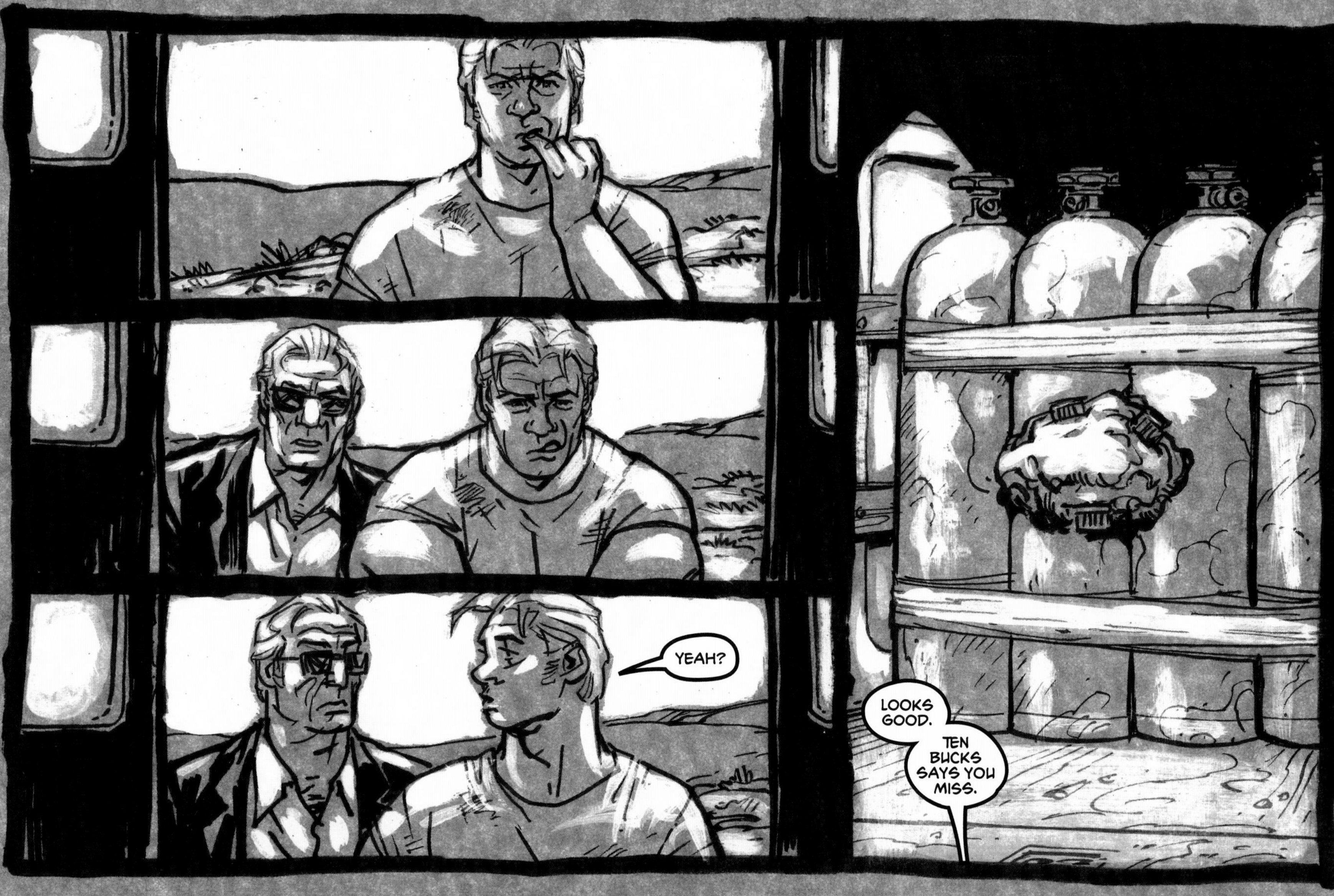
YEAH?
LOOKS GOOD.
TEN BUCKS SAYS YOU MISS.

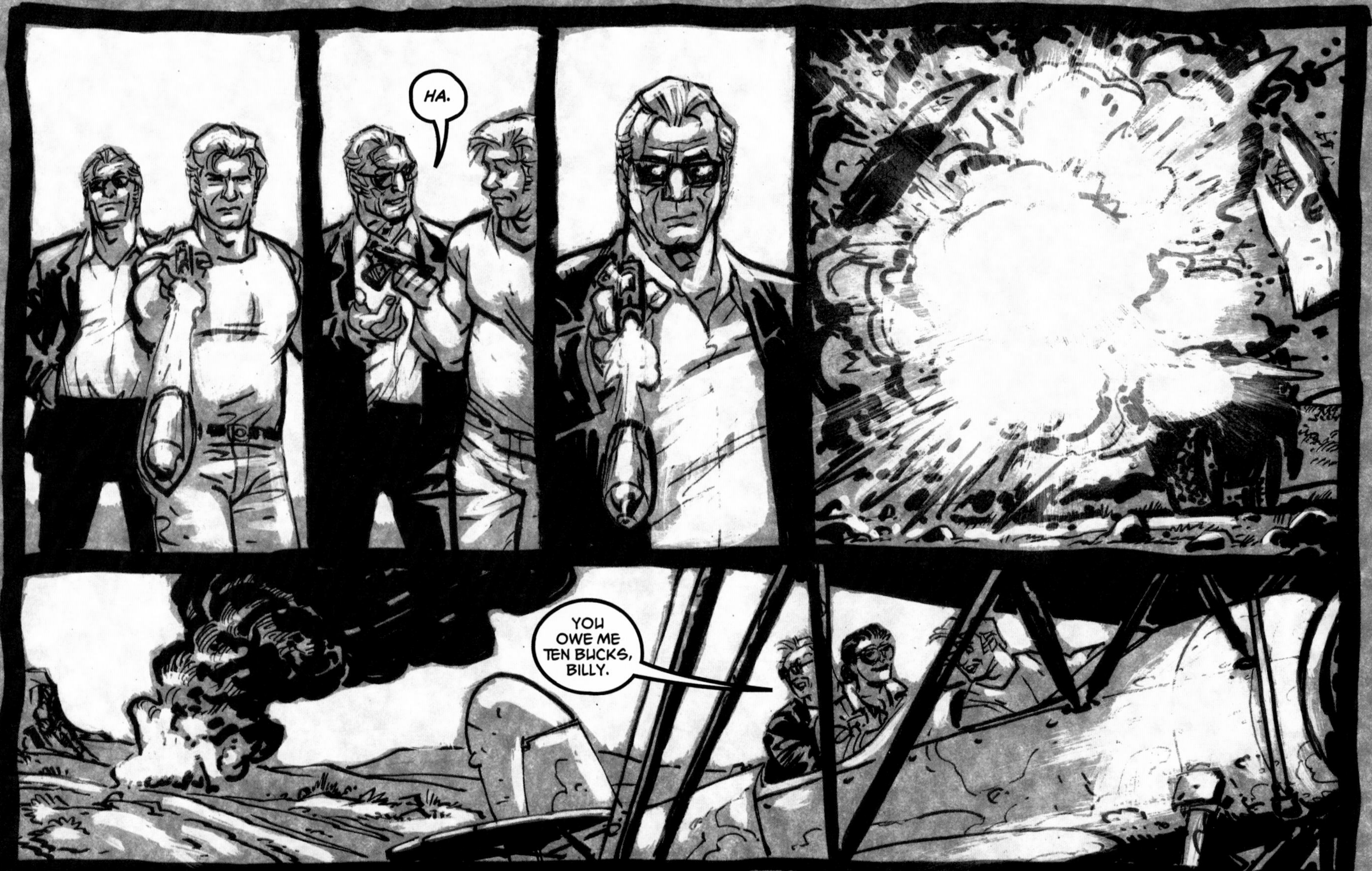
HA.
YOU OWE ME TEN BUCKS, BILLY.

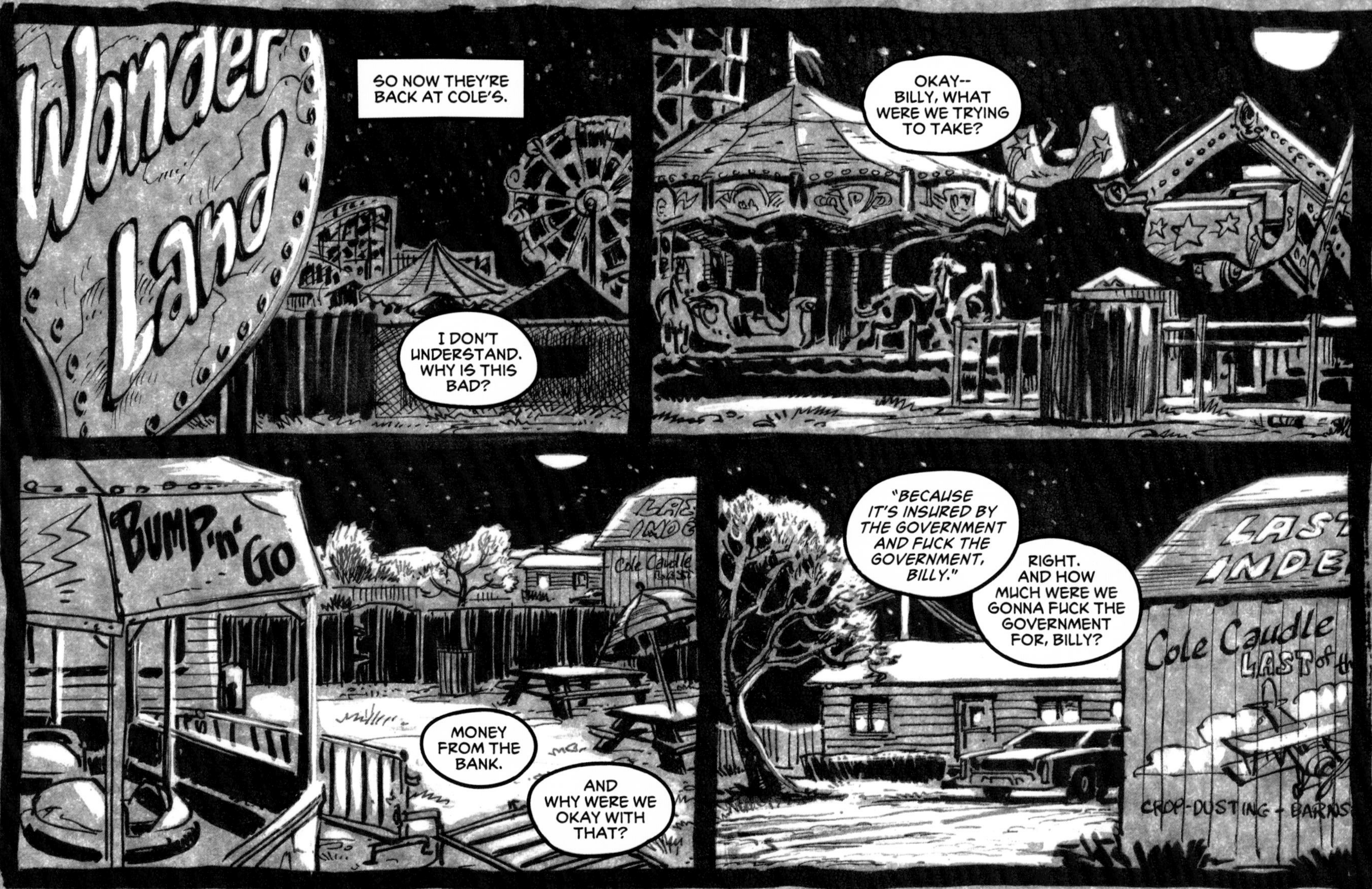
Wonder Land
SO NOW THEY'RE BACK AT COLE'S.
I DON'T UNDERSTAND. WHY IS THIS BAD?
OKAY-- BILLY, WHAT WERE WE TRYING TO TAKE?
BUMP 'n' GO
MONEY FROM THE BANK.
AND WHY WERE WE OKAY WITH THAT?
"BECAUSE IT'S INSURED BY THE GOVERNMENT AND FUCK THE GOVERNMENT, BILLY."
RIGHT. AND HOW MUCH WERE WE GONNA FUCK THE GOVERNMENT FOR, BILLY?
Cole Caudle

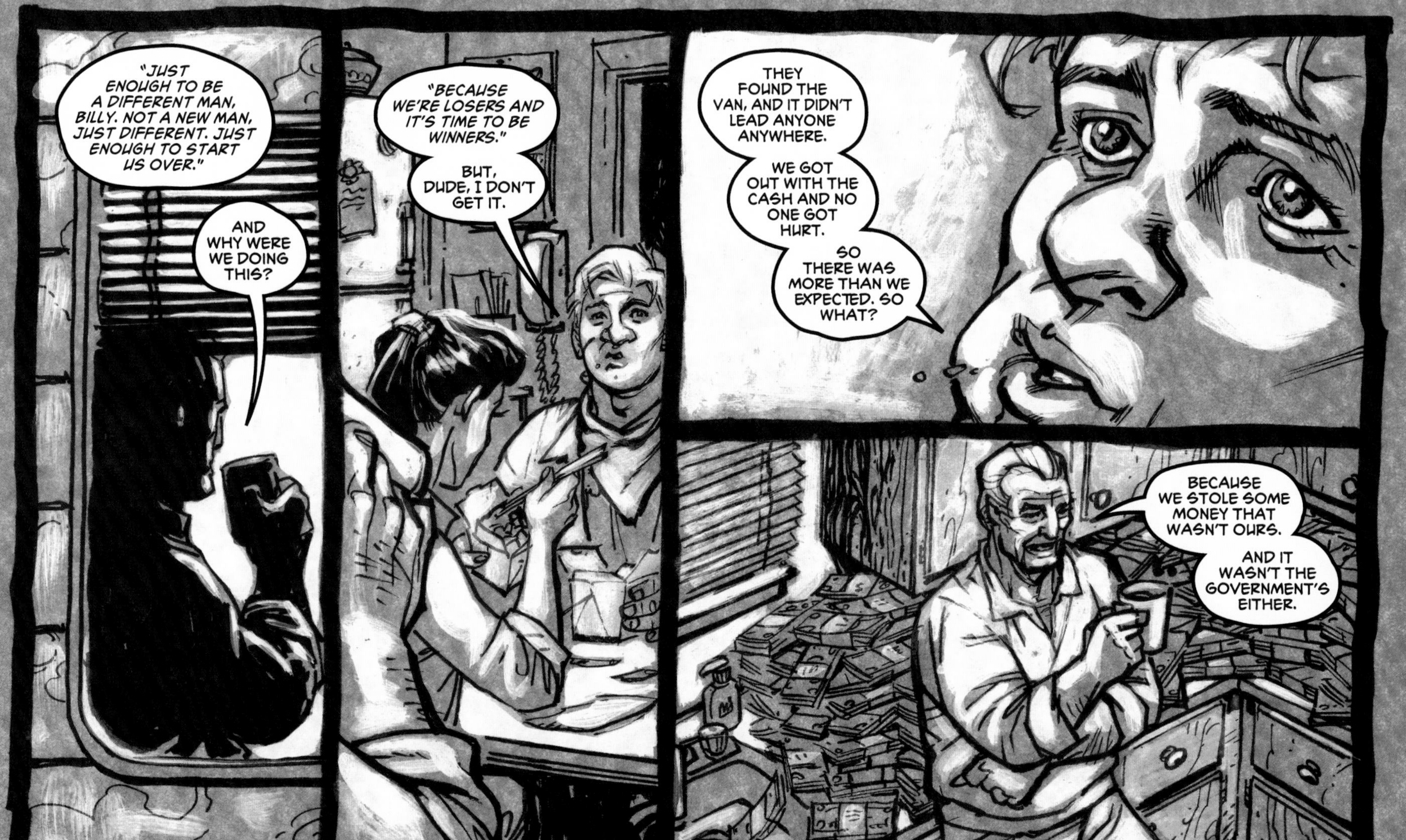
"JUST ENOUGH TO BE A DIFFERENT MAN, BILLY. NOT A NEW MAN, JUST DIFFERENT. JUST ENOUGH TO START US OVER."
AND WHY WERE WE DOING THIS?
"BECAUSE WE'RE LOSERS AND IT'S TIME TO BE WINNERS."
BUT, DUDE, I DON'T GET IT.
THEY FOUND THE VAN, AND IT DIDN'T LEAD ANYONE ANYWHERE.
WE GOT OUT WITH THE CASH AND NO ONE GOT HURT.
SO THERE WAS MORE THAN WE EXPECTED. SO WHAT?
BECAUSE WE STOLE SOME MONEY THAT WASN'T OURS.
AND IT WASN'T THE GOVERNMENT'S EITHER.

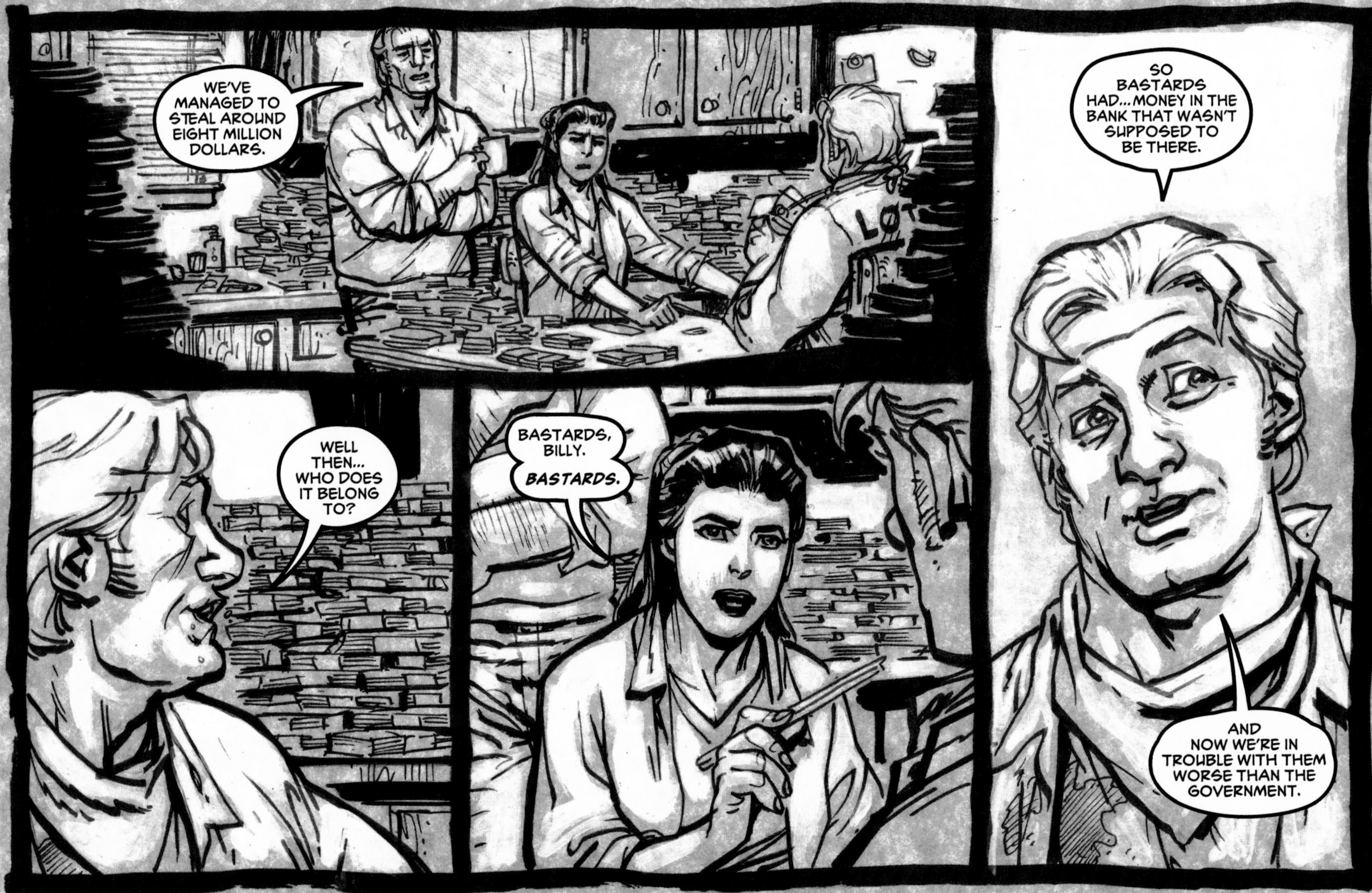
WE'VE MANAGED TO STEAL AROUND EIGHT MILLION DOLLARS.
WELL THEN... WHO DOES IT BELONG TO?
BASTARDS, BILLY.
BASTARDS.
SO BASTARDS HAD... MONEY IN THE BANK THAT WASN'T SUPPOSED TO BE THERE.
AND NOW WE'RE IN TROUBLE WITH THEM WORSE THAN THE GOVERNMENT.

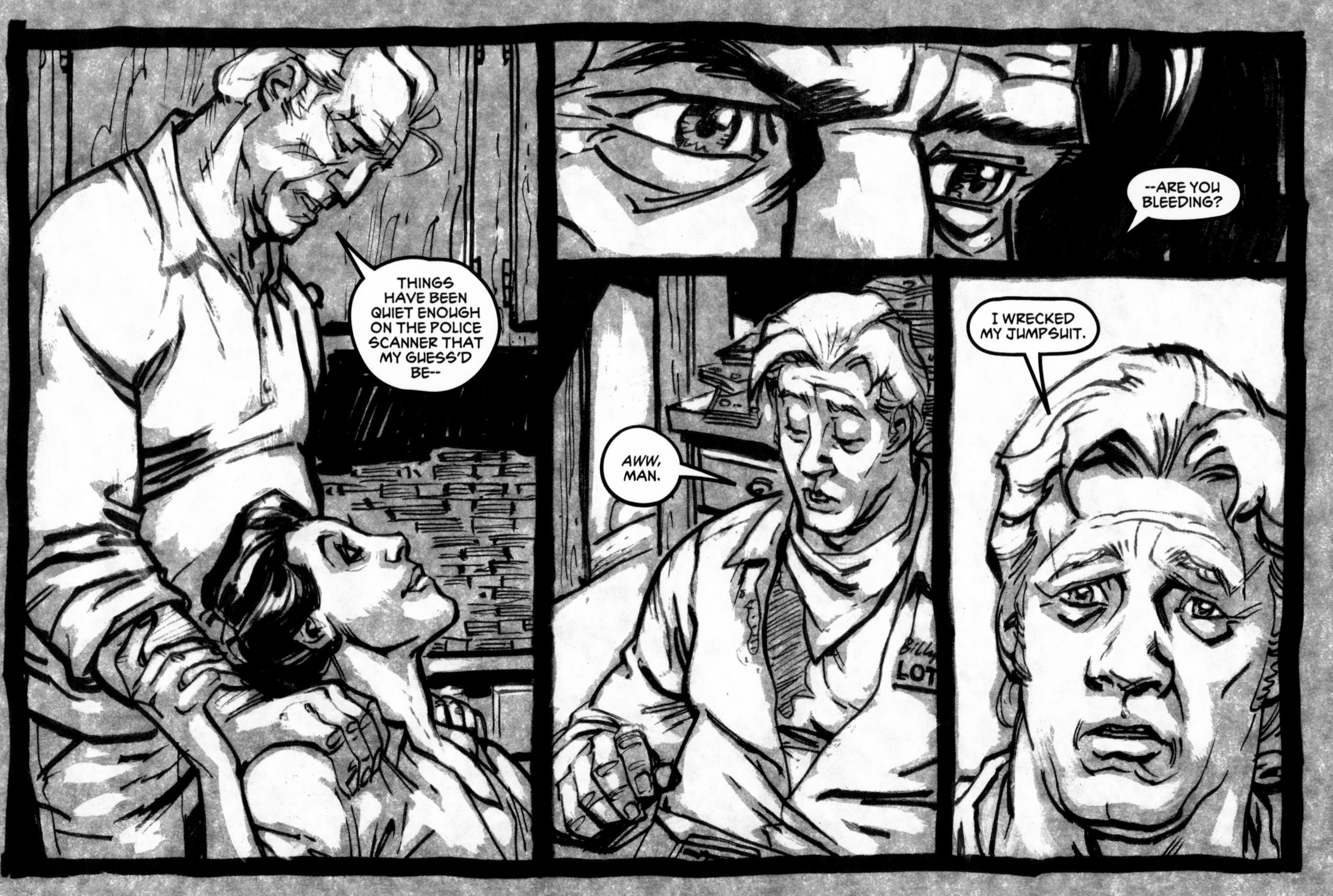
THINGS HAVE BEEN QUIET ENOUGH ON THE POLICE SCANNER THAT MY GUESS'D BE--
--ARE YOU BLEEDING?
AWW, MAN.
I WRECKED MY JUMPSUIT.

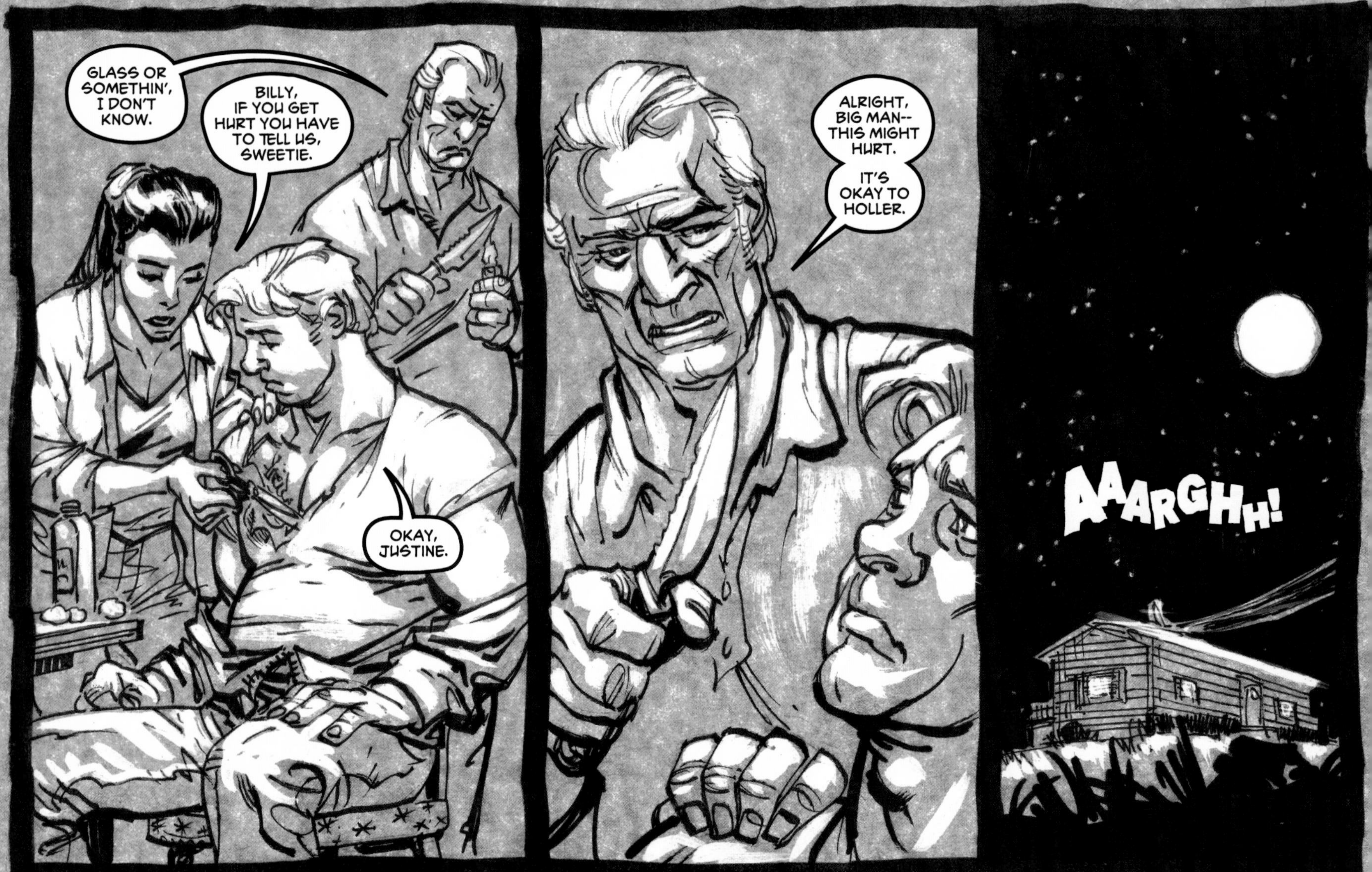
GLASS OR SOMETHIN', I DON'T KNOW.
BILLY, IF YOU GET HURT YOU HAVE TO TELL US, SWEETIE.
OKAY, JUSTINE.
ALRIGHT, BIG MAN-- THIS MIGHT HURT.
IT'S OKAY TO HOLLER.
AAARGHH!

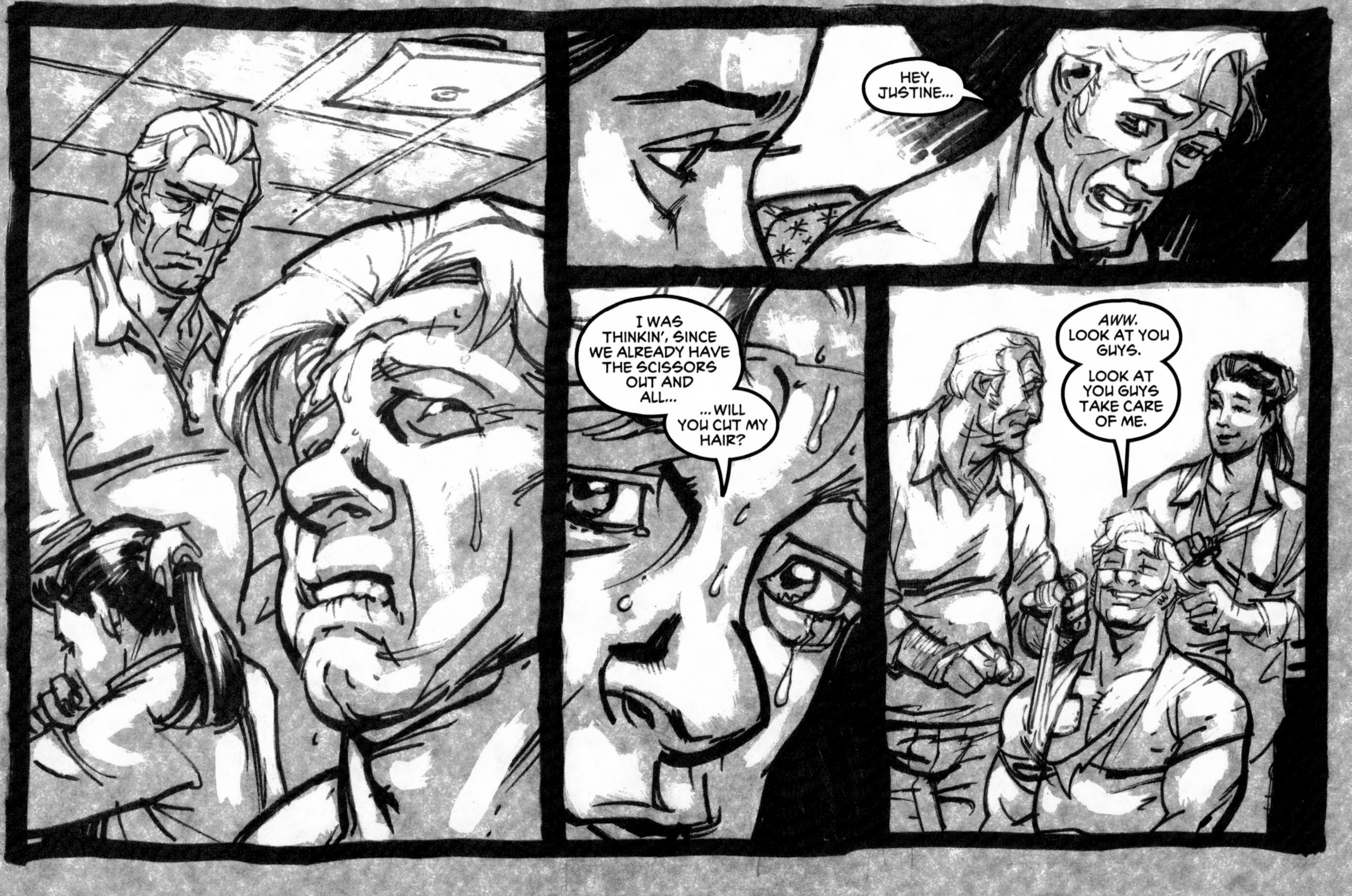
HEY, JUSTINE...
I WAS THINKIN', SINCE WE ALREADY HAVE THE SCISSORS OUT AND ALL...
...WILL YOU CUT MY HAIR?
AWW. LOOK AT YOU GUYS.
LOOK AT YOU GUYS TAKE CARE OF ME.

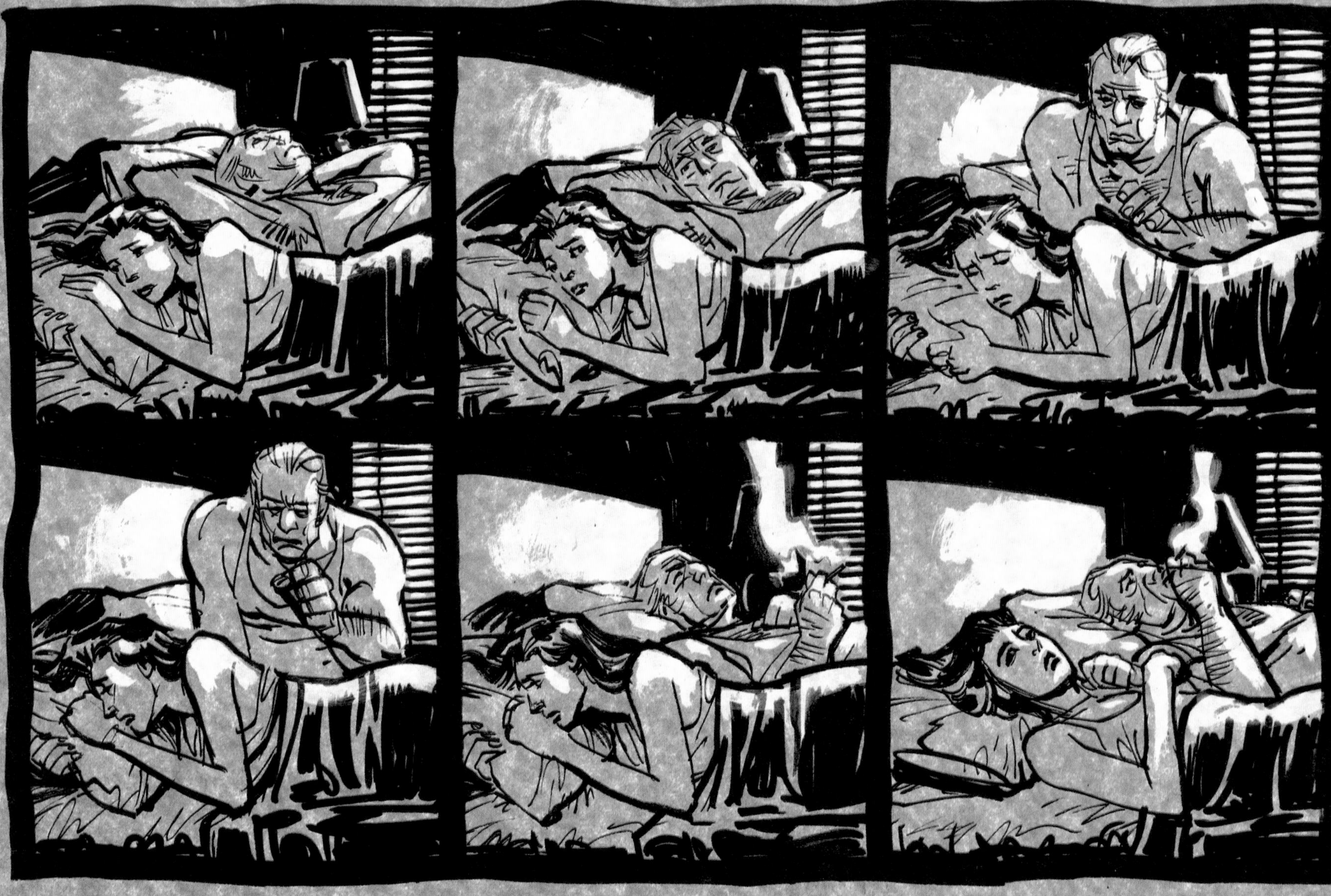

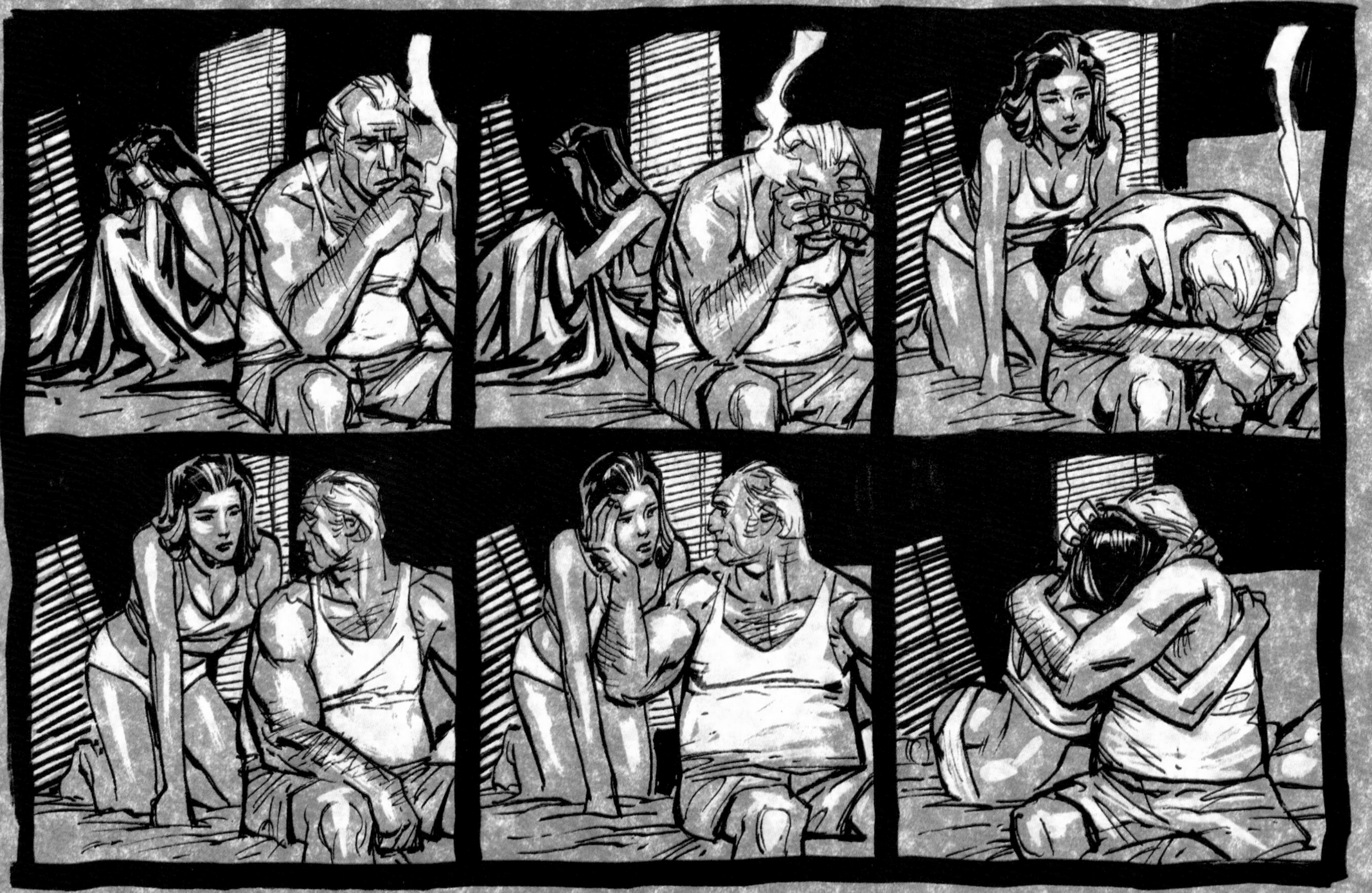

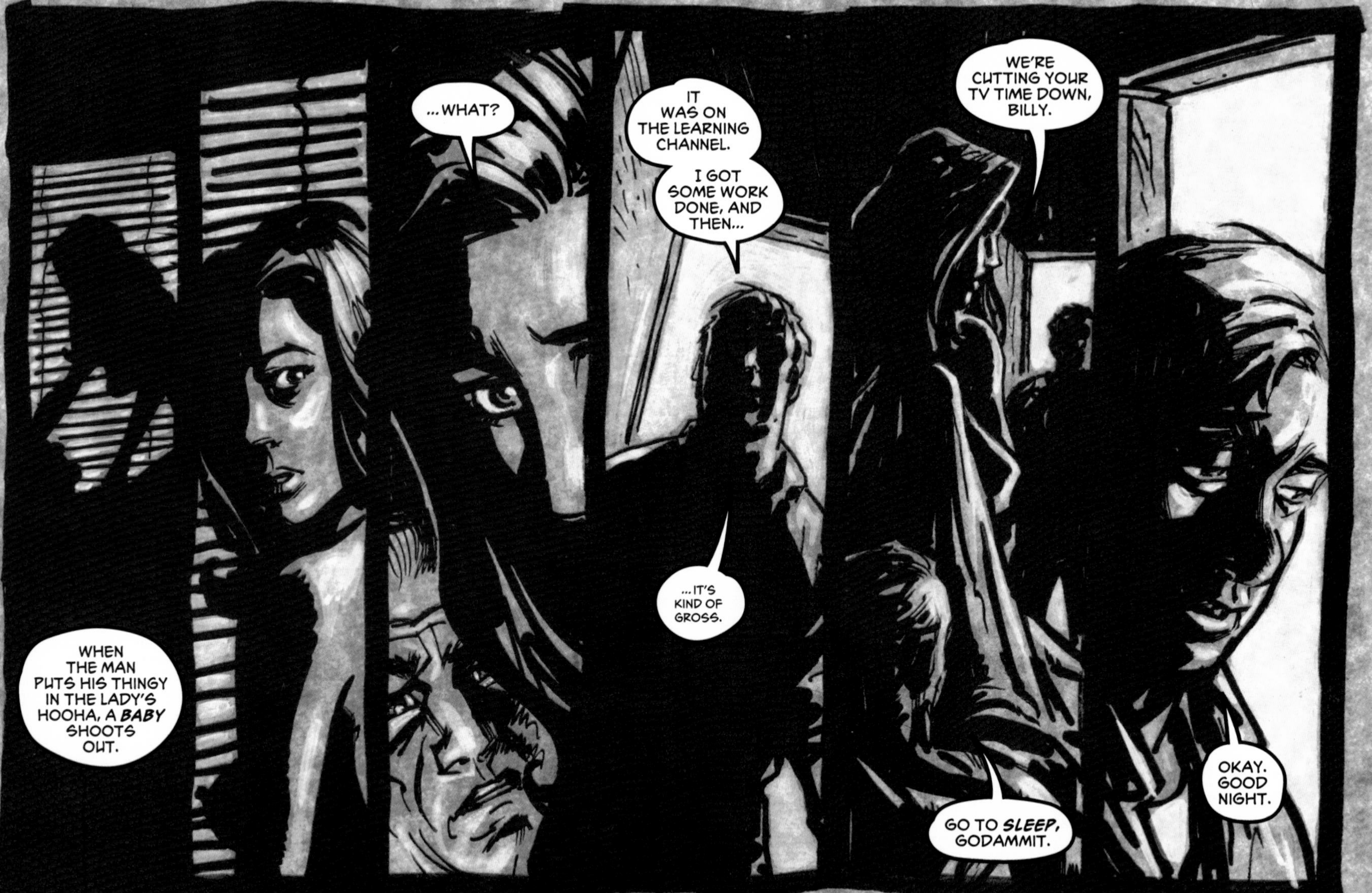
WHEN THE MAN PUTS HIS THINGY IN THE LADY'S HOOHA, A *BABY* SHOOTS OUT.
...WHAT?
IT WAS ON THE LEARNING CHANNEL.
I GOT SOME WORK DONE, AND THEN...
...IT'S KIND OF GROSS.
WE'RE CUTTING YOUR TV TIME DOWN, BILLY.
GO TO *SLEEP,* GODAMMIT.
OKAY. GOOD NIGHT.

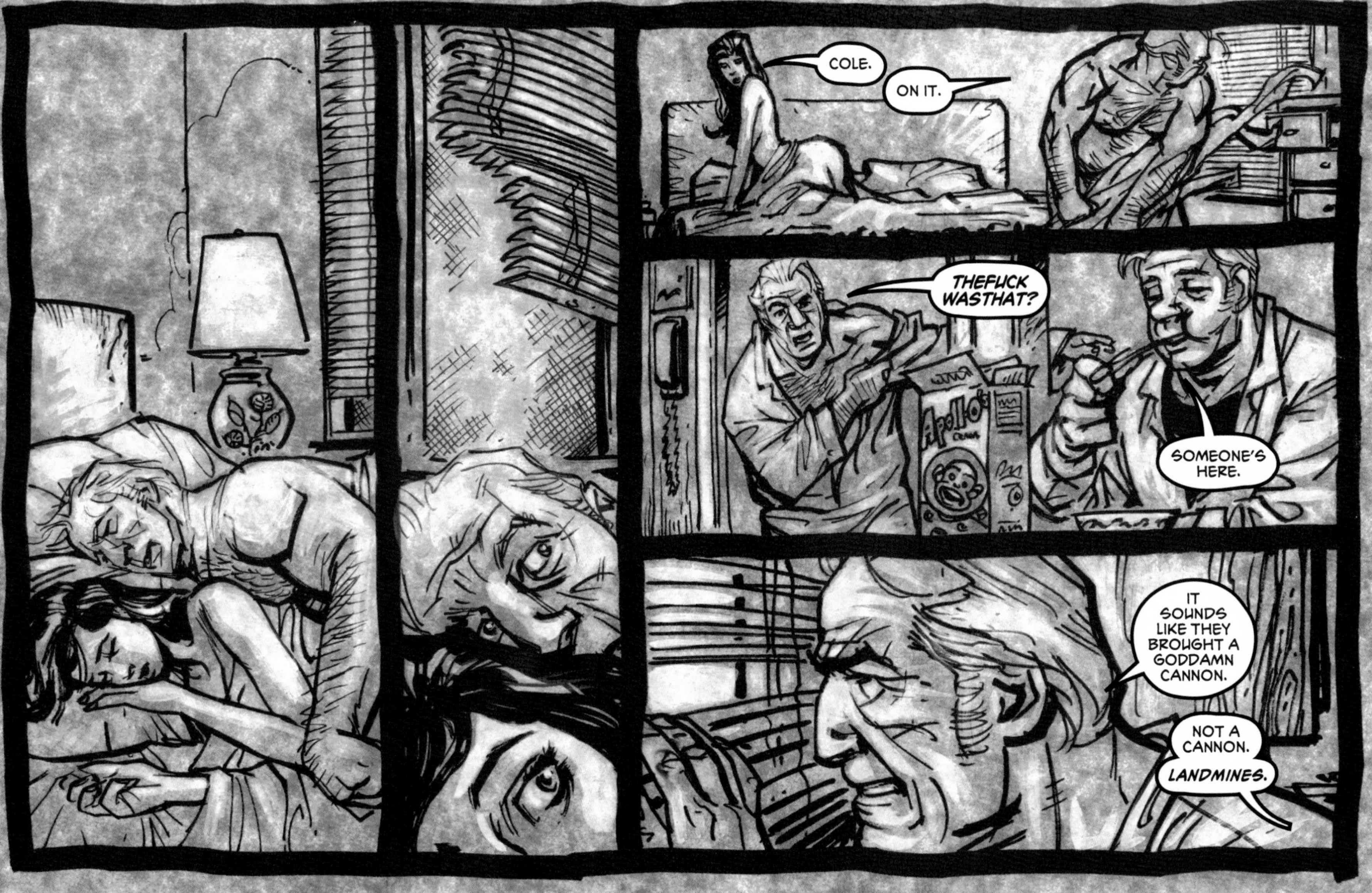
COLE.
ON IT.
THEFUCK WASTHAT?
SOMEONE'S HERE.
IT SOUNDS LIKE THEY BROUGHT A GODDAMN CANNON.
NOT A CANNON.
LANDMINES.

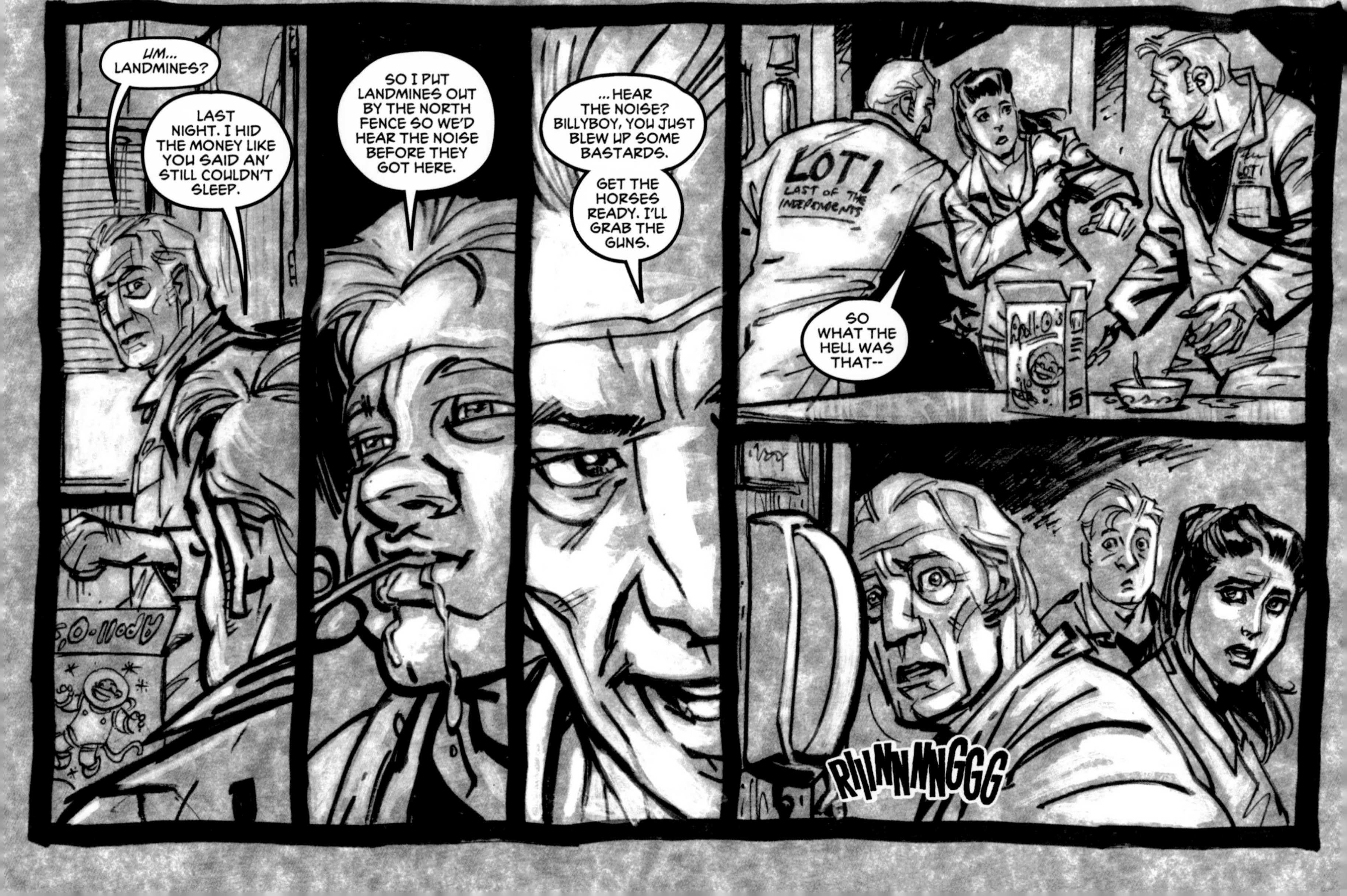
UM... LANDMINES?
LAST NIGHT. I HID THE MONEY LIKE YOU SAID AN' STILL COULDN'T SLEEP.
SO I PUT LANDMINES OUT BY THE NORTH FENCE SO WE'D HEAR THE NOISE BEFORE THEY GOT HERE.
...HEAR THE NOISE? BILLYBOY, YOU JUST BLEW UP SOME BASTARDS.
GET THE HORSES READY. I'LL GRAB THE GUNS.
LOT 1
LAST OF THE INDEPENDENTS
SO WHAT THE HELL WAS THAT--
RIIINNNNGGG

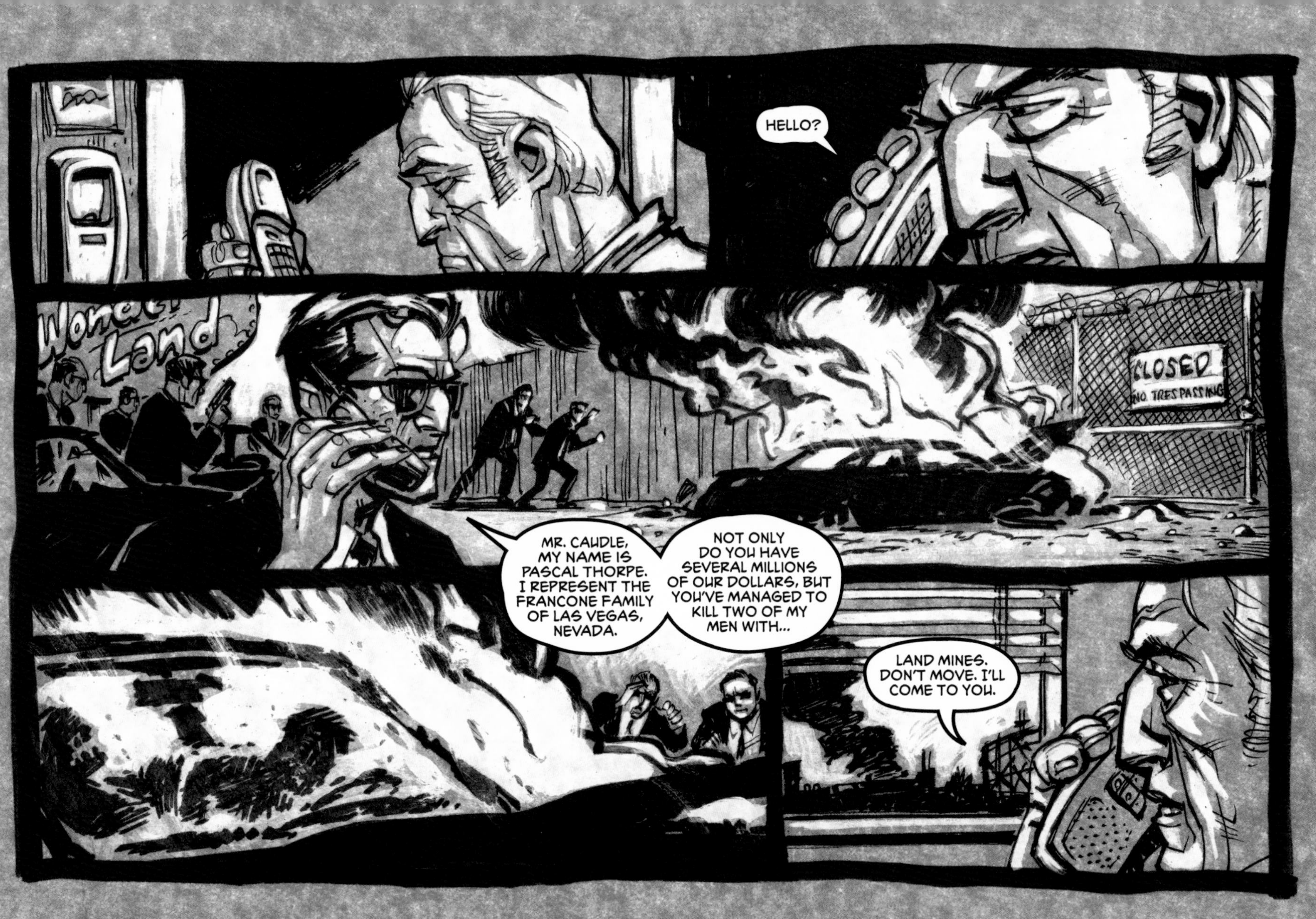
HELLO?
CLOSED
NO TRESPASSING
MR. CAUDLE, MY NAME IS PASCAL THORPE. I REPRESENT THE FRANCONE FAMILY OF LAS VEGAS, NEVADA.
NOT ONLY DO YOU HAVE SEVERAL MILLIONS OF OUR DOLLARS, BUT YOU'VE MANAGED TO KILL TWO OF MY MEN WITH...
LAND MINES. DON'T MOVE. I'LL COME TO YOU.

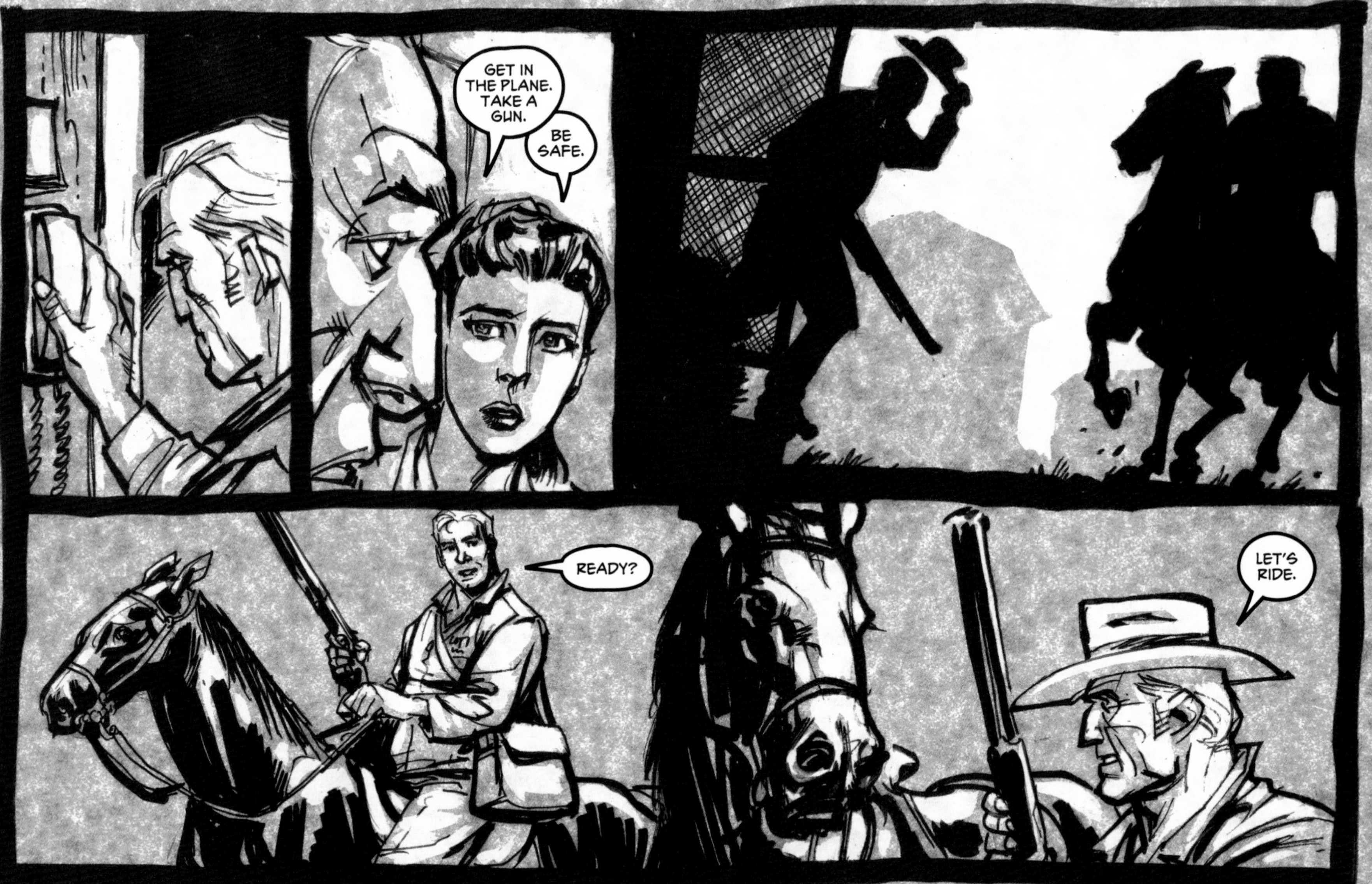
GET IN THE PLANE. TAKE A GUN.
BE SAFE.
READY?
LET'S RIDE.

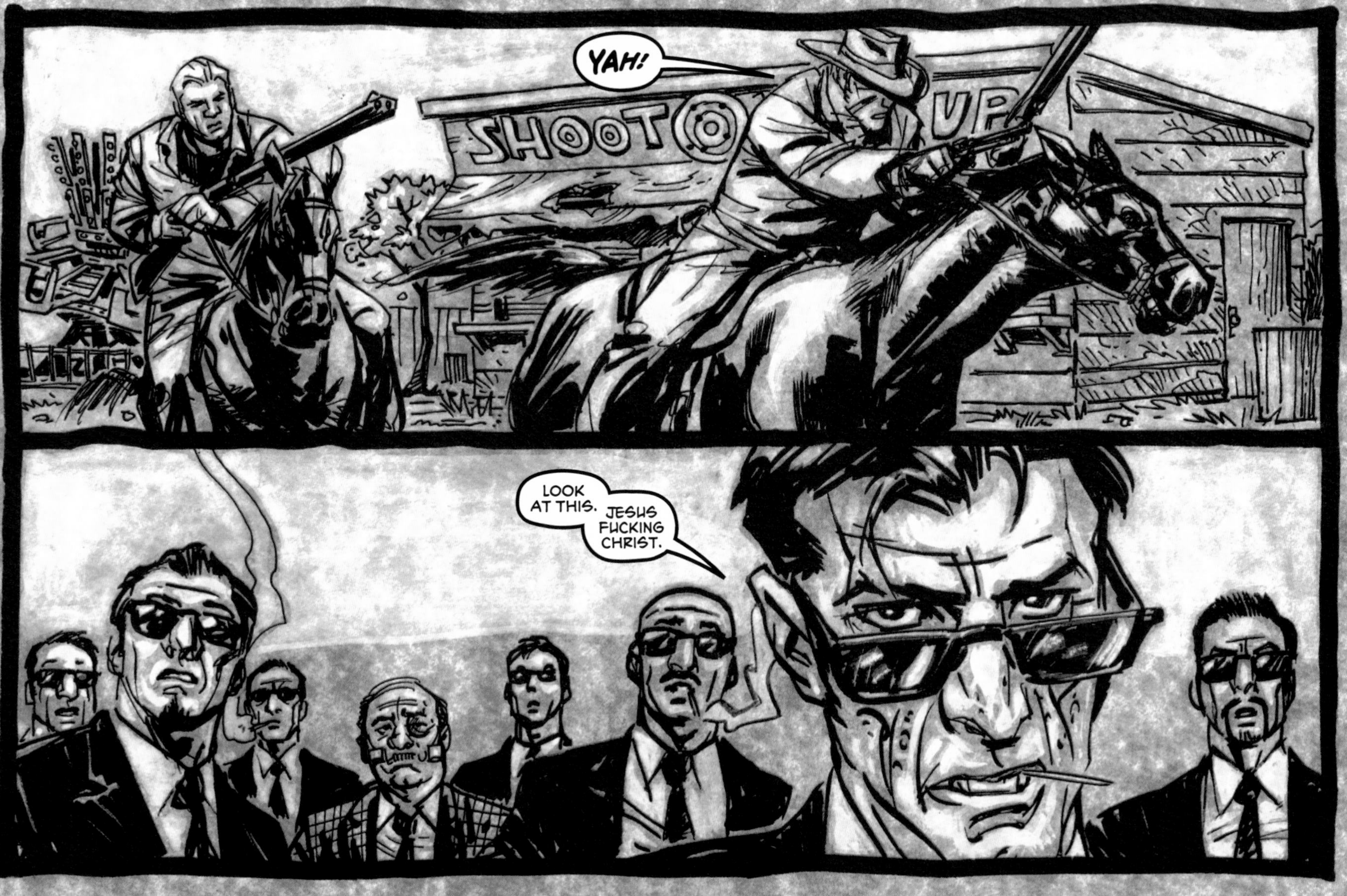
YAH!
SHOOT UP
LOOK AT THIS.
JESUS FUCKING CHRIST.

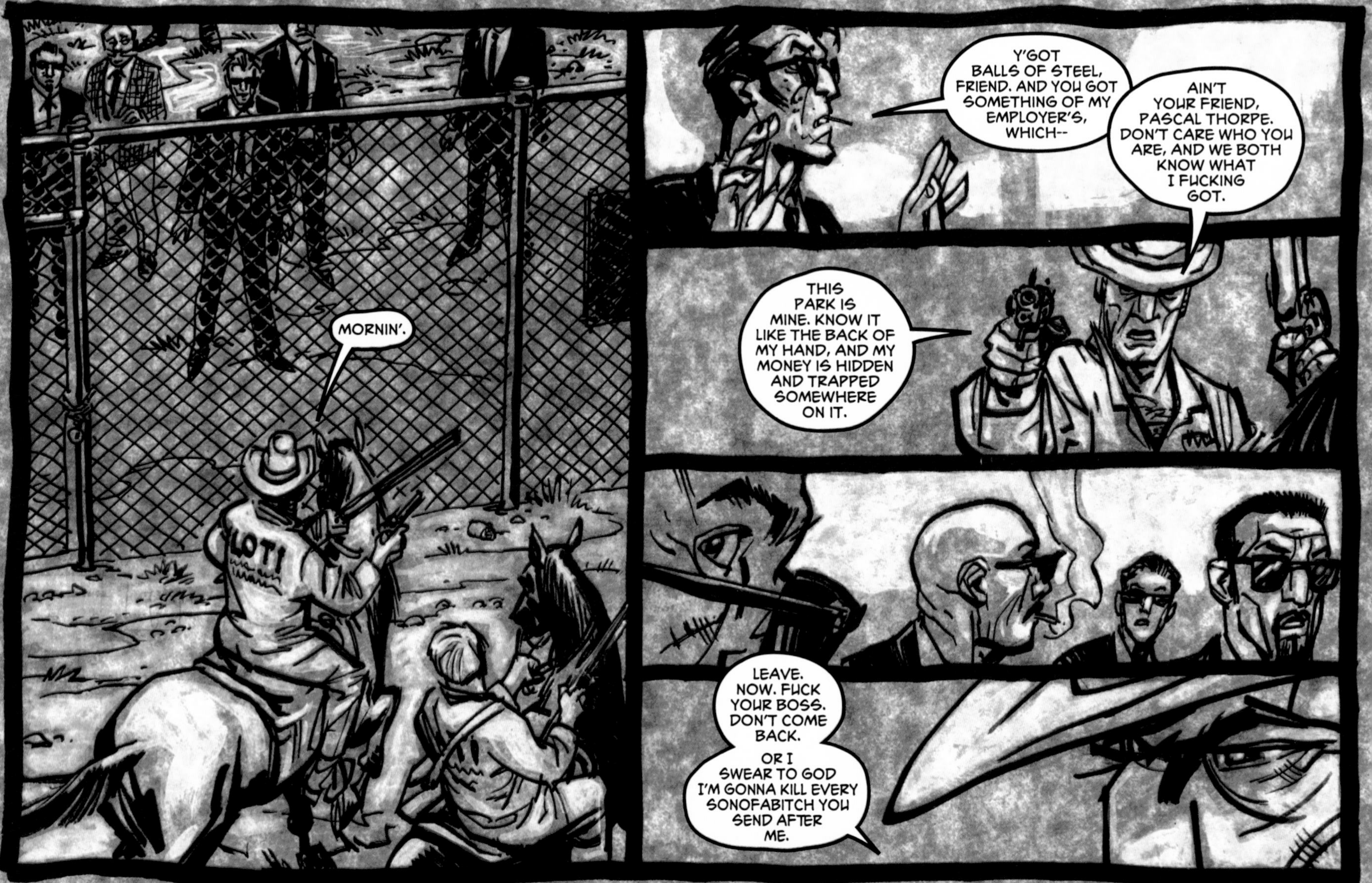
MORNIN'.
Y'GOT BALLS OF STEEL, FRIEND. AND YOU GOT SOMETHING OF MY EMPLOYER'S, WHICH--
AIN'T YOUR FRIEND, PASCAL THORPE. DON'T CARE WHO YOU ARE, AND WE BOTH KNOW WHAT I FUCKING GOT.
THIS PARK IS MINE. KNOW IT LIKE THE BACK OF MY HAND, AND MY MONEY IS HIDDEN AND TRAPPED SOMEWHERE ON IT.
LEAVE. NOW. FUCK YOUR BOSS. DON'T COME BACK.
OR I SWEAR TO GOD I'M GONNA KILL EVERY SONOFABITCH YOU SEND AFTER ME.
LOTI

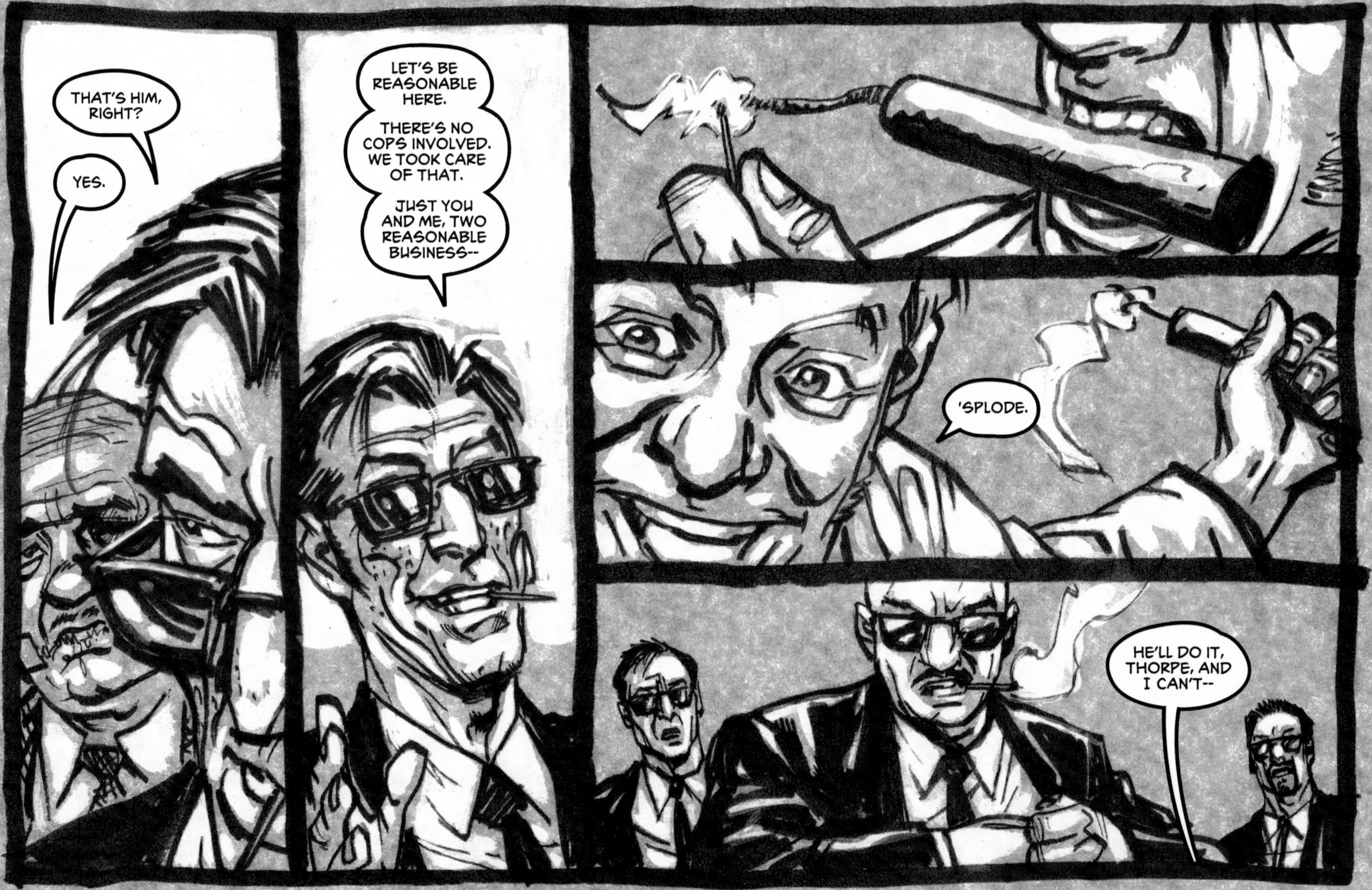
THAT'S HIM, RIGHT?
YES.
LET'S BE REASONABLE HERE.
THERE'S NO COPS INVOLVED. WE TOOK CARE OF THAT.
JUST YOU AND ME, TWO REASONABLE BUSINESS--
'SPLODE.
HE'LL DO IT, THORPE, AND I CAN'T--

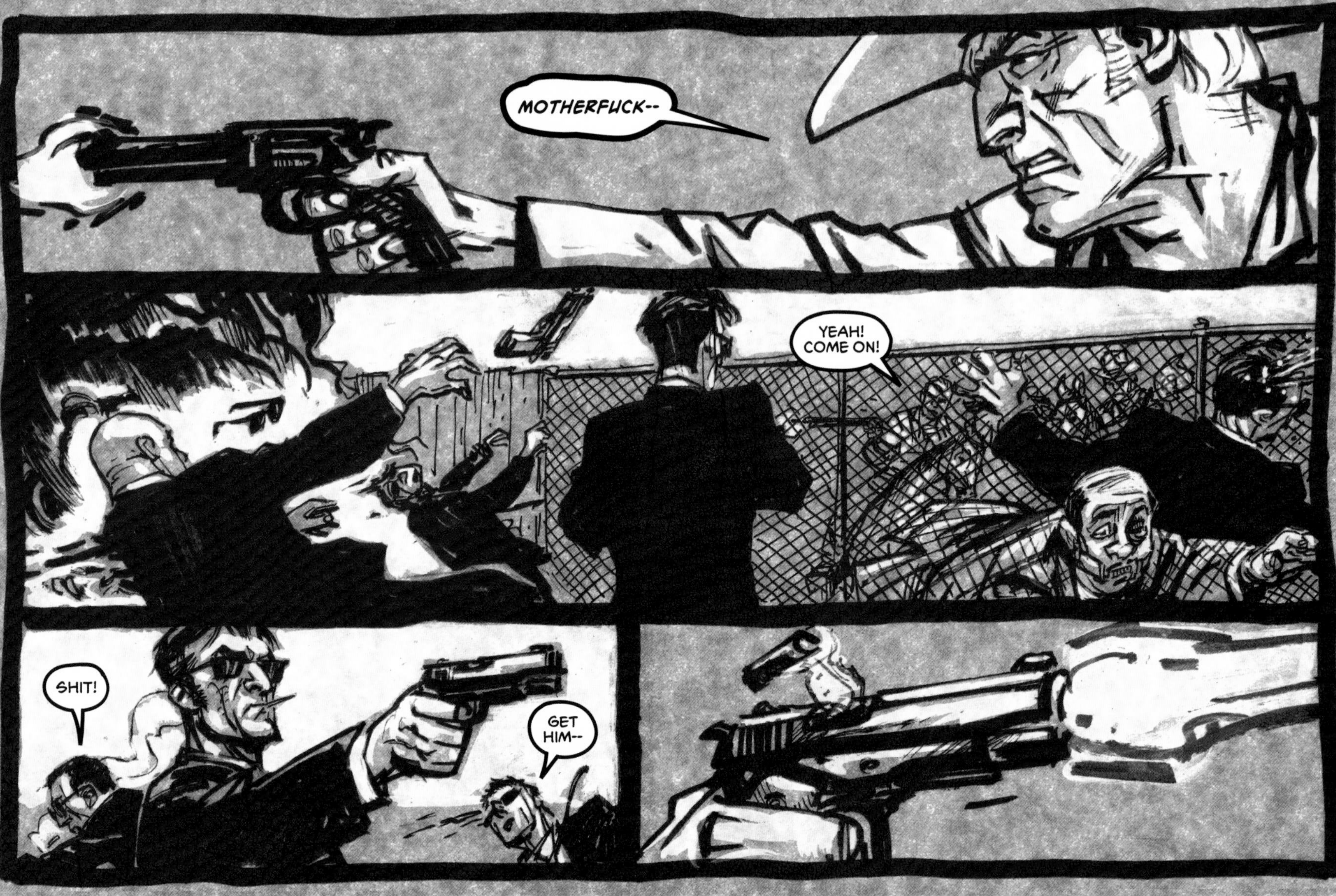
MOTHERFUCK--
YEAH! COME ON!
SHIT!
GET HIM--

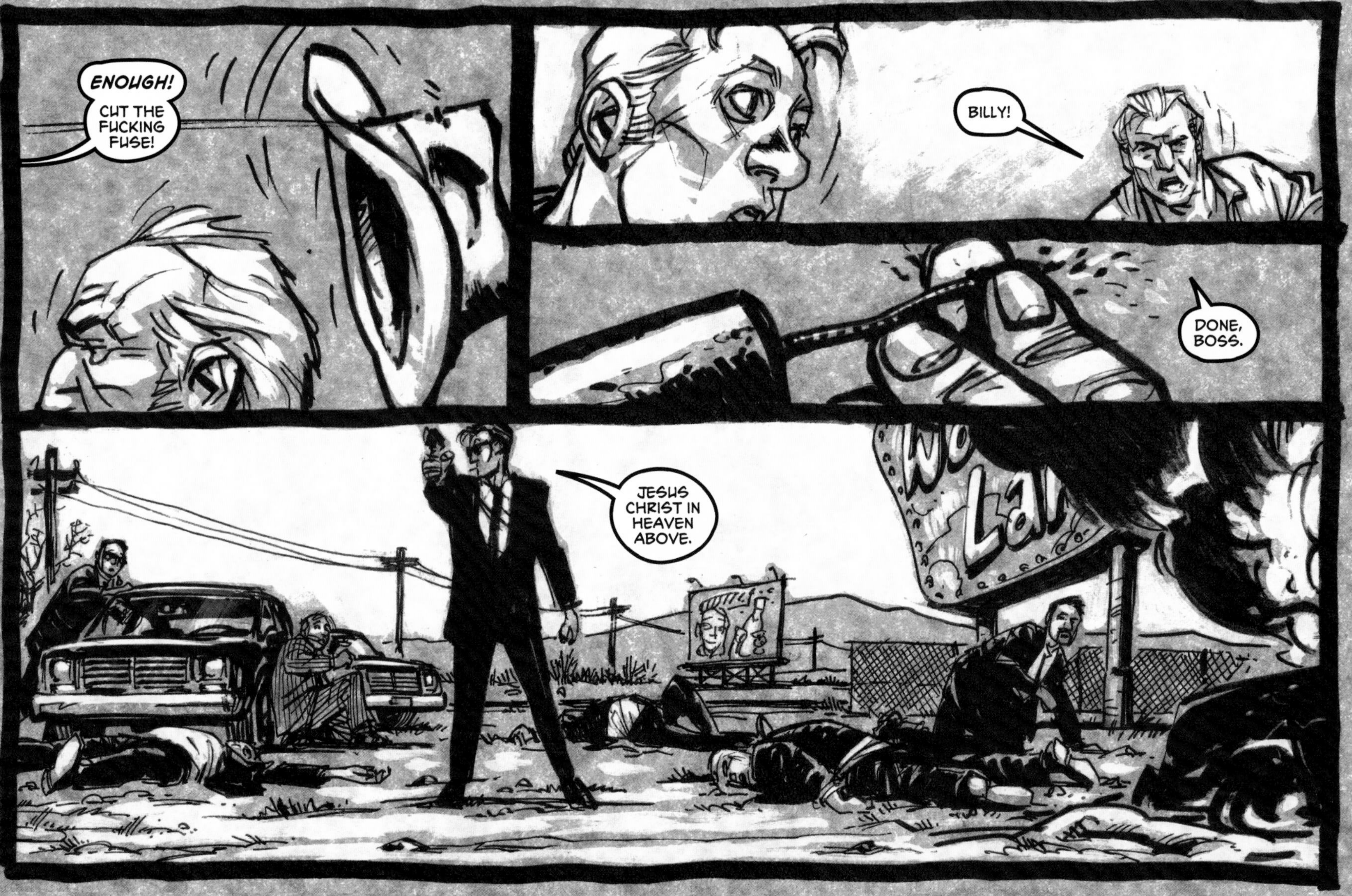
ENOUGH!
CUT THE FUCKING FUSE!
BILLY!
DONE, BOSS.
JESUS CHRIST IN HEAVEN ABOVE.

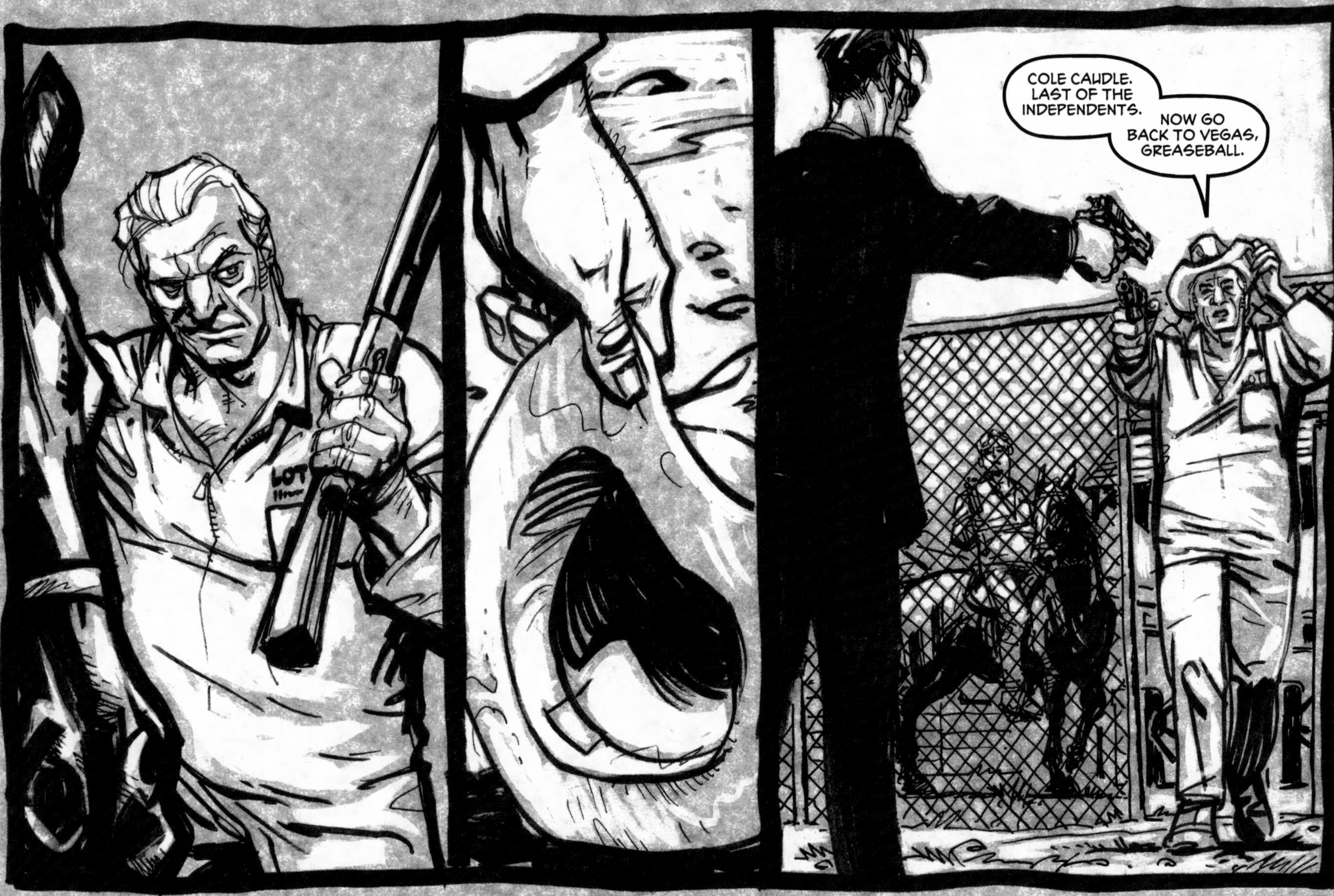
COLE CANDLE. LAST OF THE INDEPENDENTS.
NOW GO BACK TO VEGAS, GREASEBALL.

WE'LL MEET AGAIN, SUNSHINE.

LIKE HELL.

HEY, MISTER BANK MANAGER.

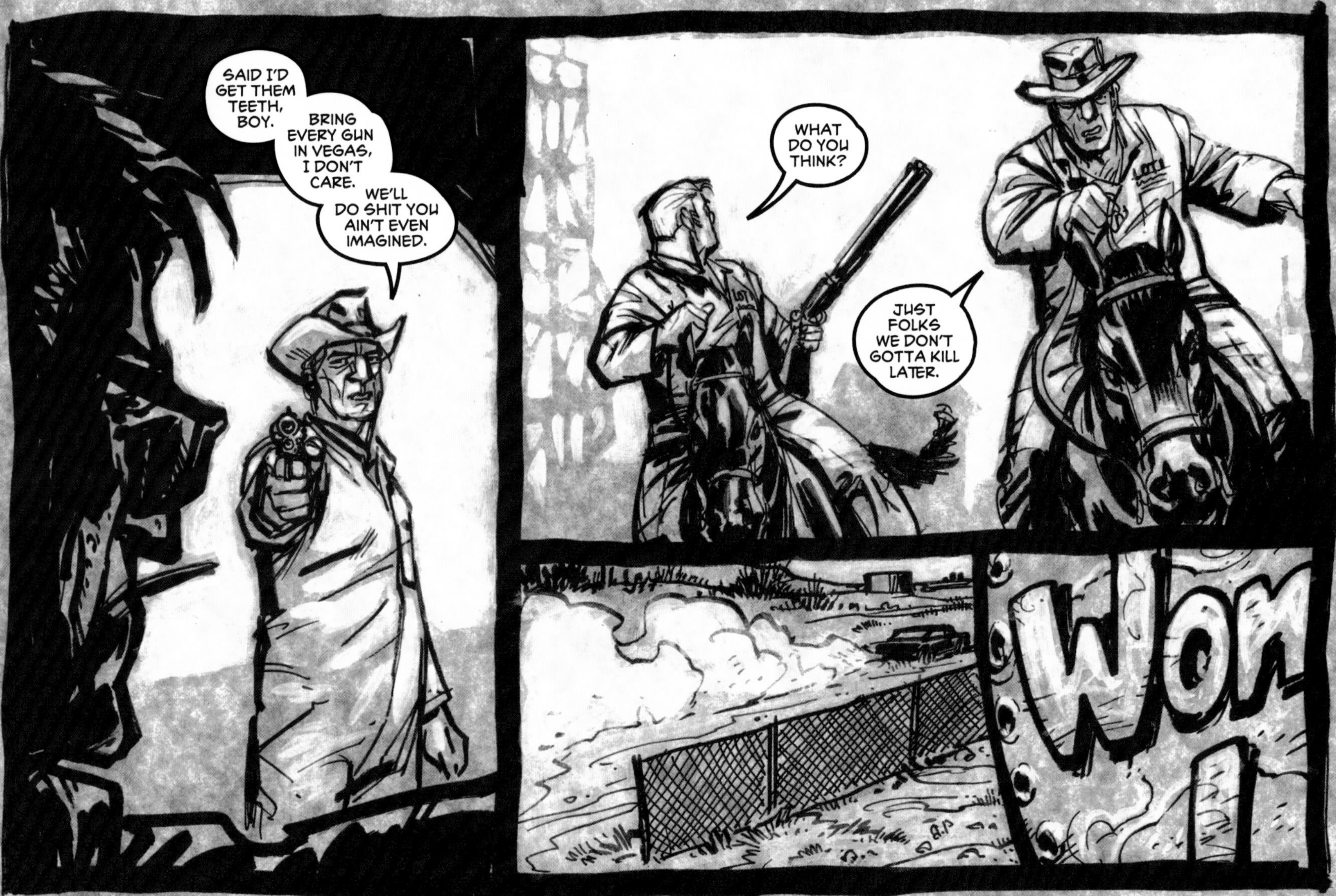
SAID I'D GET THEM TEETH, BOY.
BRING EVERY GUN IN VEGAS, I DON'T CARE.
WE'LL DO SHIT YOU AIN'T EVEN IMAGINED.
WHAT DO YOU THINK?
JUST FOLKS WE DON'T GOTTA KILL LATER.
WOM

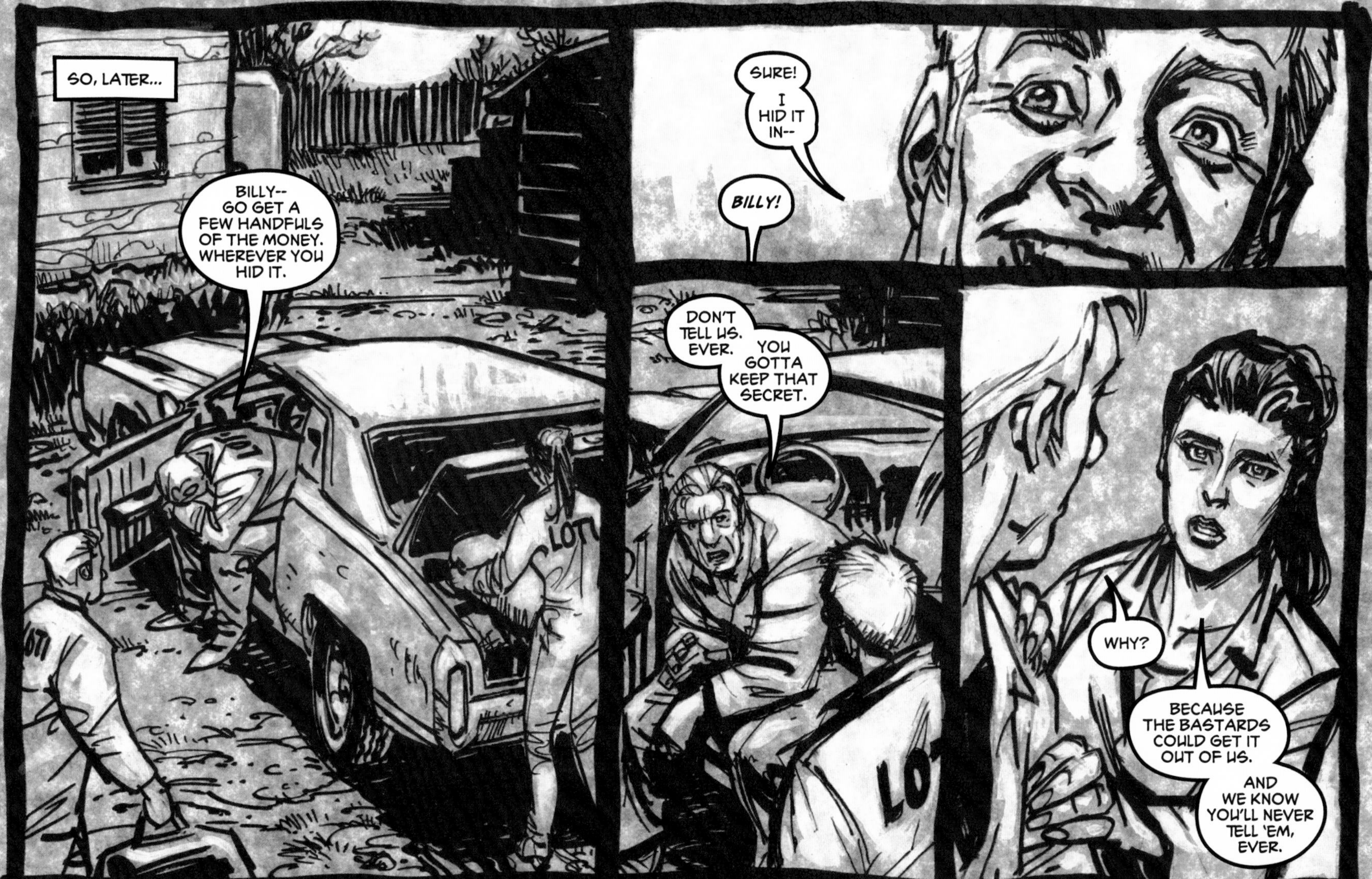
SO, LATER...
BILLY-- GO GET A FEW HANDFULS OF THE MONEY. WHEREVER YOU HID IT.
SURE!
I HID IT IN--
BILLY!
DON'T TELL US. EVER.
YOU GOTTA KEEP THAT SECRET.
LOT
WHY?
BECAUSE THE BASTARDS COULD GET IT OUT OF US.
AND WE KNOW YOU'LL NEVER TELL 'EM, EVER.

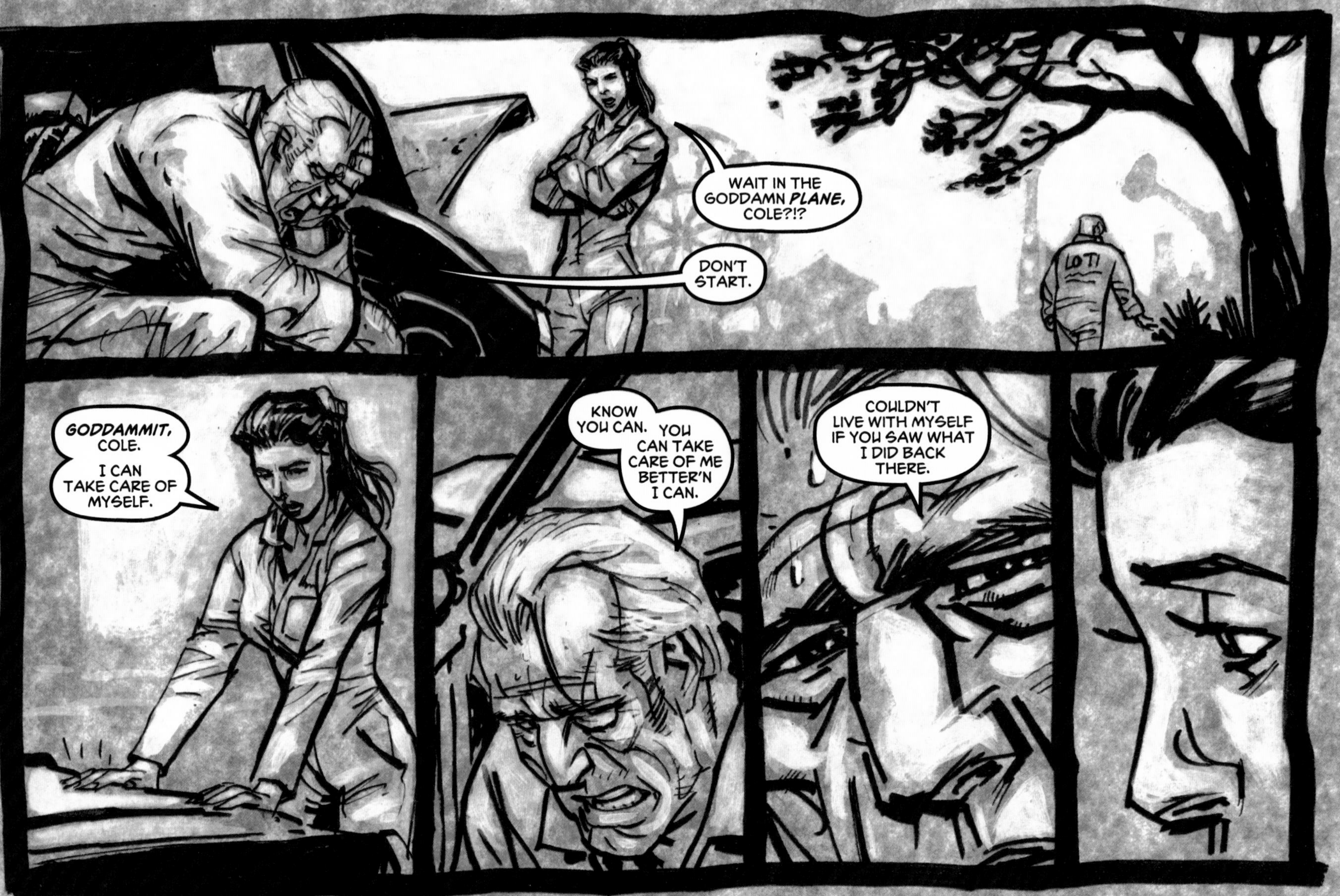
WAIT IN THE GODDAMN *PLANE*, COLE?!?
DON'T START.
LOTI
GODDAMMIT, COLE.
I CAN TAKE CARE OF MYSELF.
KNOW YOU CAN.
YOU CAN TAKE CARE OF ME BETTER'N I CAN.
COULDN'T LIVE WITH MYSELF IF YOU SAW WHAT I DID BACK THERE.

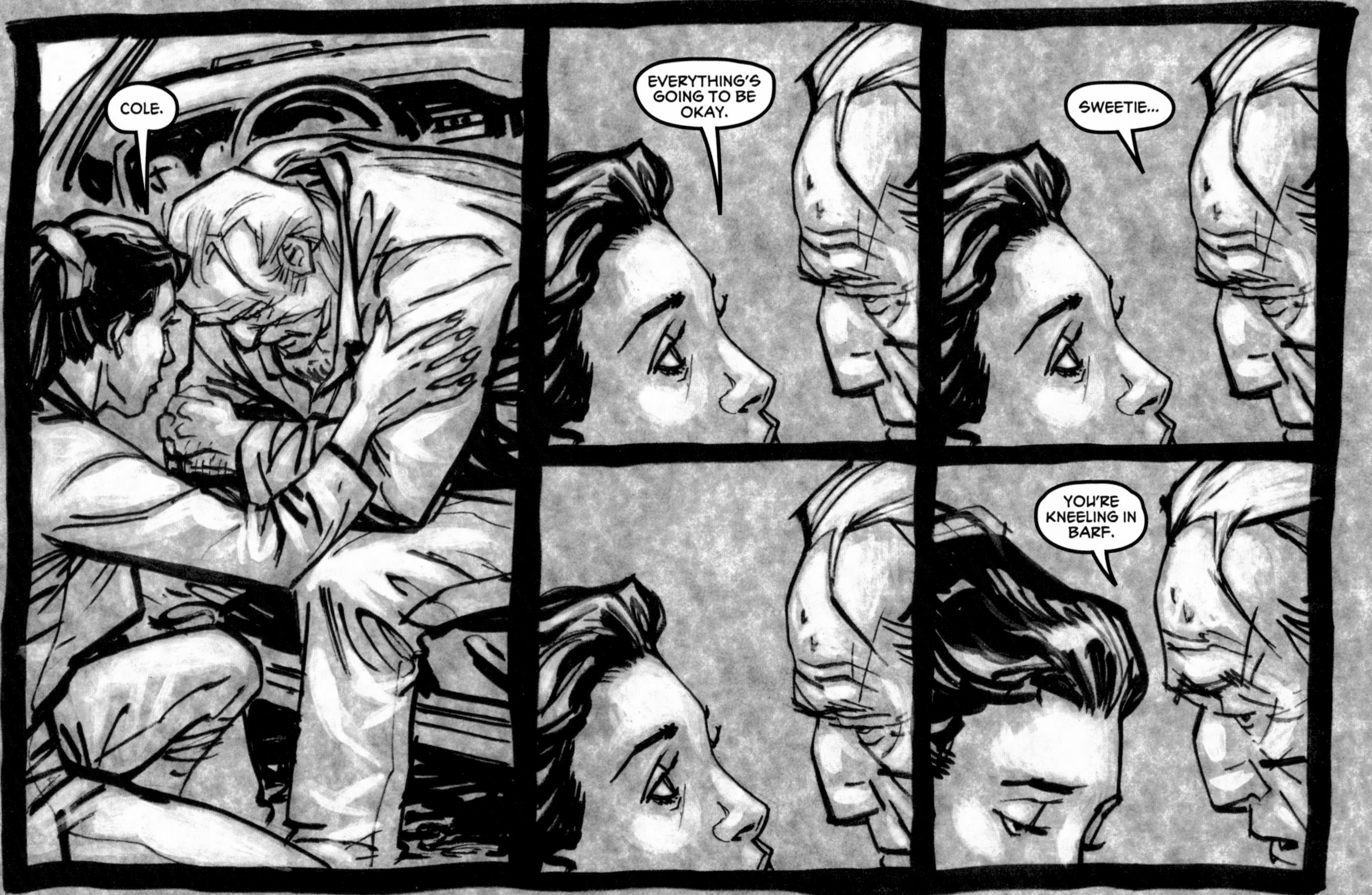
COLE.
EVERYTHING'S GOING TO BE OKAY.
SWEETIE...
YOU'RE KNEELING IN BARF.

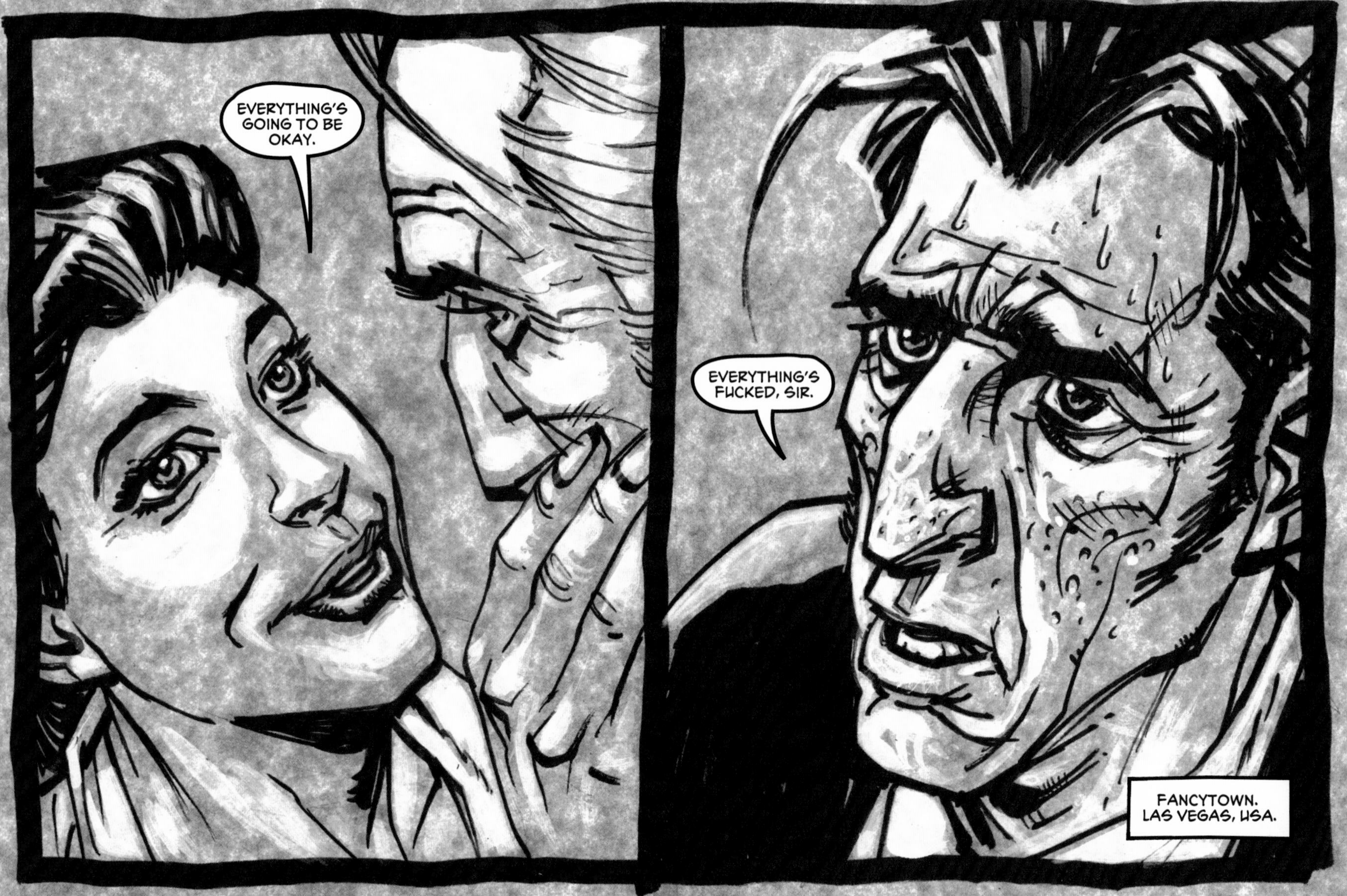
EVERYTHING'S GOING TO BE OKAY.
EVERYTHING'S FUCKED, SIR.
FANCYTOWN. LAS VEGAS, USA.

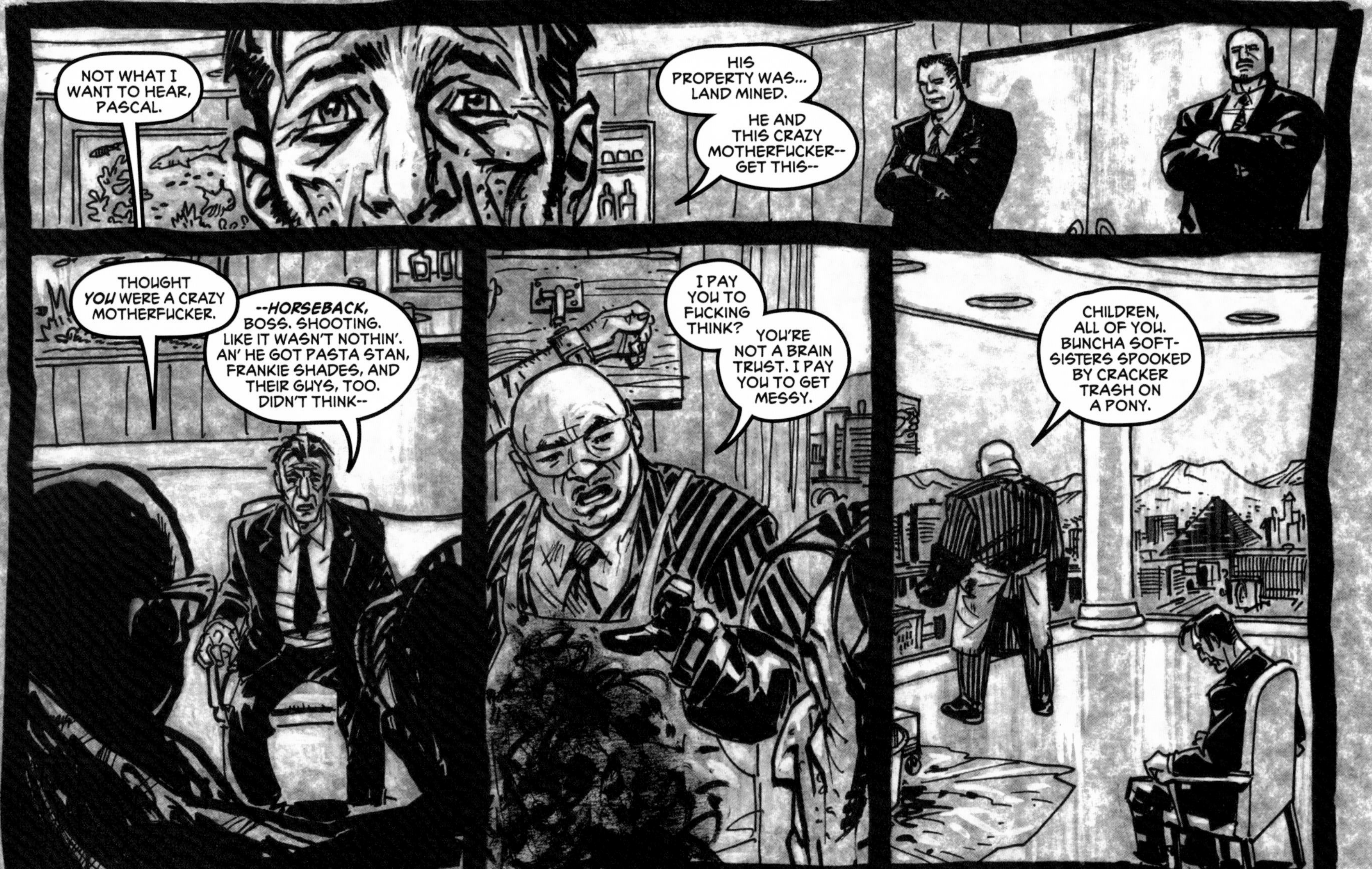
NOT WHAT I WANT TO HEAR, PASCAL.
HIS PROPERTY WAS... LAND MINED.
HE AND THIS CRAZY MOTHERFUCKER-- GET THIS--
--HORSEBACK, BOSS. SHOOTING. LIKE IT WASN'T NOTHIN'. AN' HE GOT PASTA STAN, FRANKIE SHADES, AND THEIR GUYS, TOO. DIDN'T THINK--
THOUGHT YOU WERE A CRAZY MOTHERFUCKER.
I PAY YOU TO FUCKING THINK?
YOU'RE NOT A BRAIN TRUST. I PAY YOU TO GET MESSY.
CHILDREN, ALL OF YOU. BUNCHA SOFT-SISTERS SPOOKED BY CRACKER TRASH ON A PONY.

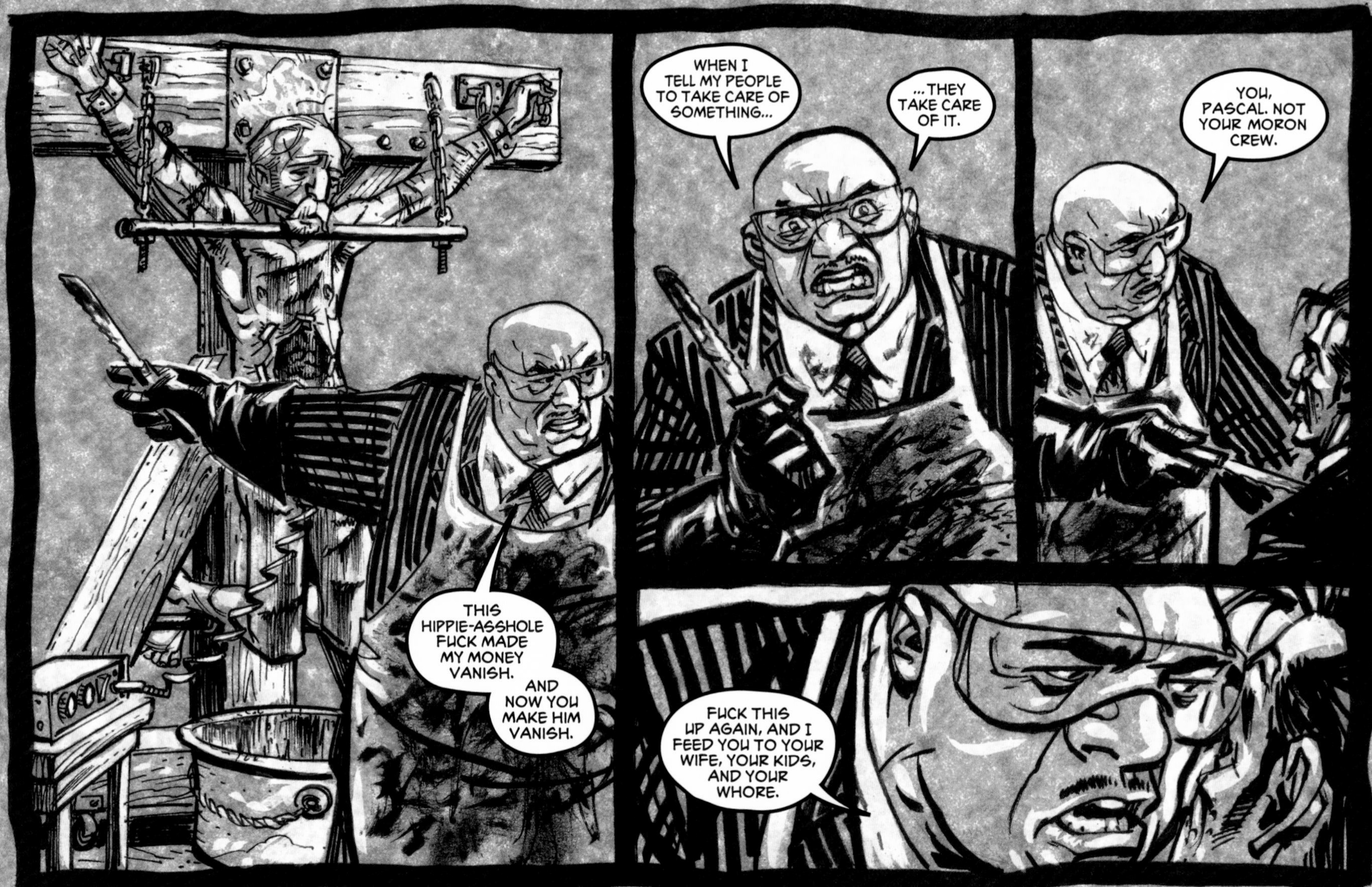
THIS HIPPIE-ASSHOLE FUCK MADE MY MONEY VANISH.
AND NOW YOU MAKE HIM VANISH.
WHEN I TELL MY PEOPLE TO TAKE CARE OF SOMETHING...
...THEY TAKE CARE OF IT.
YOU, PASCAL. NOT YOUR MORON CREW.
FUCK THIS UP AGAIN, AND I FEED YOU TO YOUR WIFE, YOUR KIDS, AND YOUR WHORE.

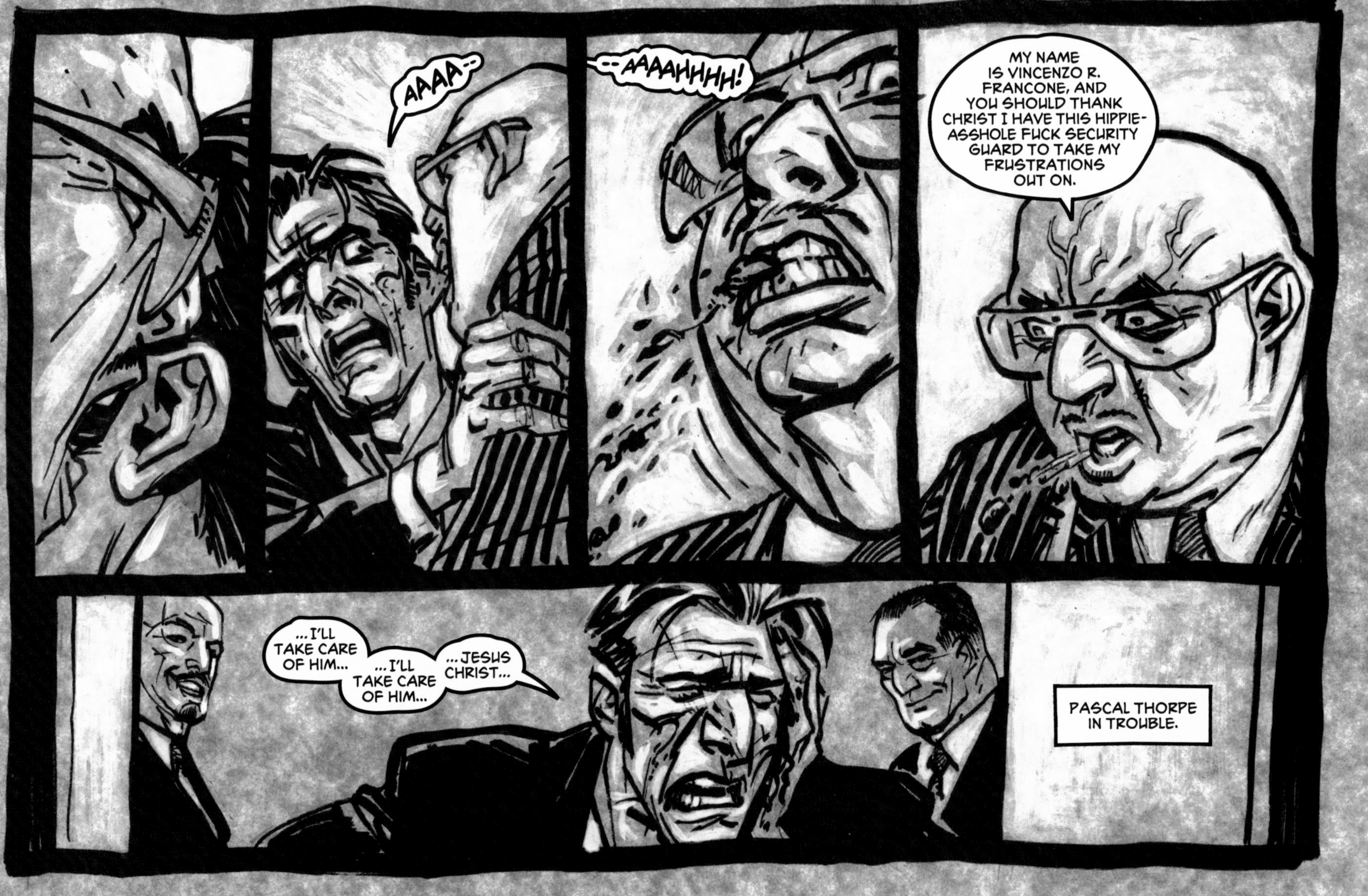
AAAA--
--AAAAHHHH!
MY NAME IS VINCENZO R. FRANCONE, AND YOU SHOULD THANK CHRIST I HAVE THIS HIPPIE-ASSHOLE FUCK SECURITY GUARD TO TAKE MY FRUSTRATIONS OUT ON.
...I'LL TAKE CARE OF HIM...
...I'LL TAKE CARE OF HIM...
...JESUS CHRIST...
PASCAL THORPE IN TROUBLE.

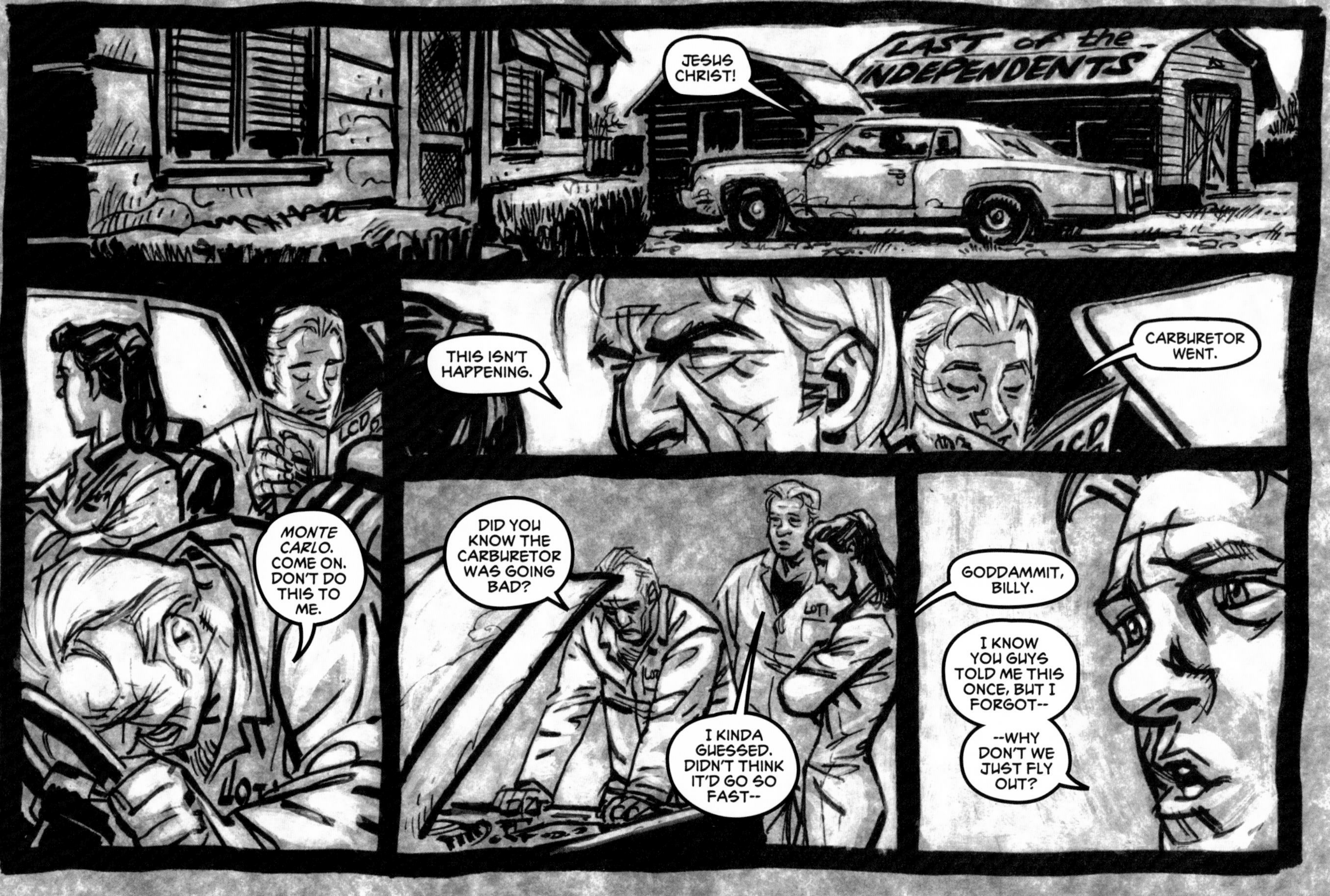
LAST of the INDEPENDENTS
JESUS CHRIST!
THIS ISN'T HAPPENING.
CARBURETOR WENT.
MONTE CARLO. COME ON. DON'T DO THIS TO ME.
DID YOU KNOW THE CARBURETOR WAS GOING BAD?
I KINDA GUESSED. DIDN'T THINK IT'D GO SO FAST--
GODDAMMIT, BILLY.
I KNOW YOU GUYS TOLD ME THIS ONCE, BUT I FORGOT--
--WHY DON'T WE JUST FLY OUT?

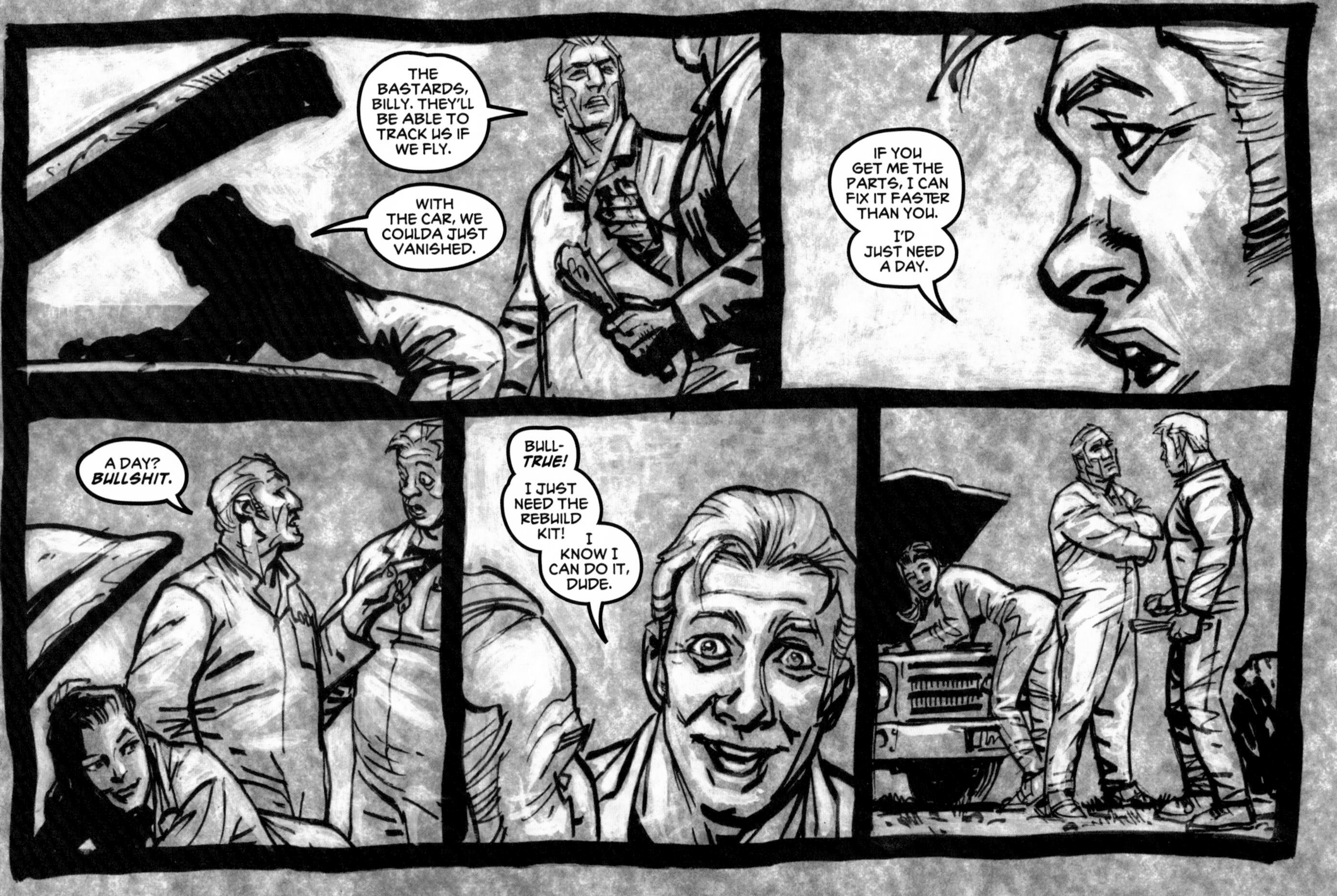
THE BASTARDS, BILLY. THEY'LL BE ABLE TO TRACK US IF WE FLY.
WITH THE CAR, WE COULDA JUST VANISHED.
IF YOU GET ME THE PARTS, I CAN FIX IT FASTER THAN YOU.
I'D JUST NEED A DAY.
A DAY? *BULLSHIT.*
BULL-*TRUE!*
I JUST NEED THE REBUILD KIT!
I KNOW I CAN DO IT, DUDE.

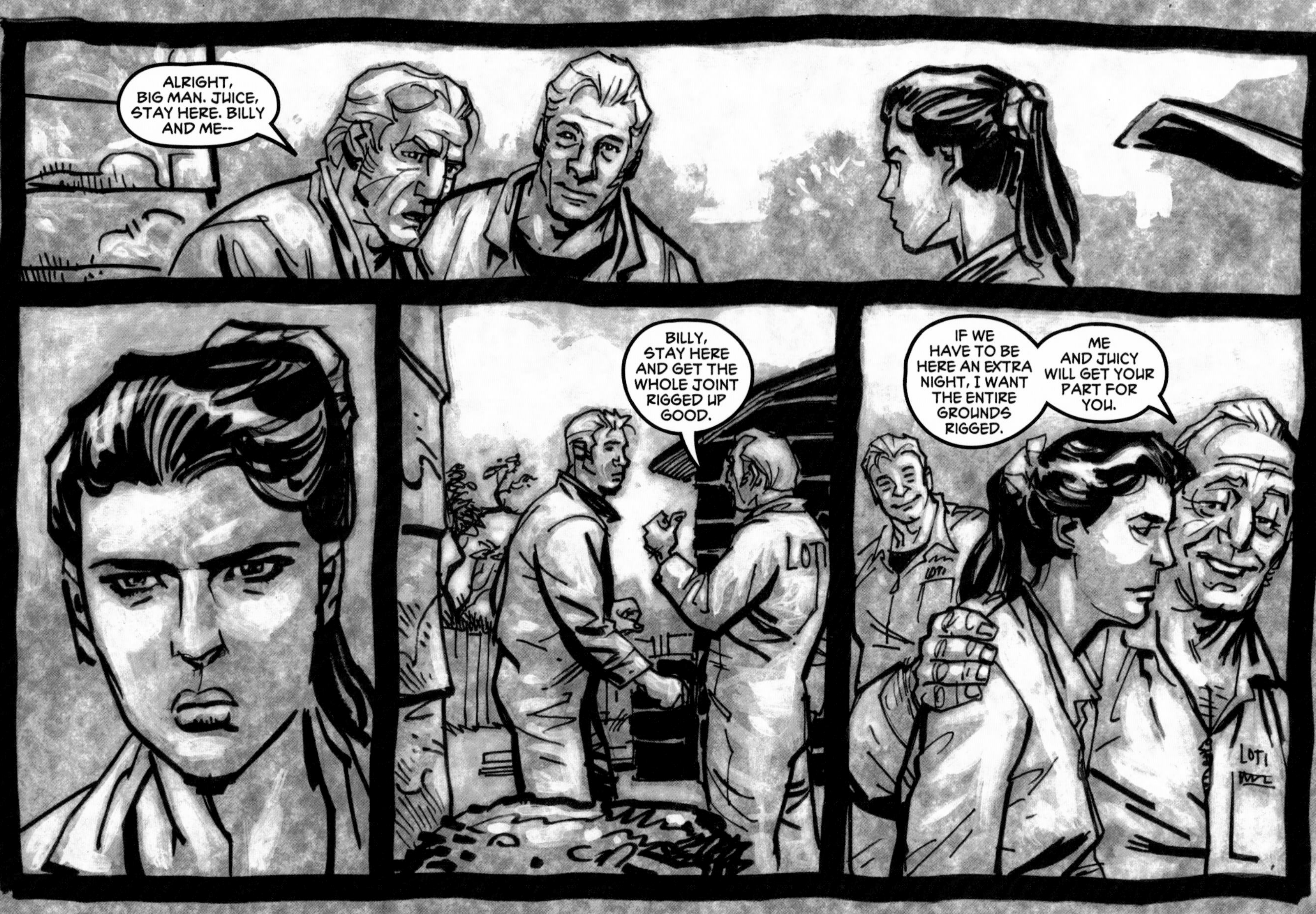
ALRIGHT, BIG MAN. JUICE, STAY HERE. BILLY AND ME--
BILLY, STAY HERE AND GET THE WHOLE JOINT RIGGED UP GOOD.
IF WE HAVE TO BE HERE AN EXTRA NIGHT, I WANT THE ENTIRE GROUNDS RIGGED.
ME AND JUICY WILL GET YOUR PART FOR YOU.
LOTI
LOTI
LOTI

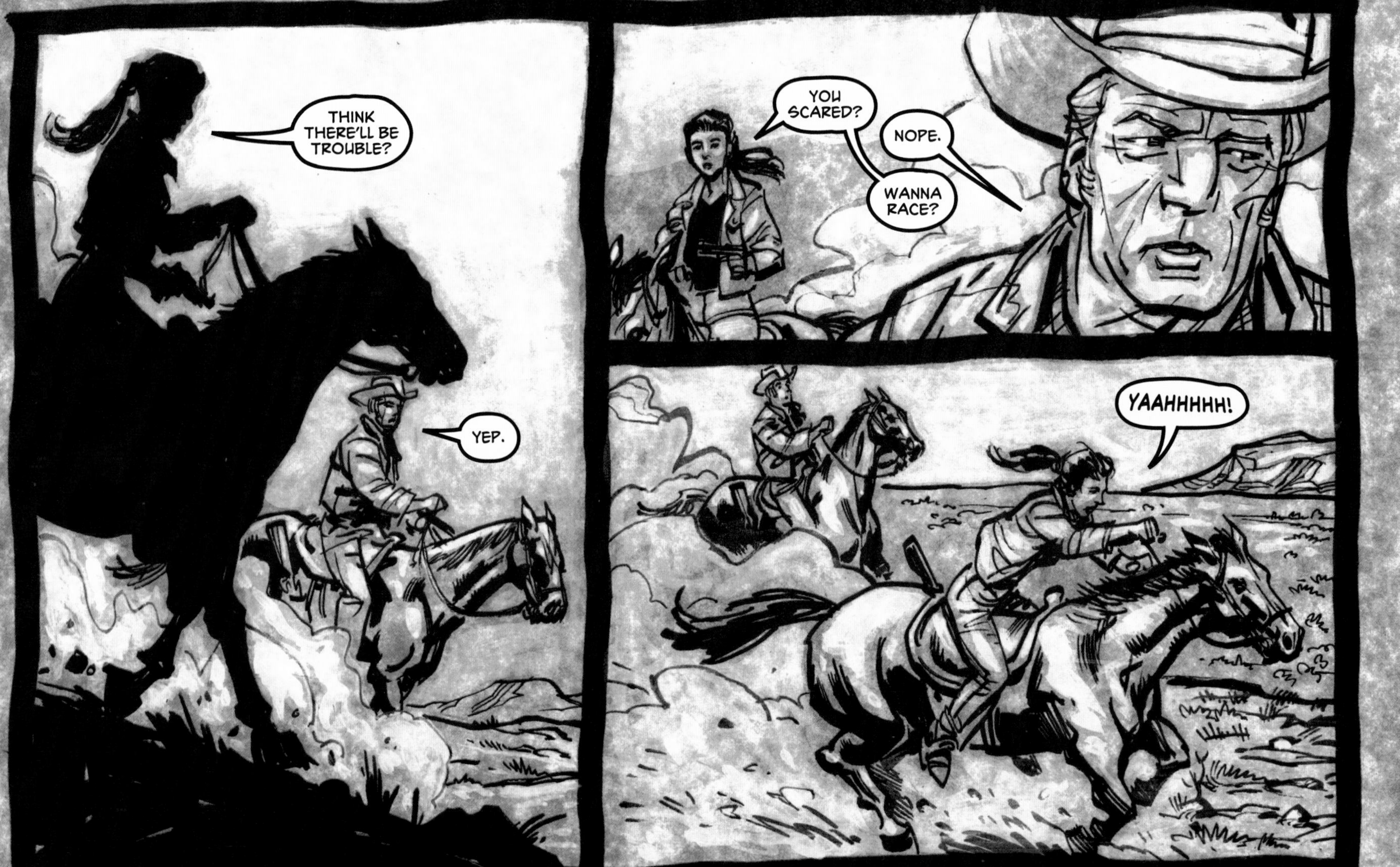
THINK THERE'LL BE TROUBLE?
YEP.
YOU SCARED?
NOPE.
WANNA RACE?
YAAHHHHH!

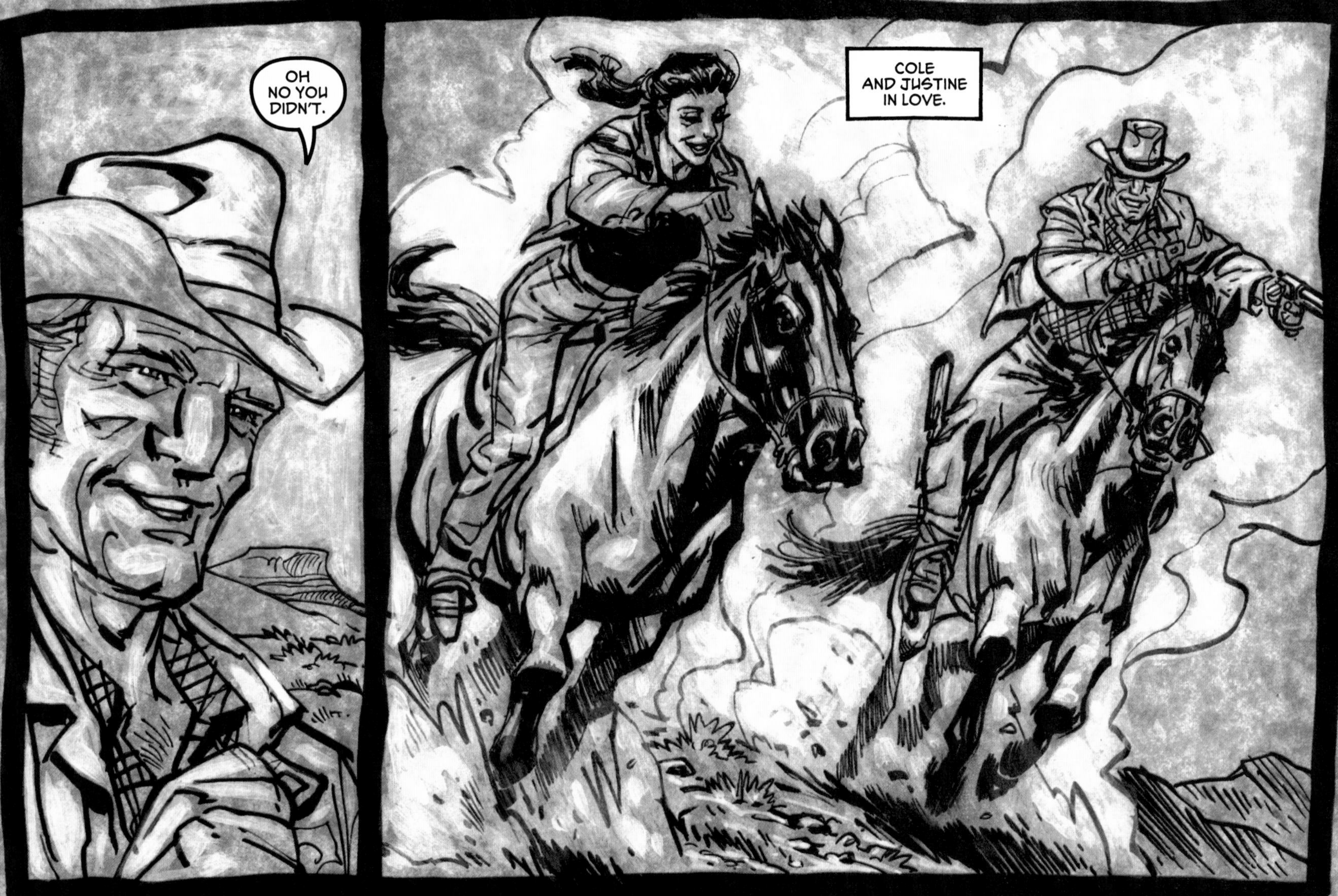
OH NO YOU DIDN'T.
COLE AND JUSTINE IN LOVE.

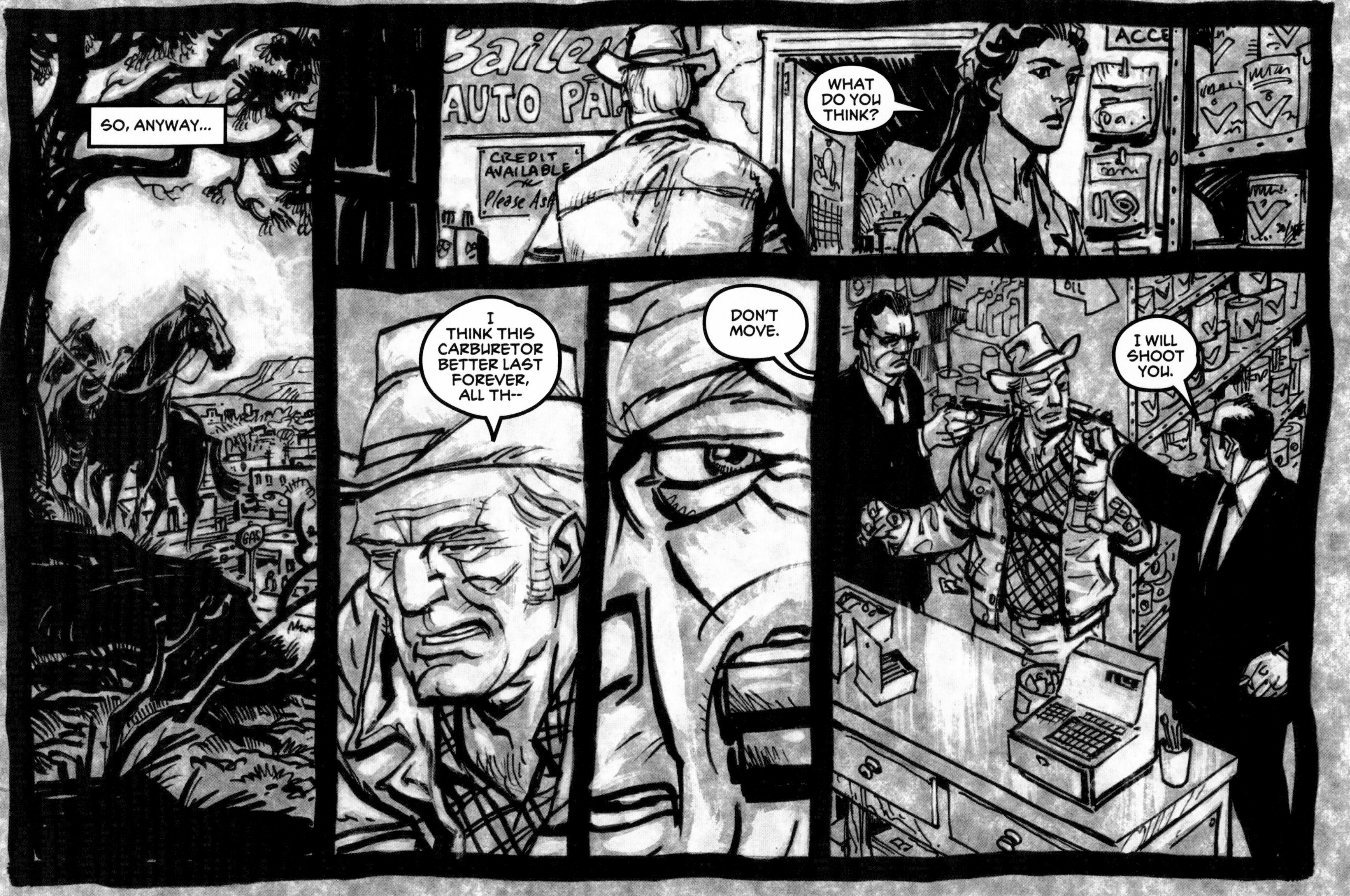
SO, ANYWAY...
Bailey AUTO PA
CREDIT AVAILABLE Please Ask
WHAT DO YOU THINK?
I THINK THIS CARBURETOR BETTER LAST FOREVER, ALL TH--
DON'T MOVE.
I WILL SHOOT YOU.

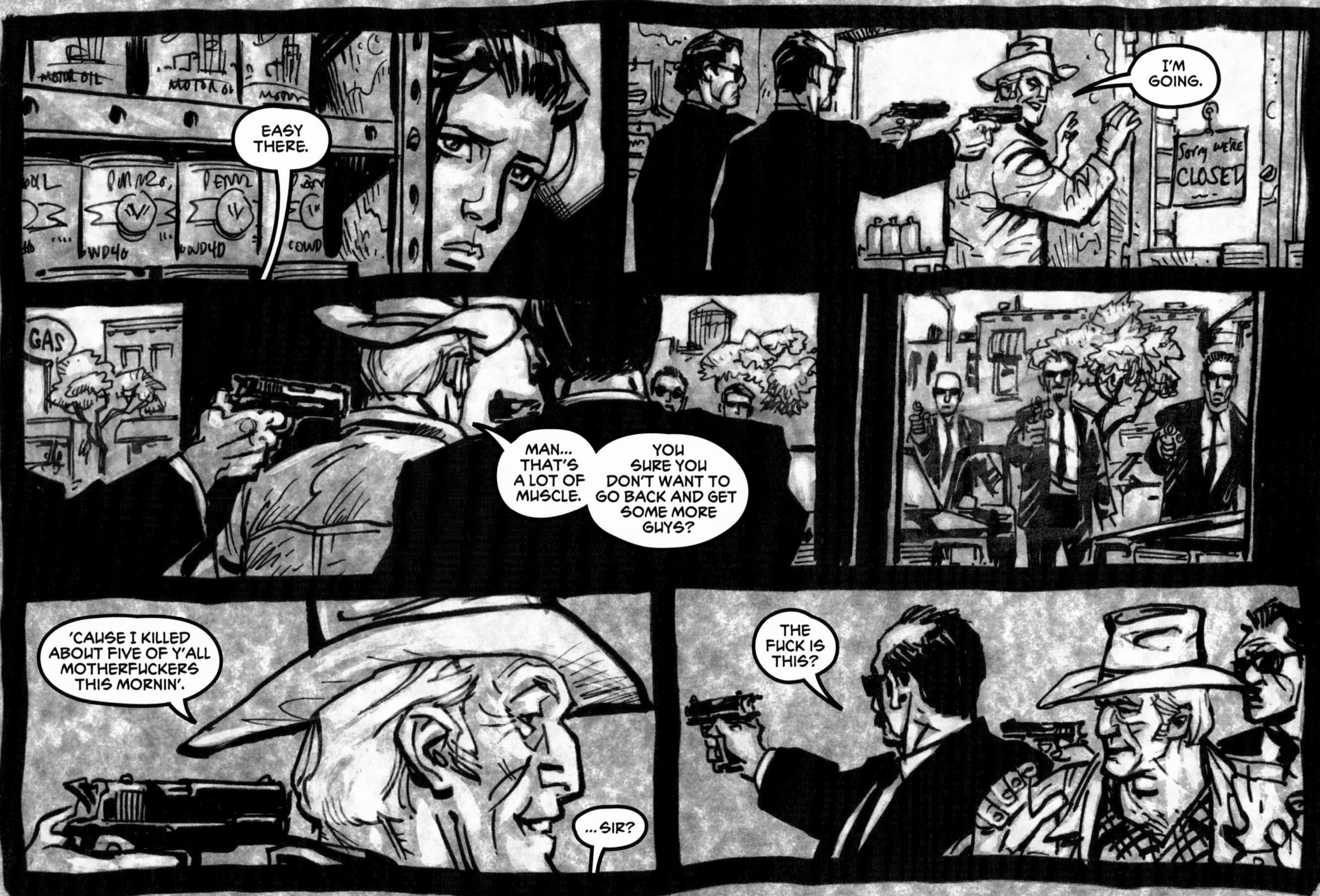
EASY THERE.
I'M GOING.
Sorry we're CLOSED
GAS
MAN... THAT'S A LOT OF MUSCLE.
YOU SURE YOU DON'T WANT TO GO BACK AND GET SOME MORE GUYS?
'CAUSE I KILLED ABOUT FIVE OF Y'ALL MOTHERFUCKERS THIS MORNIN'.
...SIR?
THE FUCK IS THIS?

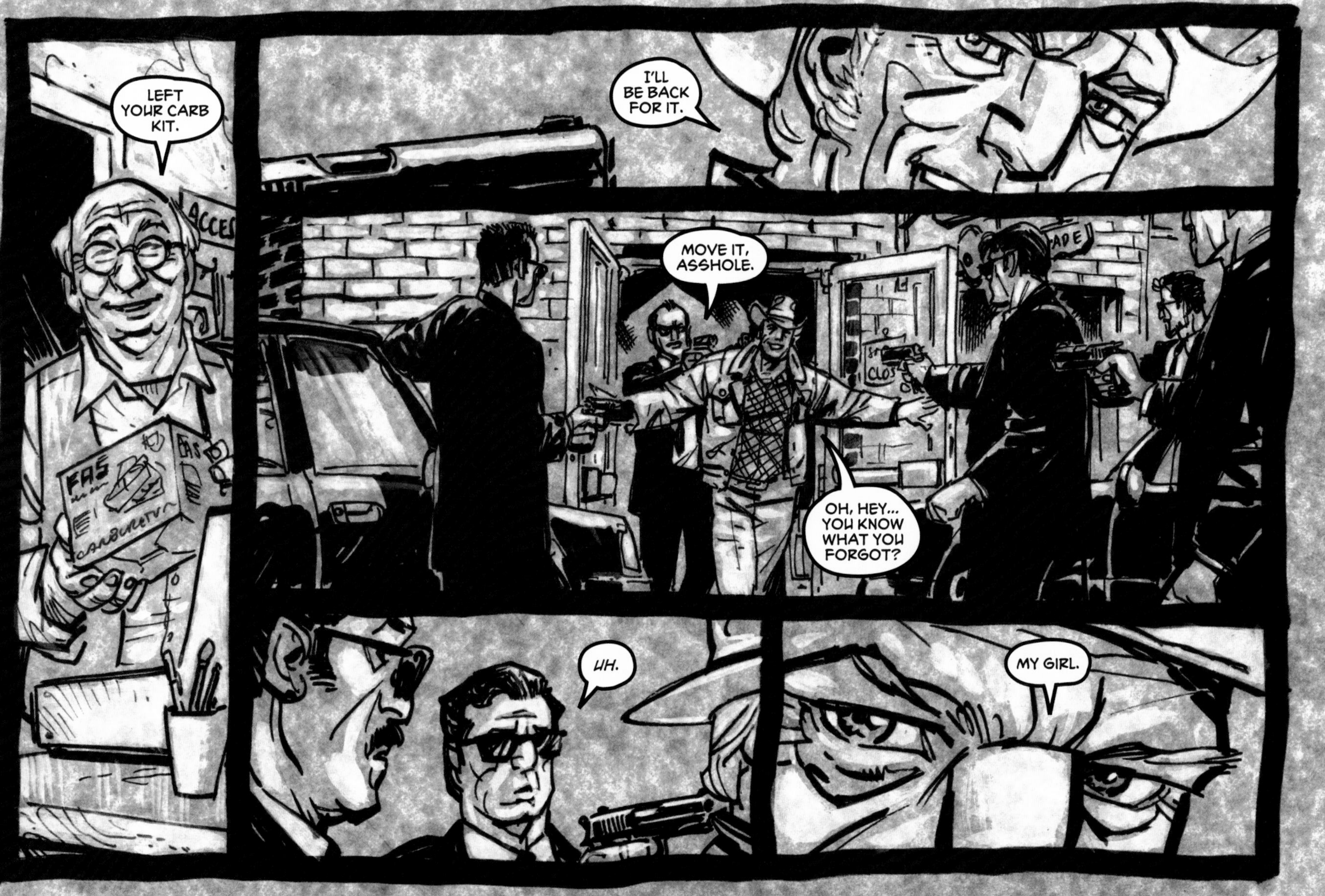
LEFT YOUR CARB KIT.
I'LL BE BACK FOR IT.
MOVE IT, ASSHOLE.
OH, HEY... YOU KNOW WHAT YOU FORGOT?
UH.
MY GIRL.

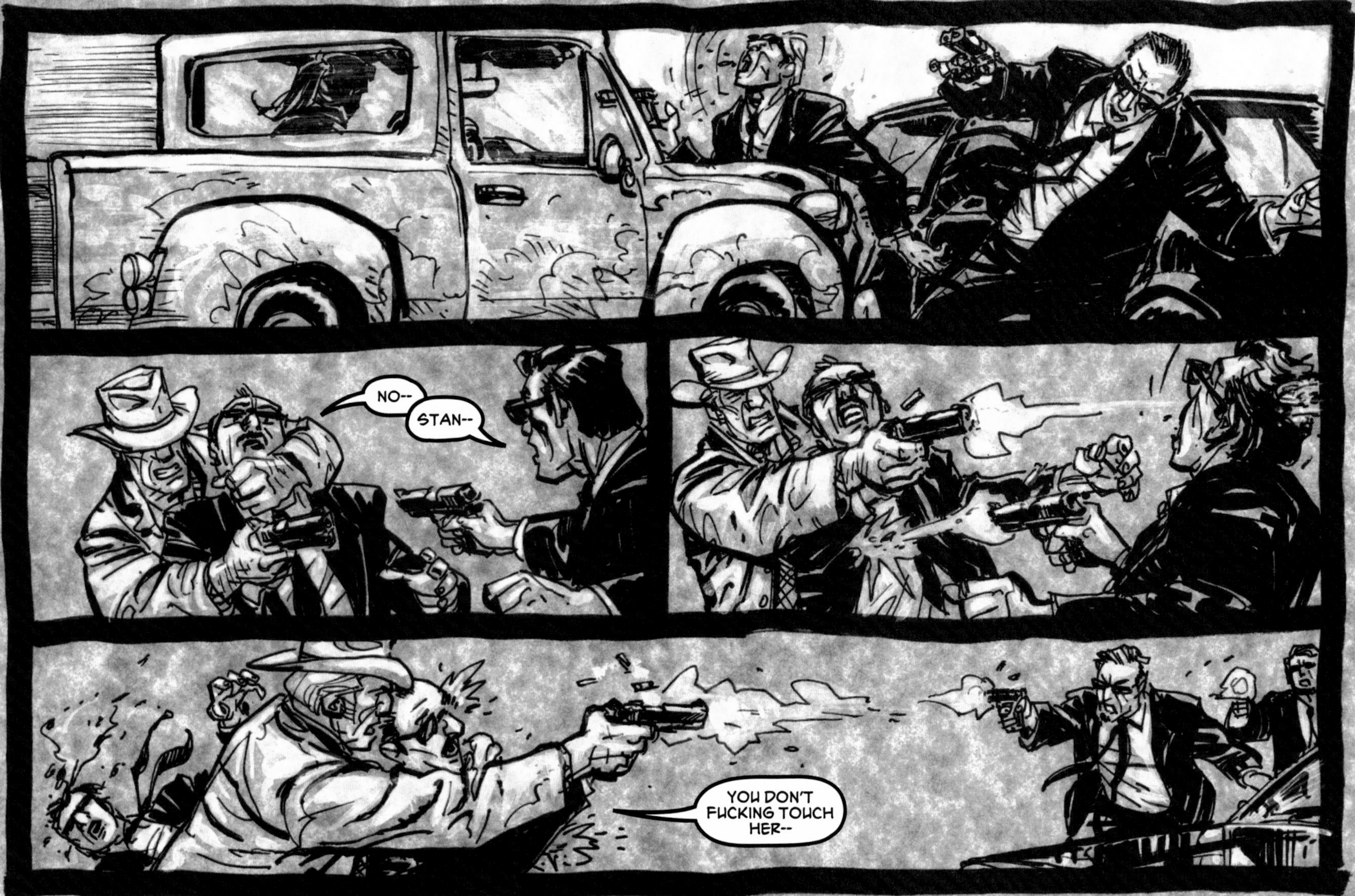
NO--
STAN--
YOU DON'T FUCKING TOUCH HER--

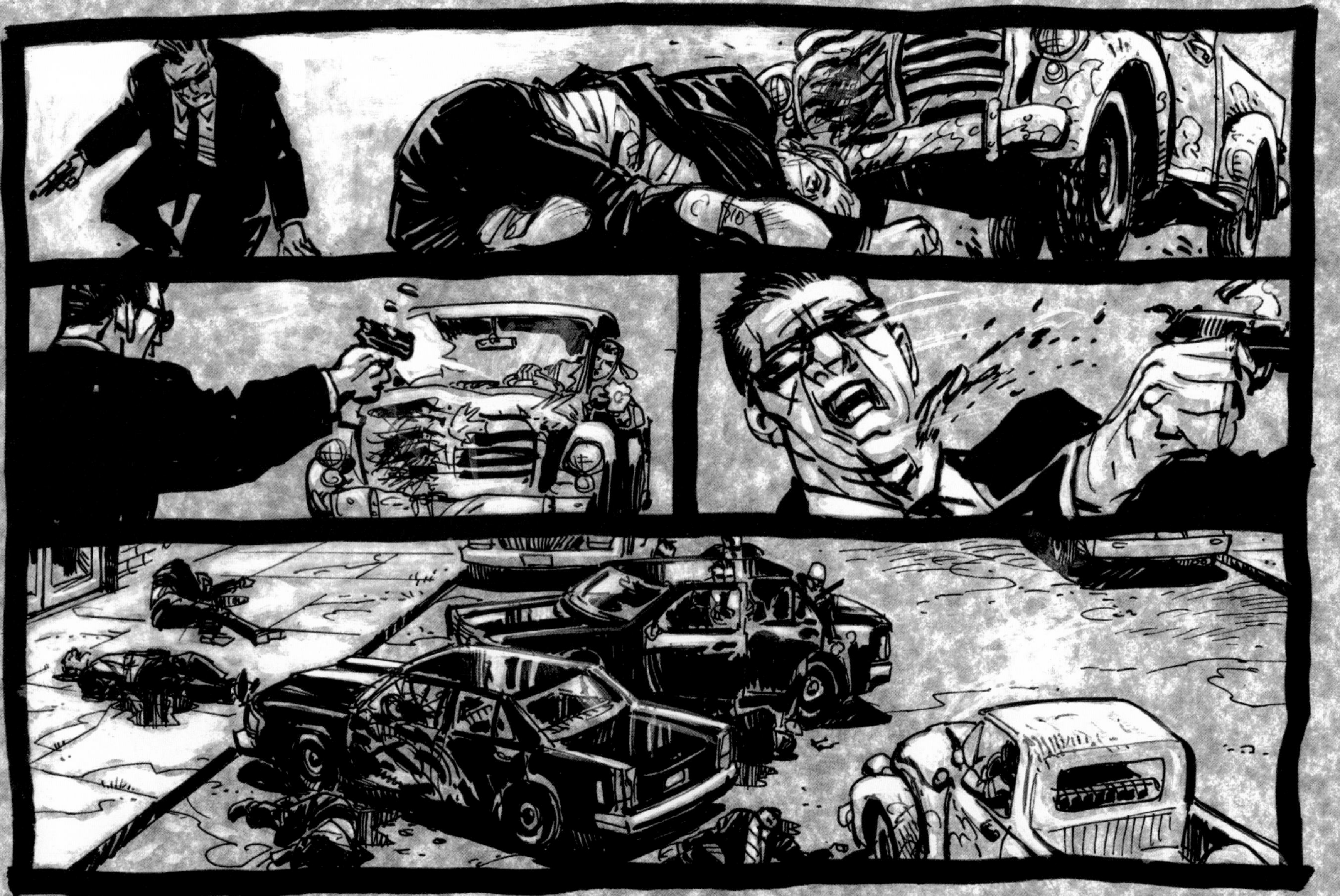

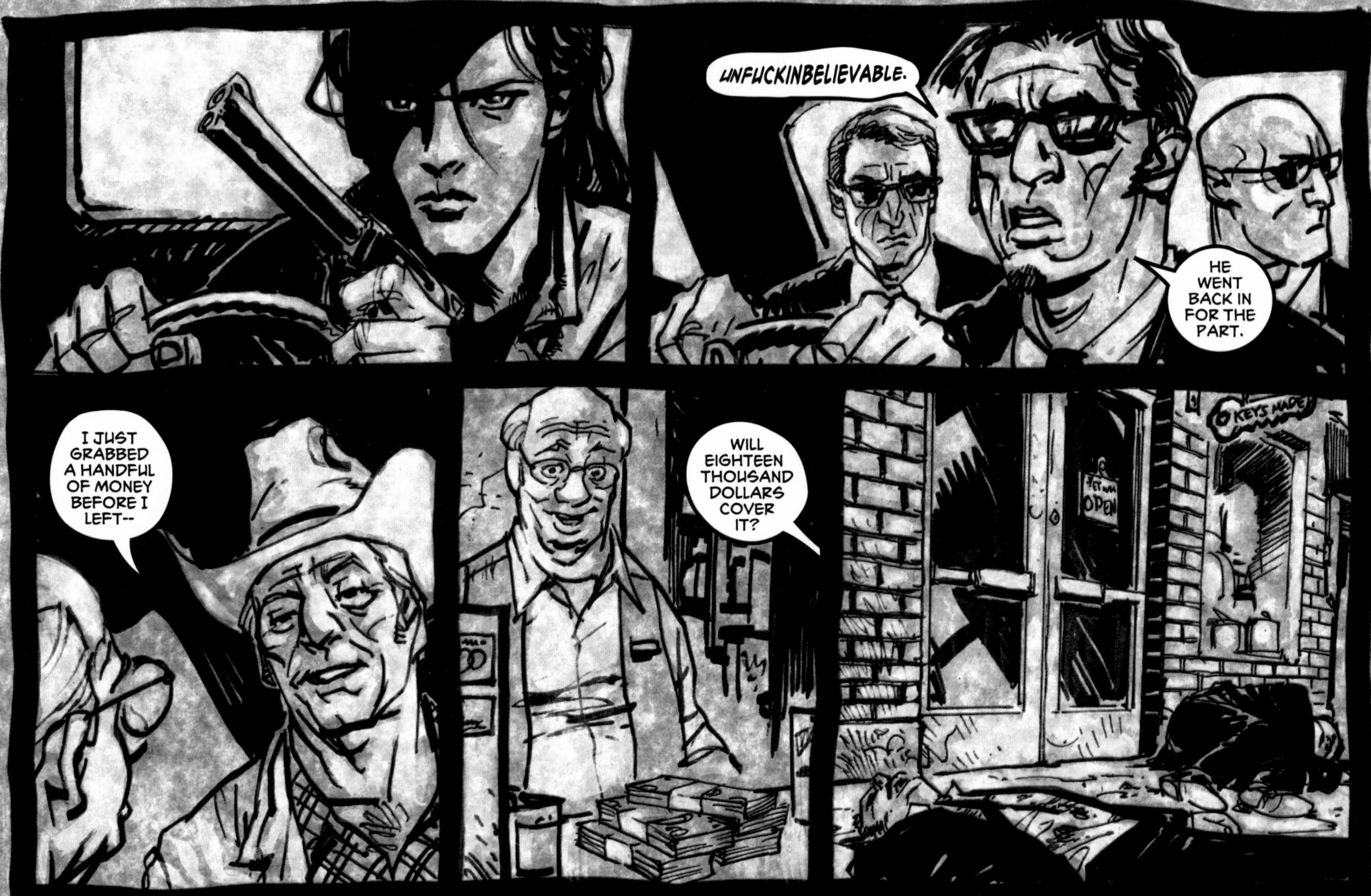
UNFUCKINBELIEVABLE.
HE WENT BACK IN FOR THE PART.
I JUST GRABBED A HANDFUL OF MONEY BEFORE I LEFT--
WILL EIGHTEEN THOUSAND DOLLARS COVER IT?
KEYS MADE
OPEN

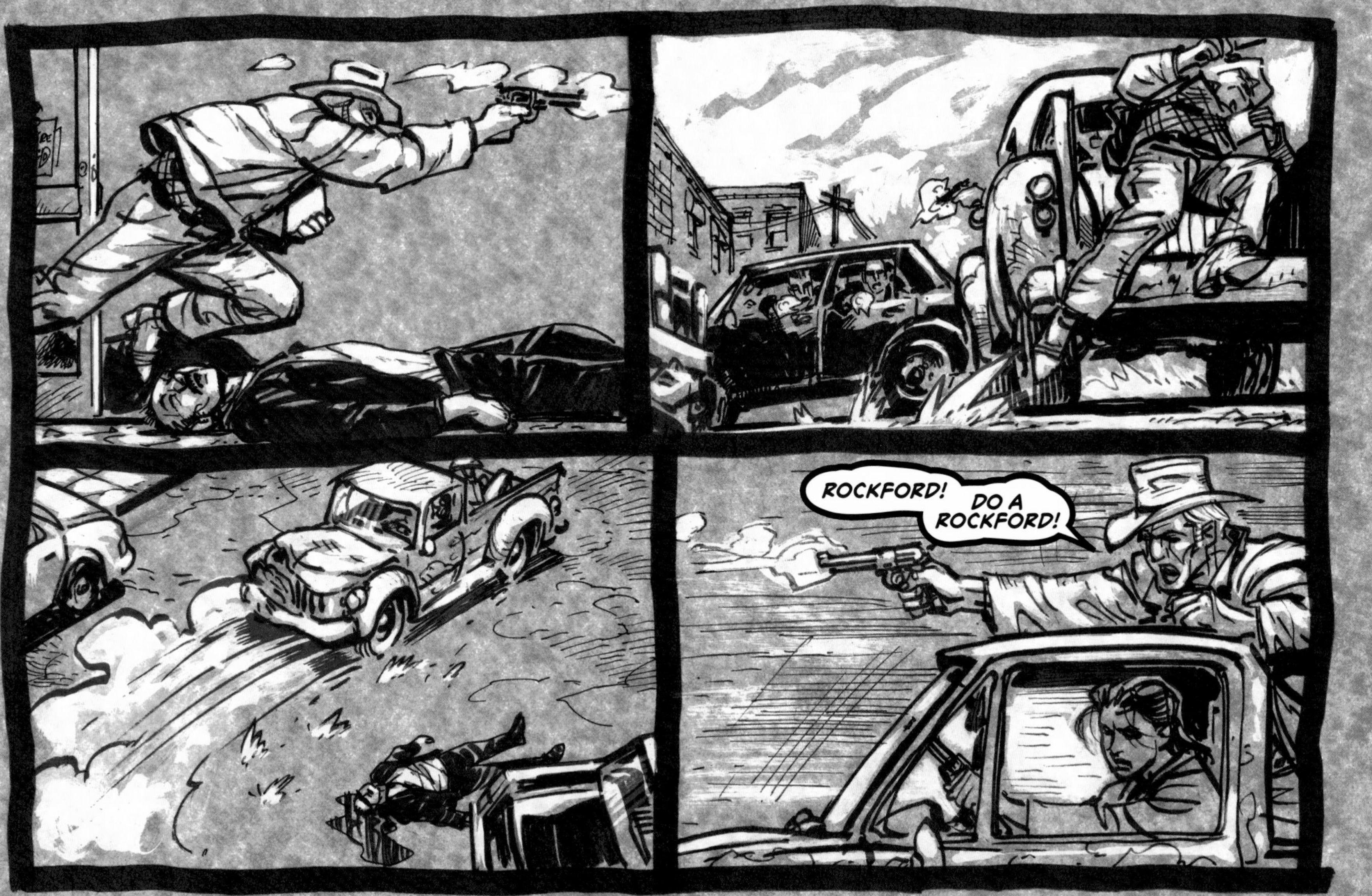
ROCKFORD!
DO A ROCKFORD!

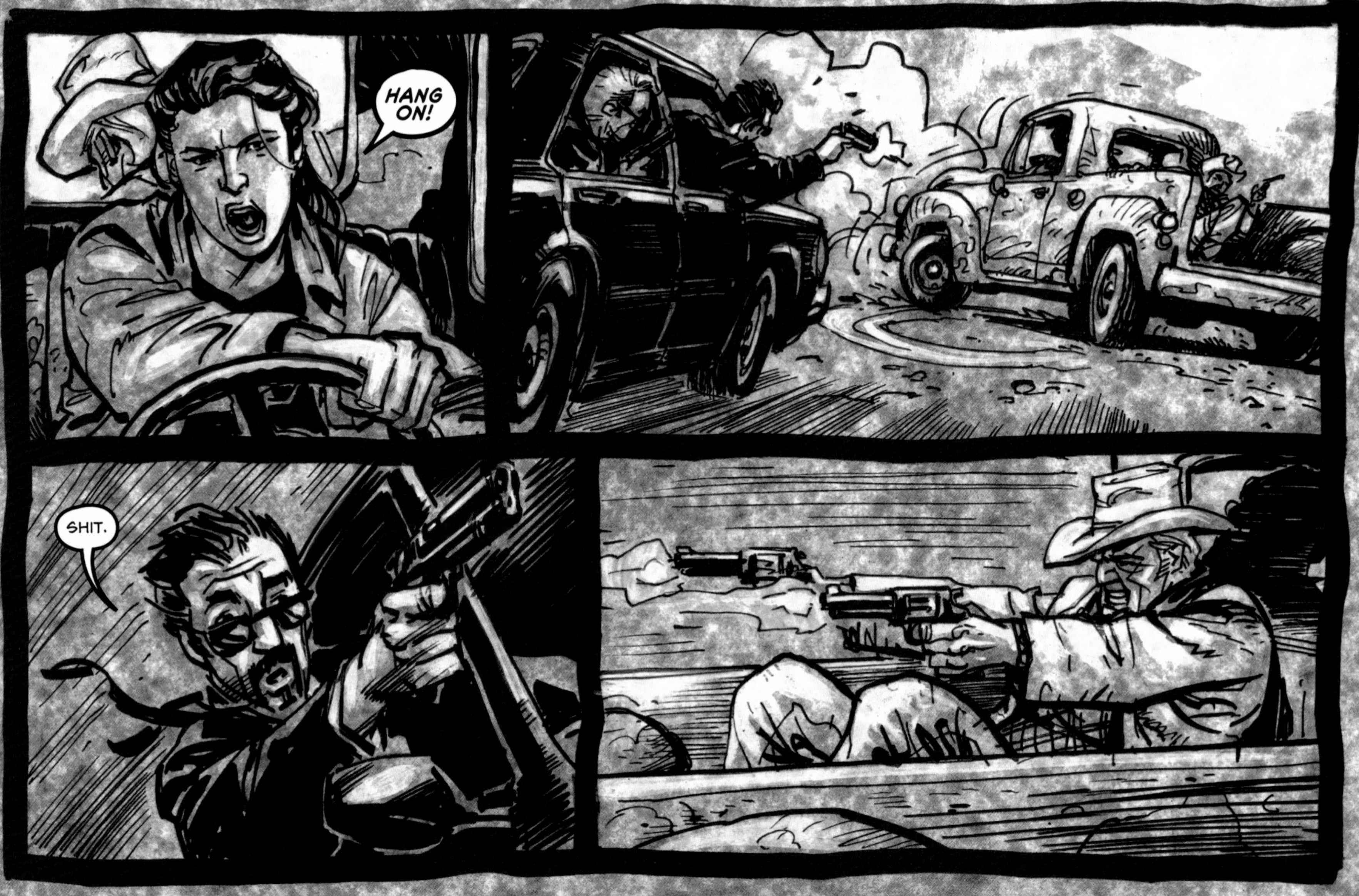
HANG ON!
SHIT.

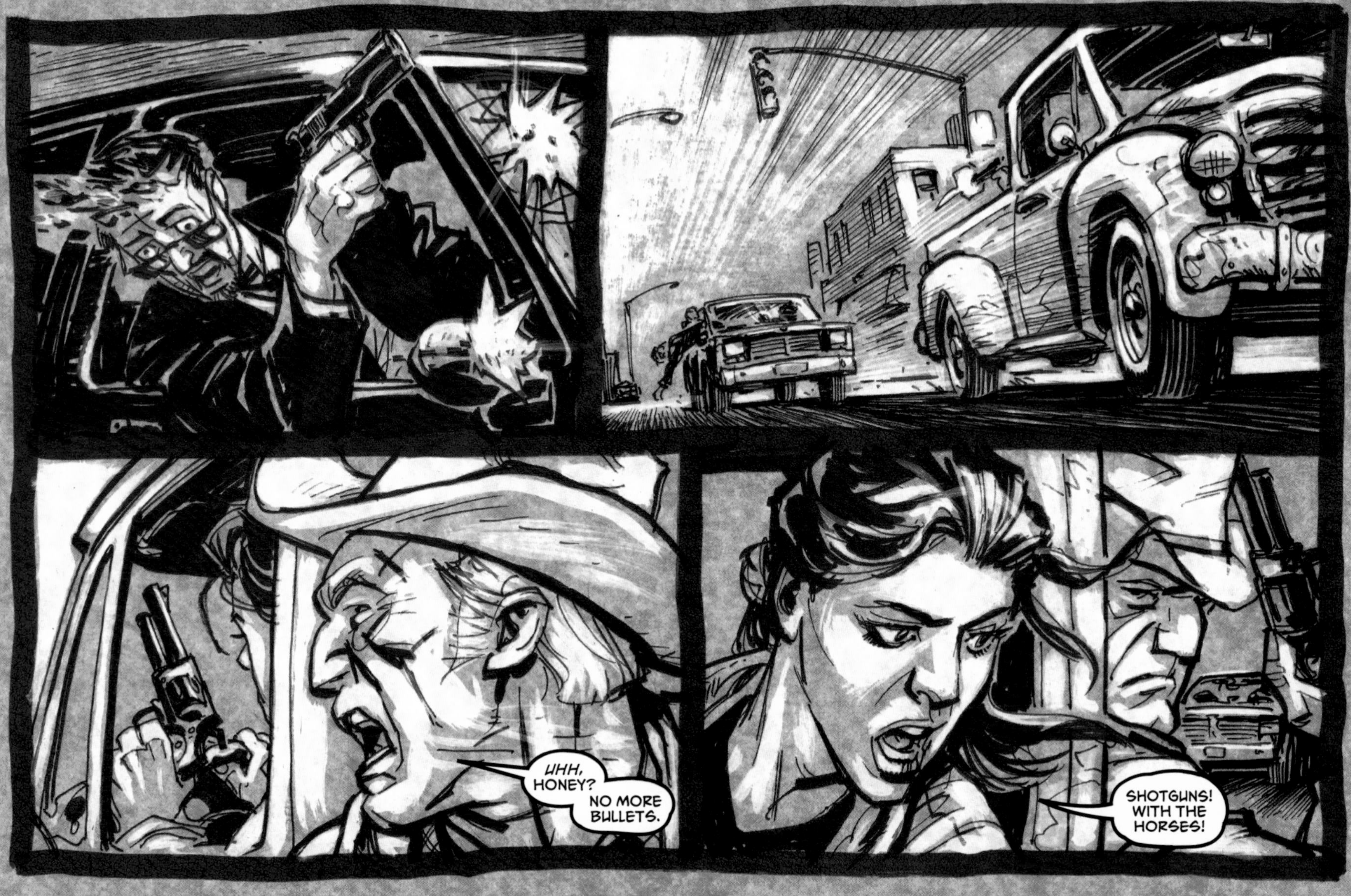
UHH, HONEY? NO MORE BULLETS.
SHOTGUNS! WITH THE HORSES!

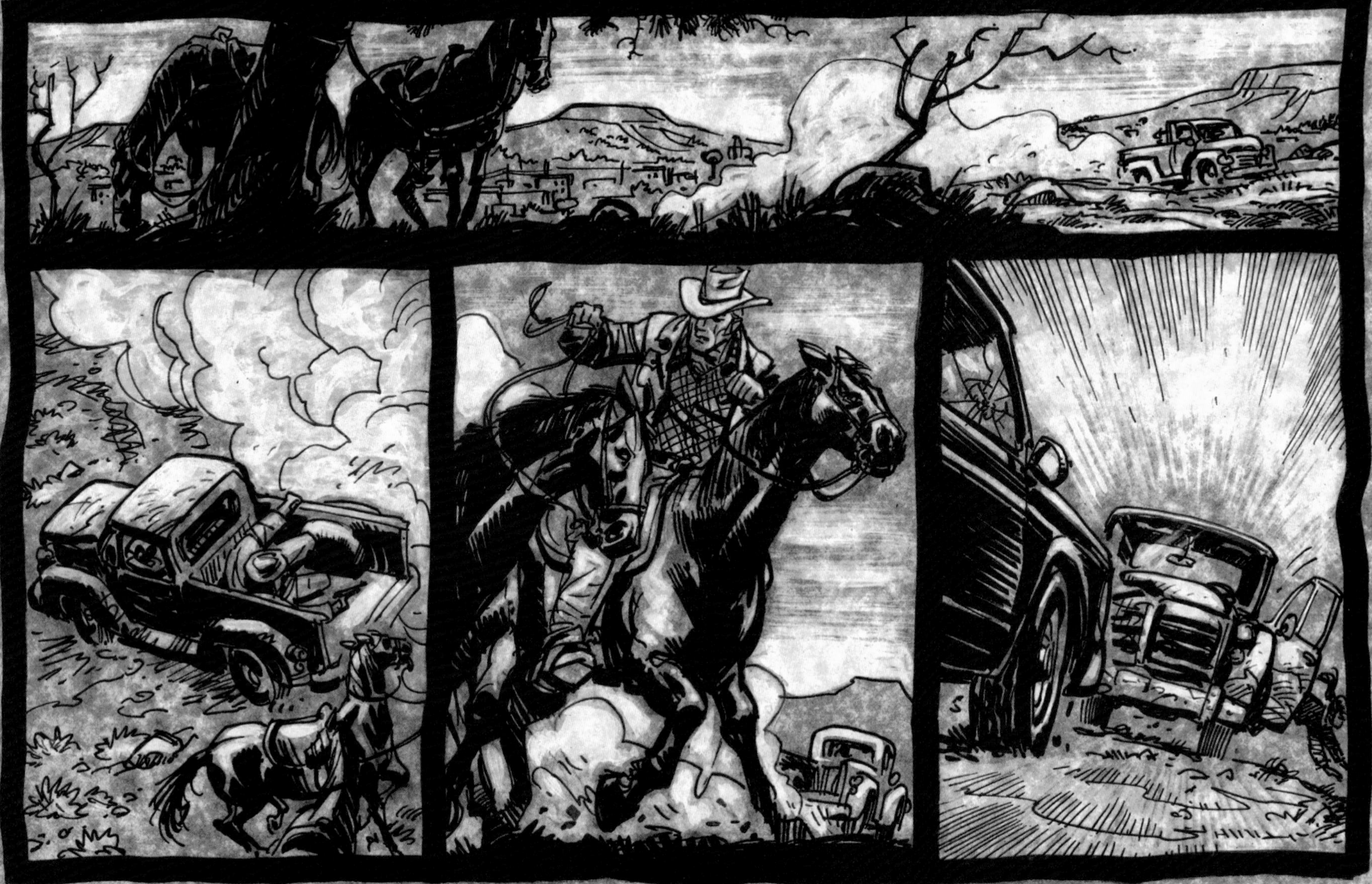

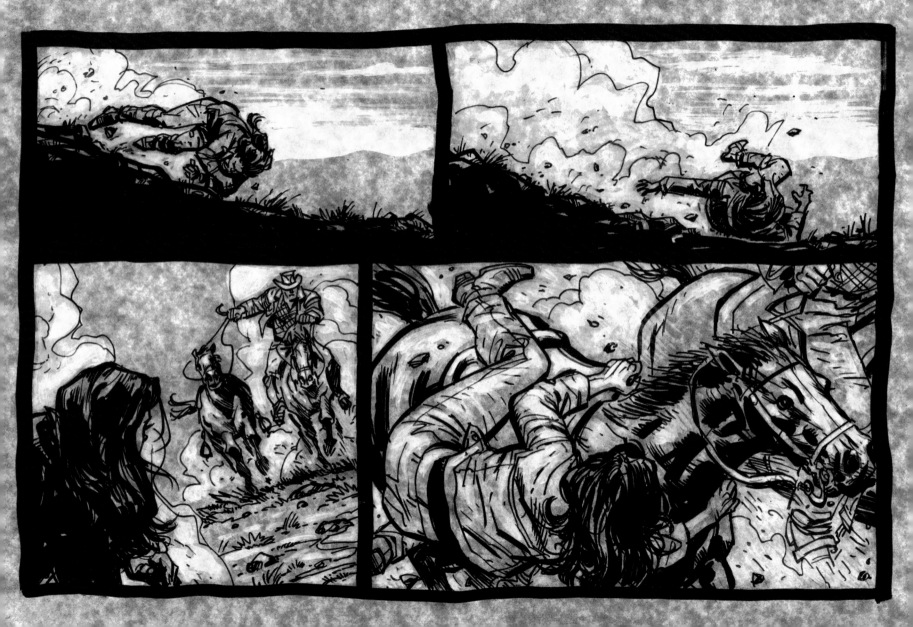

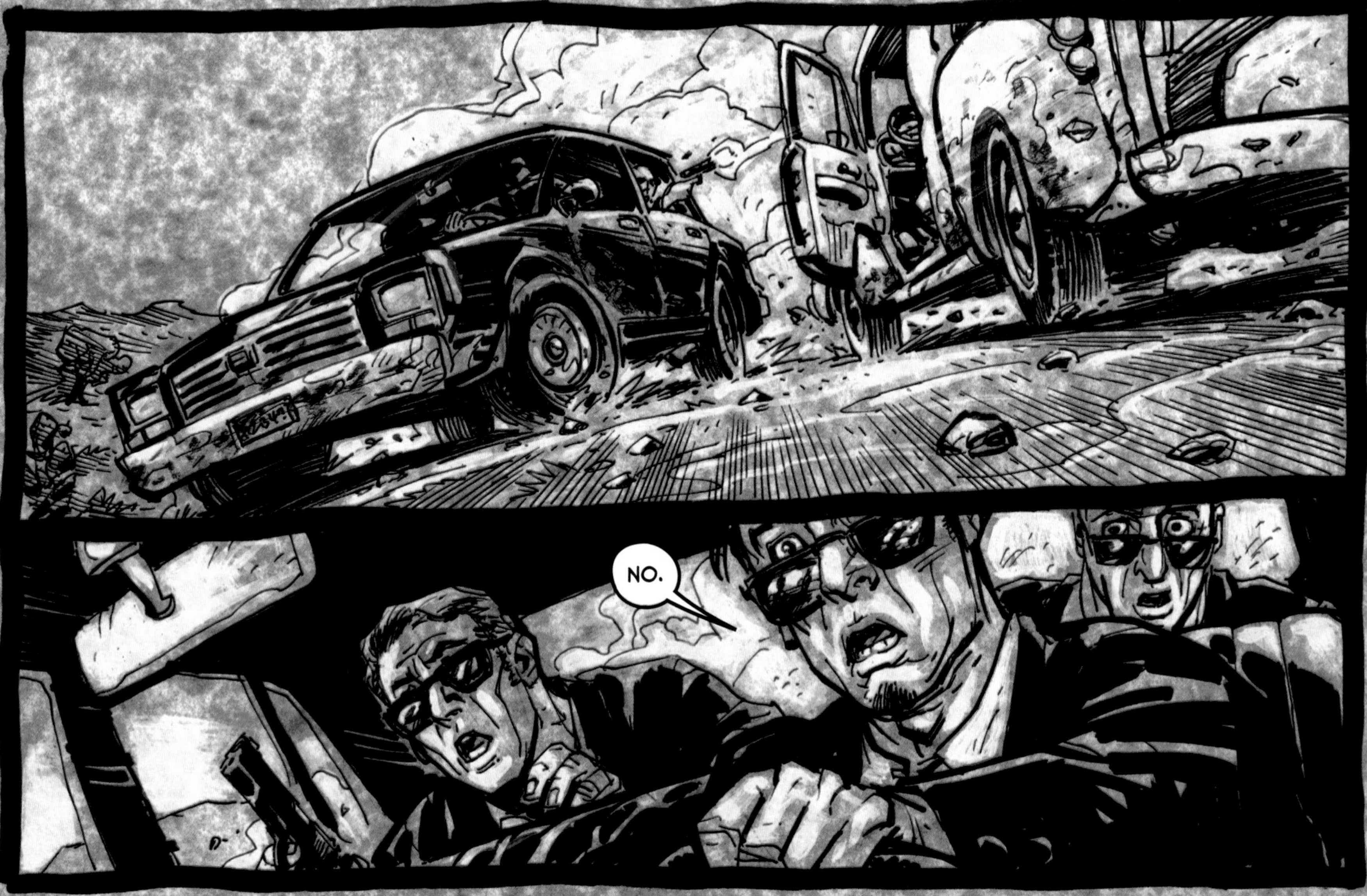
NO.

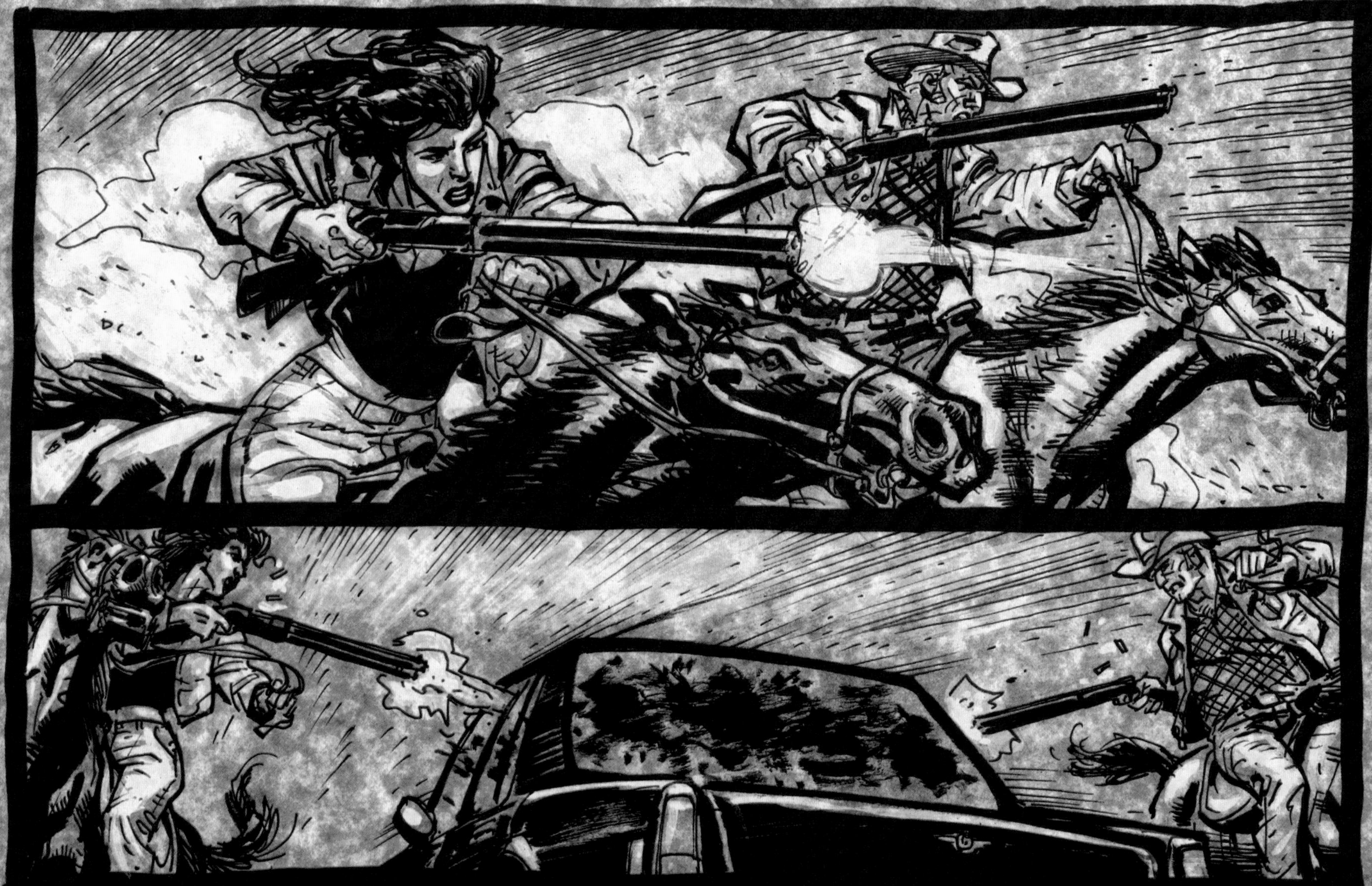

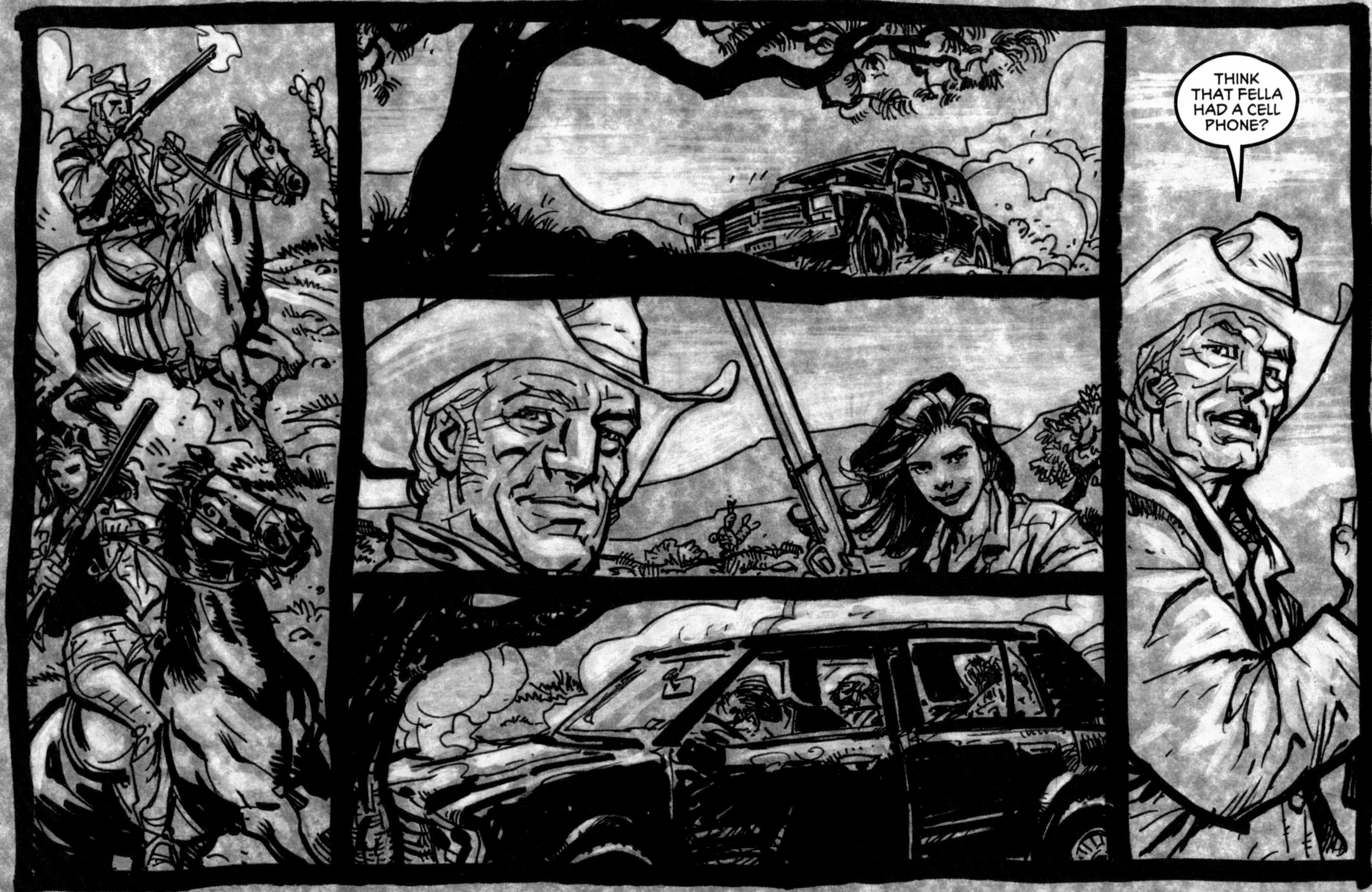
THINK THAT FELLA HAD A CELL PHONE?

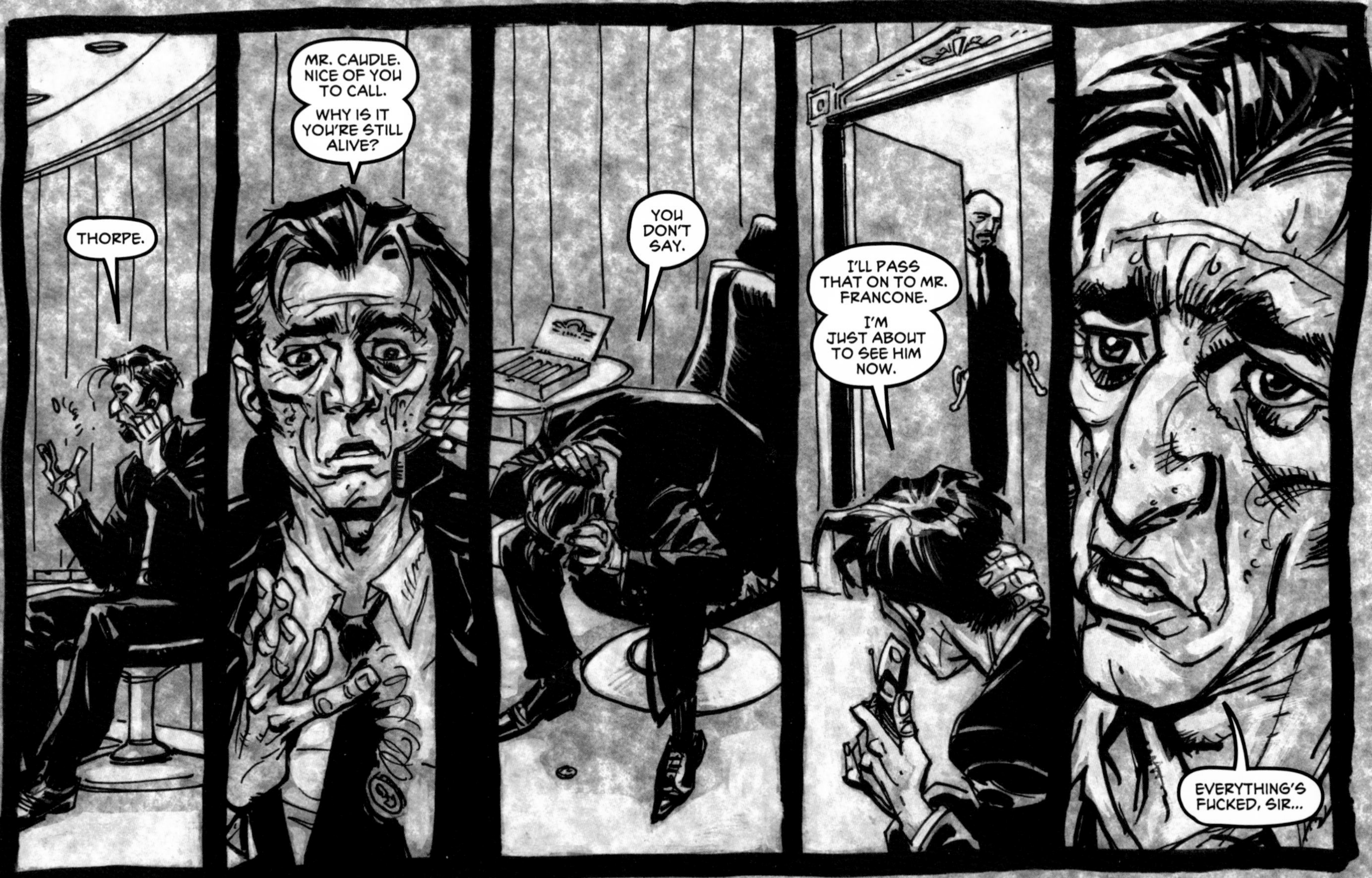
THORPE.
MR. CAUDLE. NICE OF YOU TO CALL.
WHY IS IT YOU'RE STILL ALIVE?
YOU DON'T SAY.
I'LL PASS THAT ON TO MR. FRANCONE.
I'M JUST ABOUT TO SEE HIM NOW.
EVERYTHING'S FUCKED, SIR...

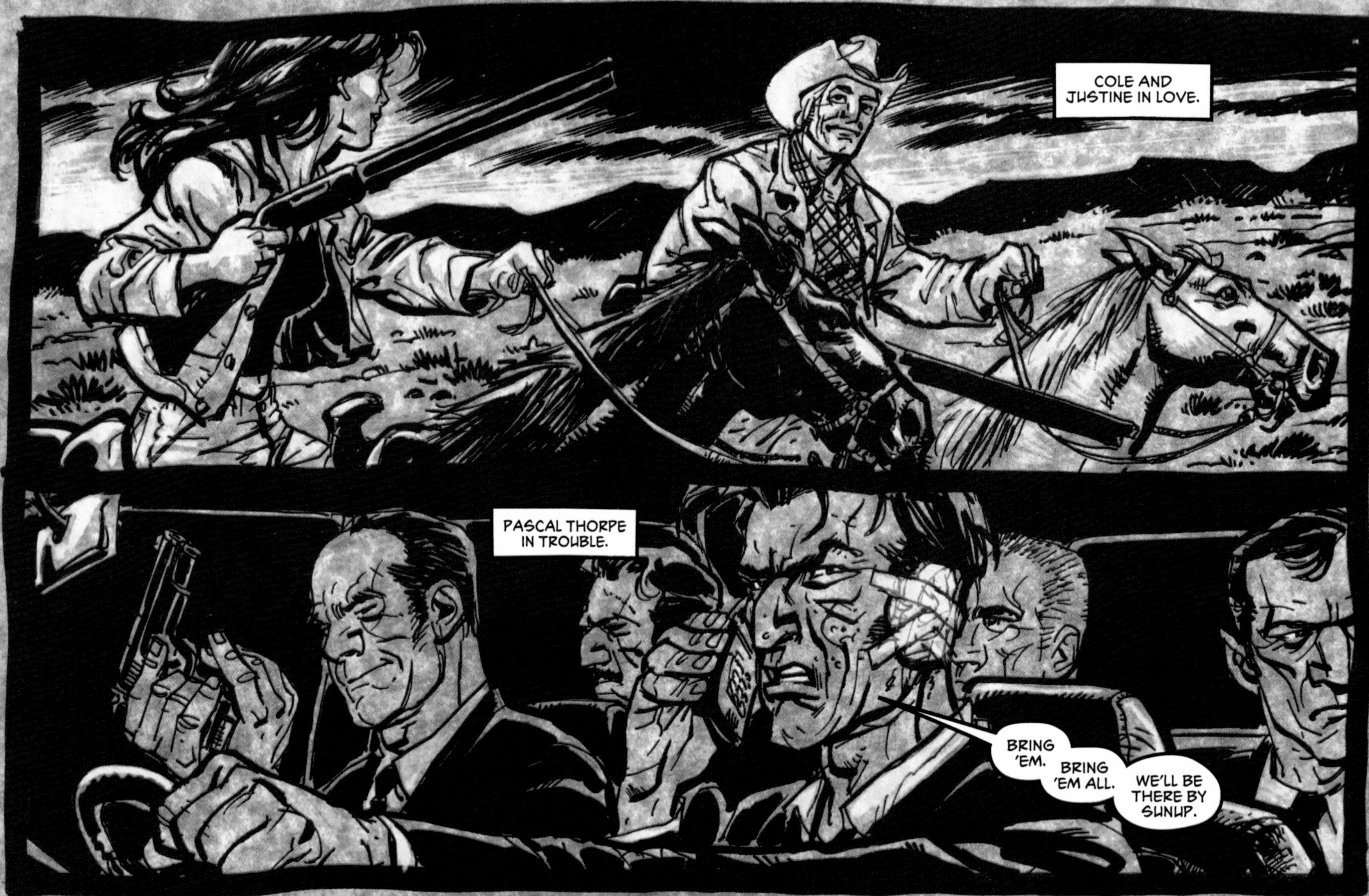
COLE AND JUSTINE IN LOVE.
PASCAL THORPE IN TROUBLE.
BRING 'EM.
BRING 'EM ALL.
WE'LL BE THERE BY SUNUP.

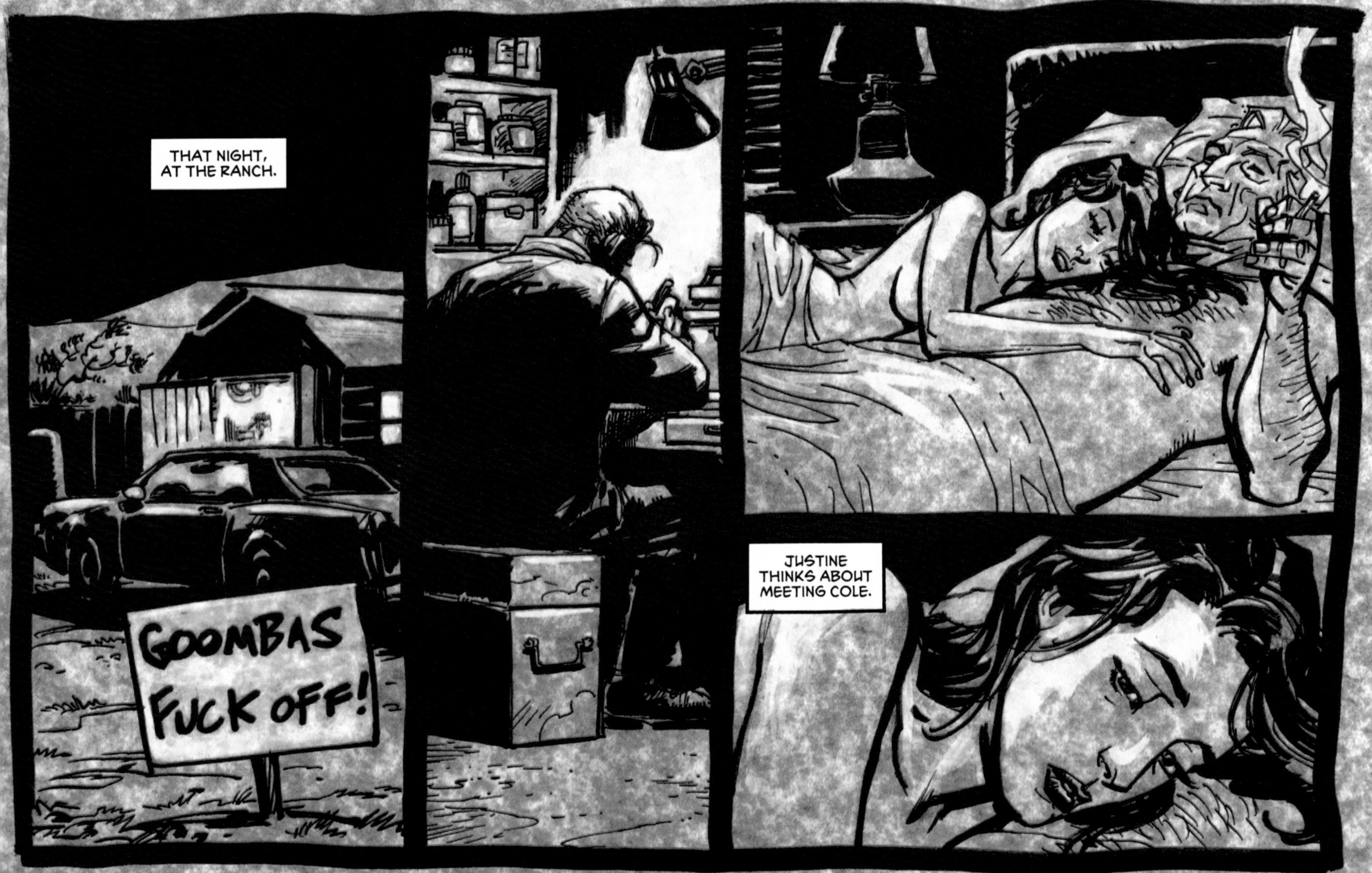
THAT NIGHT, AT THE RANCH.
GOOMBAS FUCK OFF!
JUSTINE THINKS ABOUT MEETING COLE.

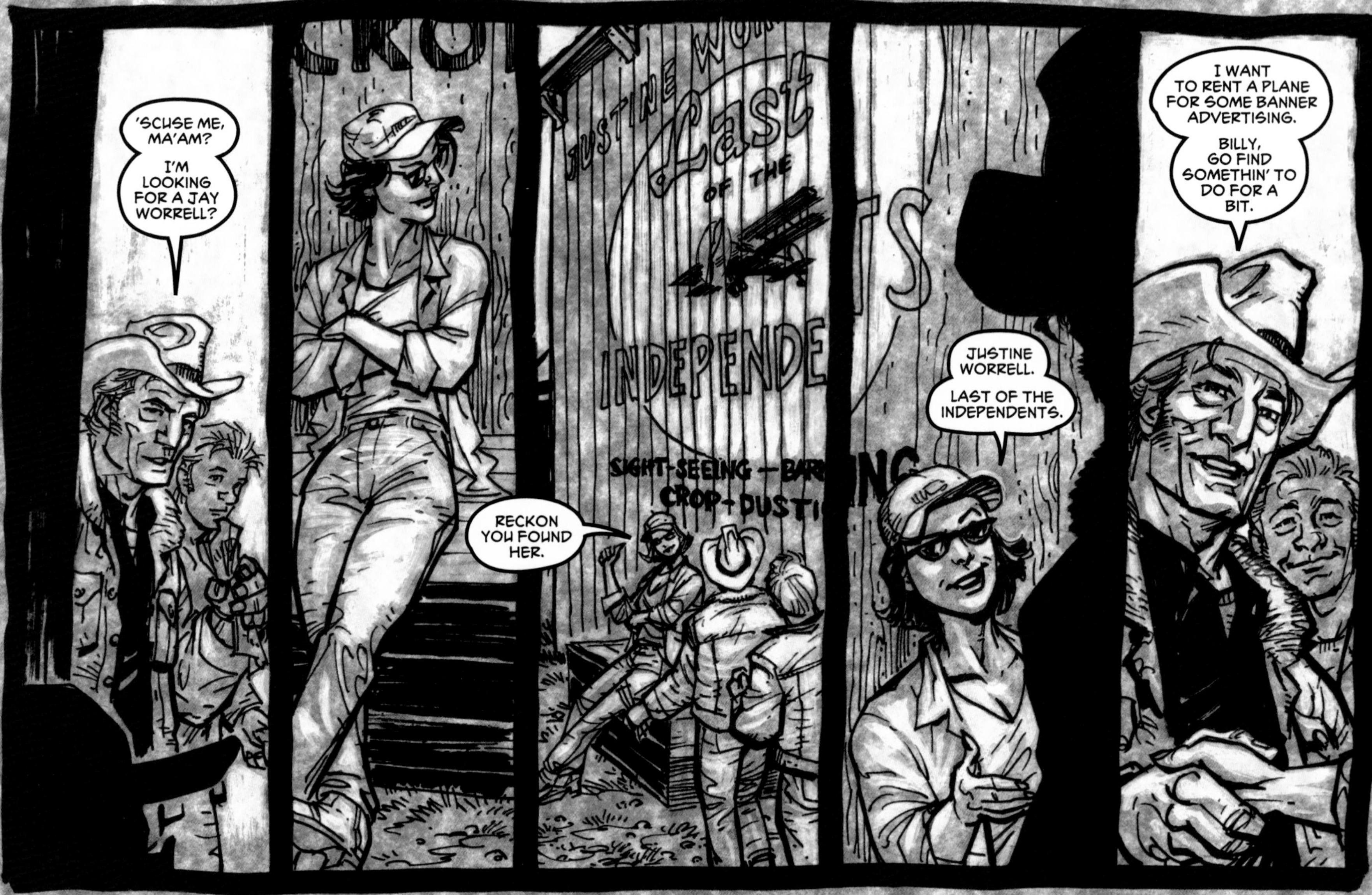
'SCUSE ME, MA'AM?
I'M LOOKING FOR A JAY WORRELL?
JUSTINE WOR
Last OF THE
INDEPENDE
SIGHT-SEEING — BAR
CROP-DUSTI
RECKON YOU FOUND HER.
JUSTINE WORRELL.
LAST OF THE INDEPENDENTS.
I WANT TO RENT A PLANE FOR SOME BANNER ADVERTISING.
BILLY, GO FIND SOMETHIN' TO DO FOR A BIT.

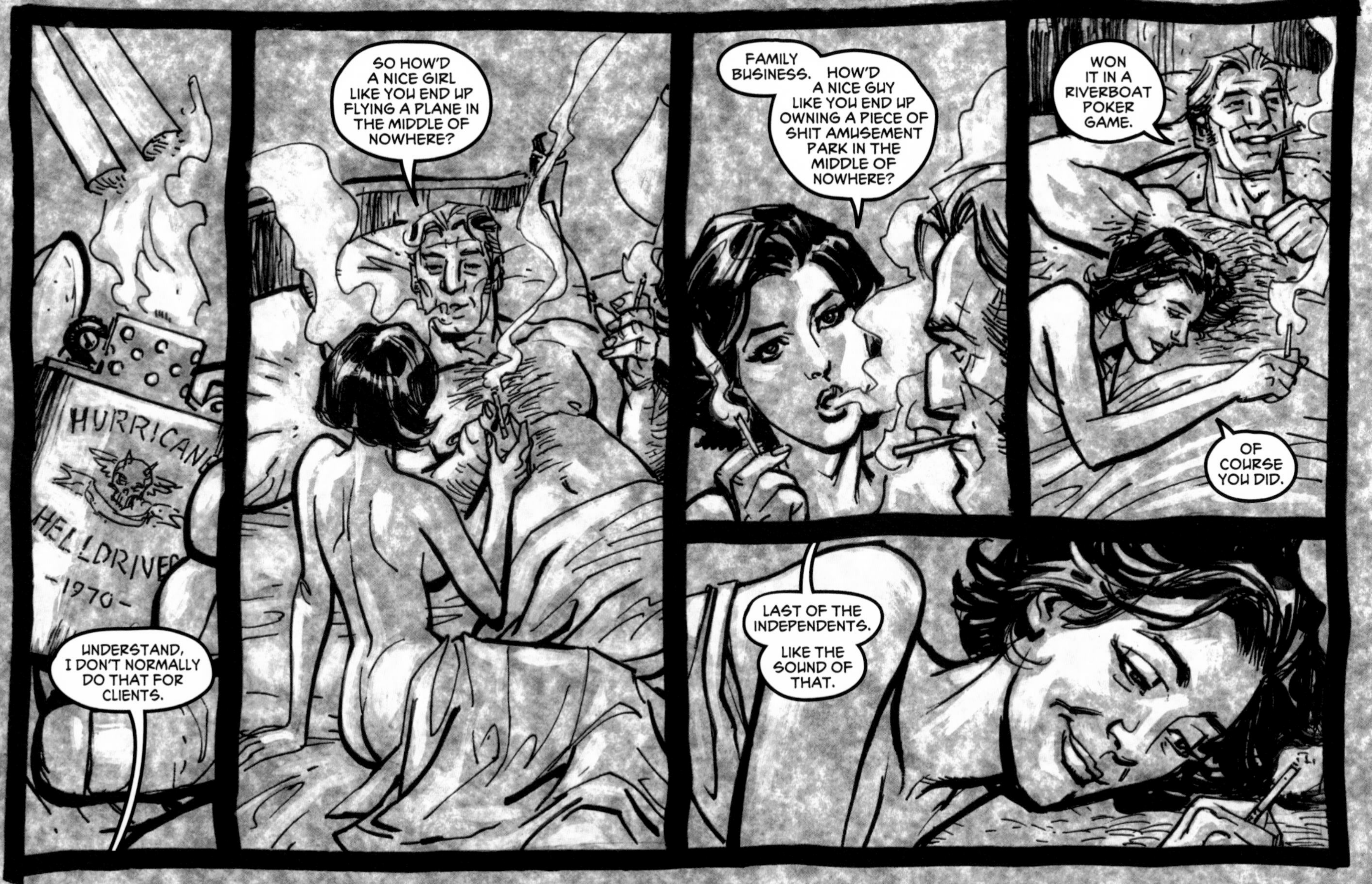
HURRICANE
HELLDRIVE
-1970-
UNDERSTAND, I DON'T NORMALLY DO THAT FOR CLIENTS.
SO HOW'D A NICE GIRL LIKE YOU END UP FLYING A PLANE IN THE MIDDLE OF NOWHERE?
FAMILY BUSINESS.
HOW'D A NICE GUY LIKE YOU END UP OWNING A PIECE OF SHIT AMUSEMENT PARK IN THE MIDDLE OF NOWHERE?
WON IT IN A RIVERBOAT POKER GAME.
OF COURSE YOU DID.
LAST OF THE INDEPENDENTS.
LIKE THE SOUND OF THAT.

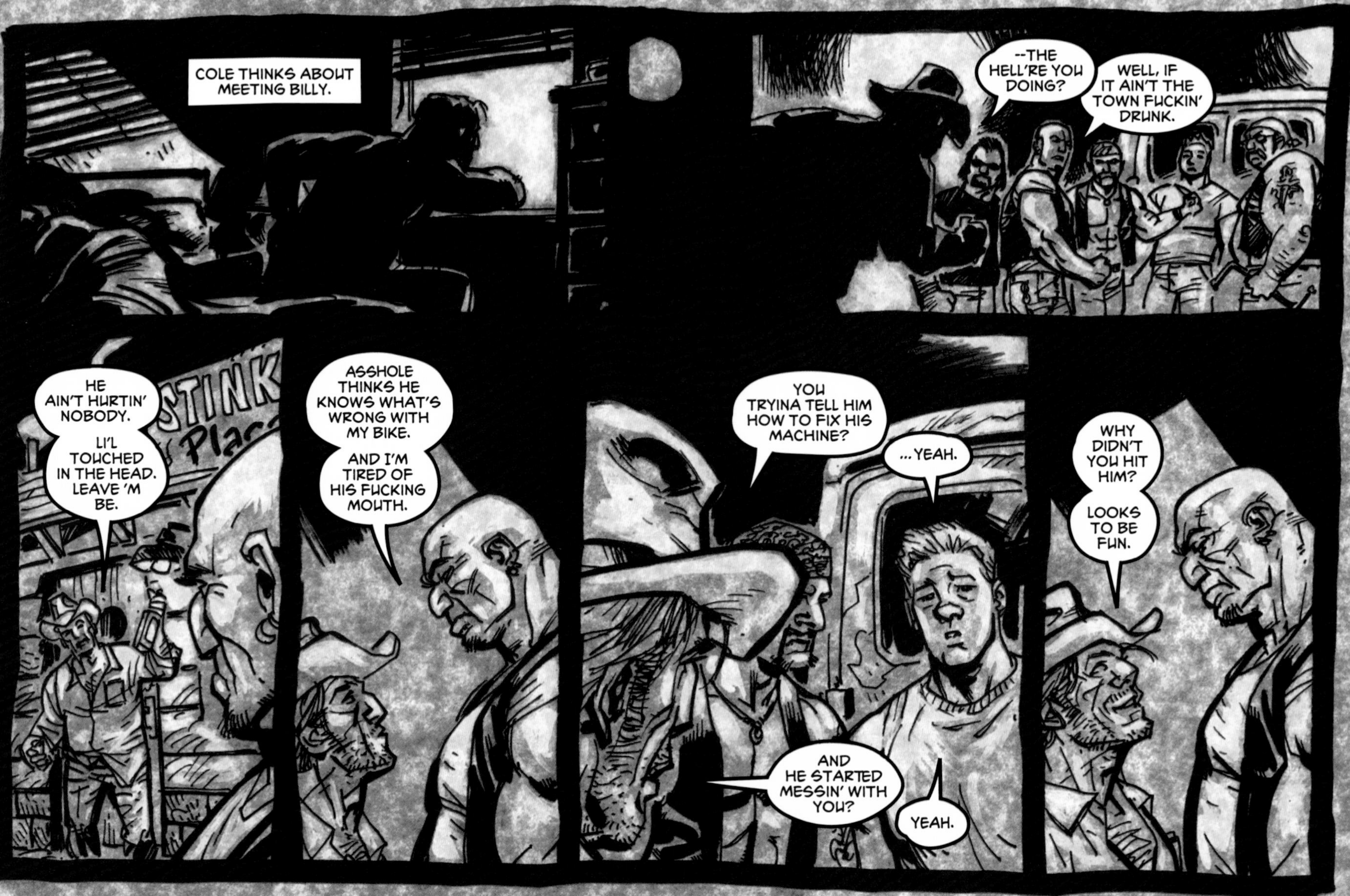
COLE THINKS ABOUT MEETING BILLY.
--THE HELL'RE YOU DOING?
WELL, IF IT AIN'T THE TOWN FUCKIN' DRUNK.
STINK Place
HE AIN'T HURTIN' NOBODY.
LI'L TOUCHED IN THE HEAD. LEAVE 'M BE.
ASSHOLE THINKS HE KNOWS WHAT'S WRONG WITH MY BIKE.
AND I'M TIRED OF HIS FUCKING MOUTH.
YOU TRYINA TELL HIM HOW TO FIX HIS MACHINE?
...YEAH.
AND HE STARTED MESSIN' WITH YOU?
YEAH.
WHY DIDN'T YOU HIT HIM?
LOOKS TO BE FUN.

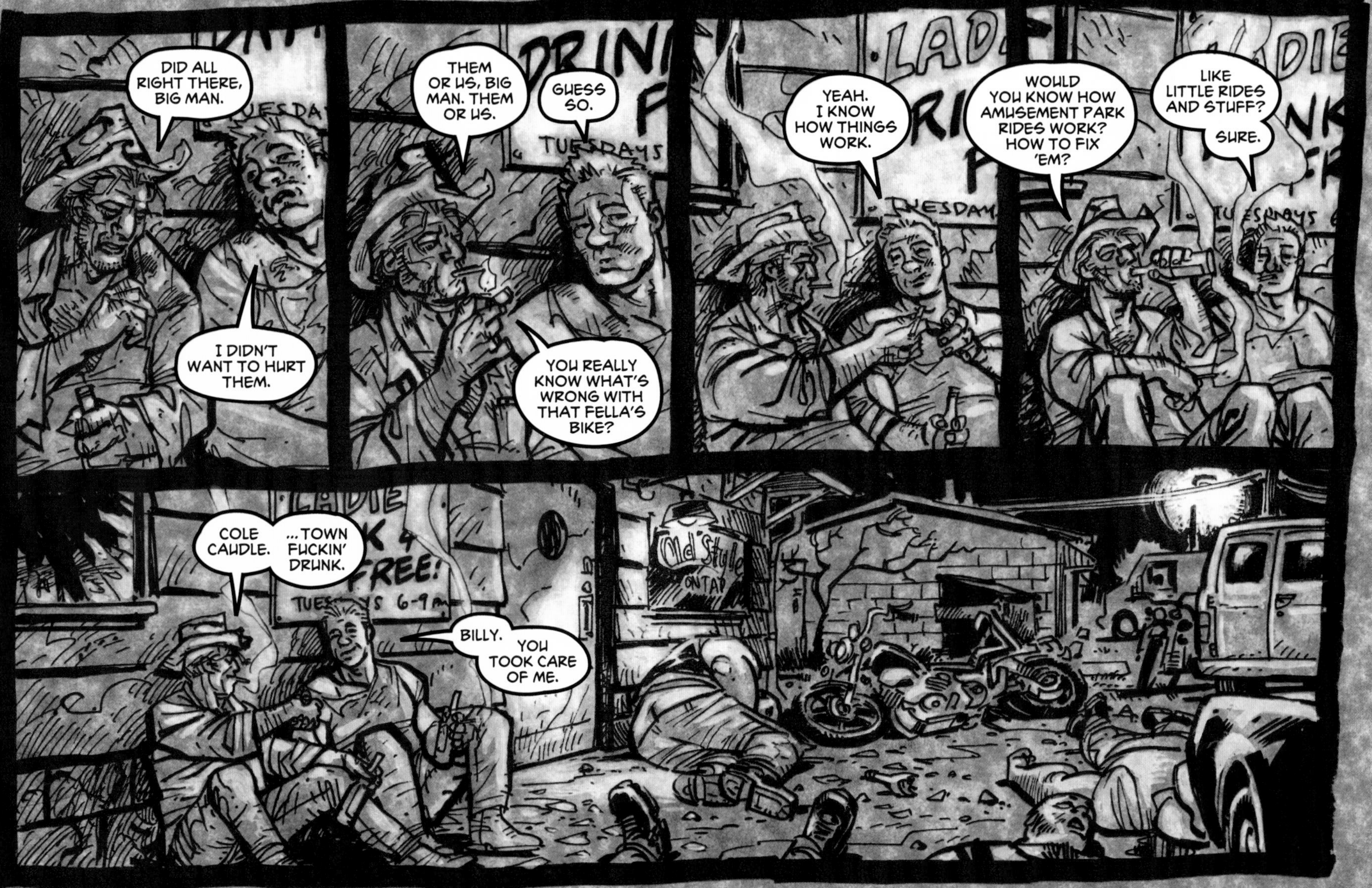
DID ALL RIGHT THERE, BIG MAN.
I DIDN'T WANT TO HURT THEM.
THEM OR US, BIG MAN. THEM OR US.
GUESS SO.
YOU REALLY KNOW WHAT'S WRONG WITH THAT FELLA'S BIKE?
YEAH. I KNOW HOW THINGS WORK.
WOULD YOU KNOW HOW AMUSEMENT PARK RIDES WORK? HOW TO FIX 'EM?
LIKE LITTLE RIDES AND STUFF?
SURE.
COLE CAUDLE.
...TOWN FUCKIN' DRUNK.
BILLY.
YOU TOOK CARE OF ME.
Old Style ON TAP

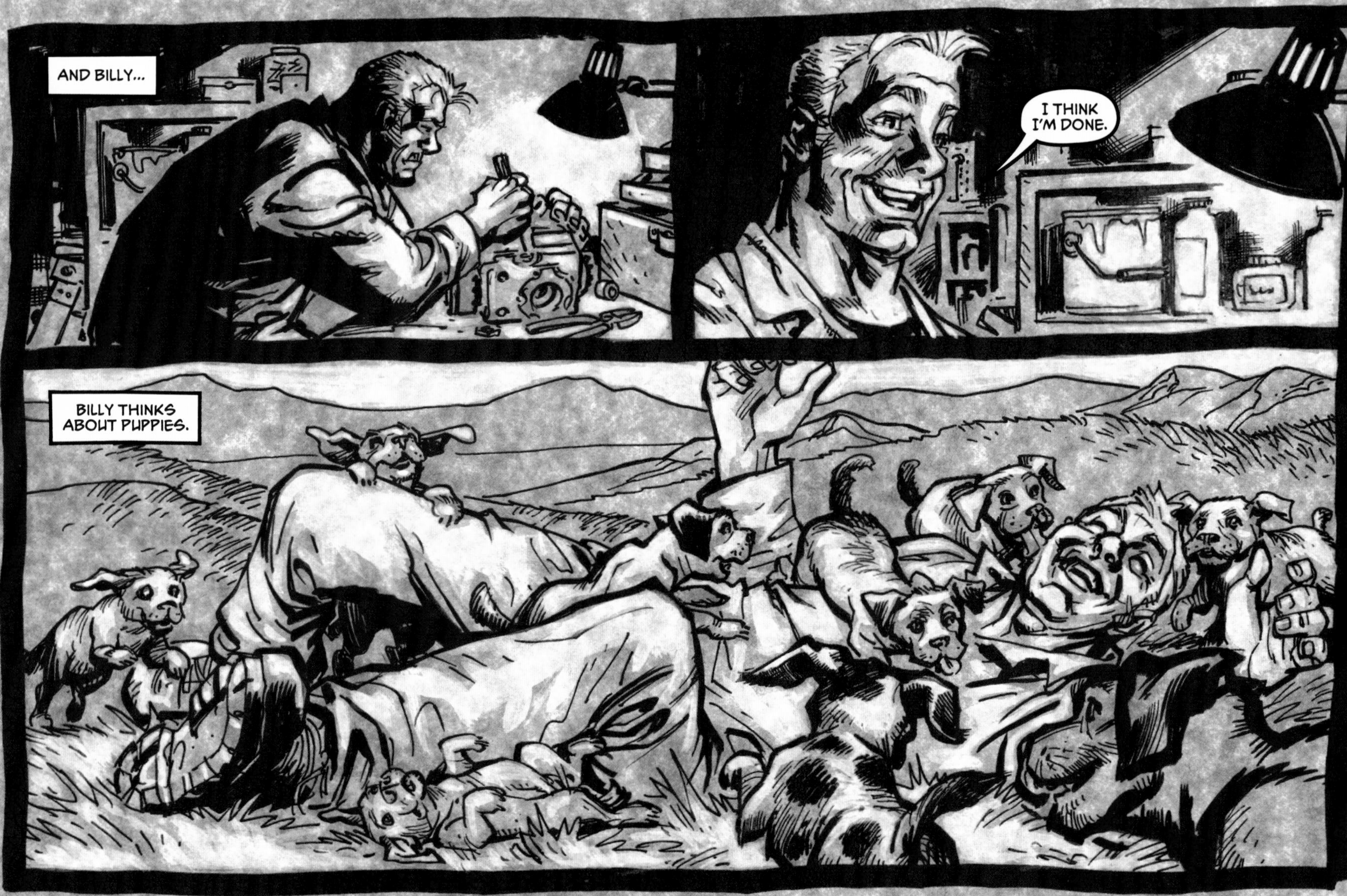
AND BILLY...
I THINK I'M DONE.
BILLY THINKS ABOUT PUPPIES.

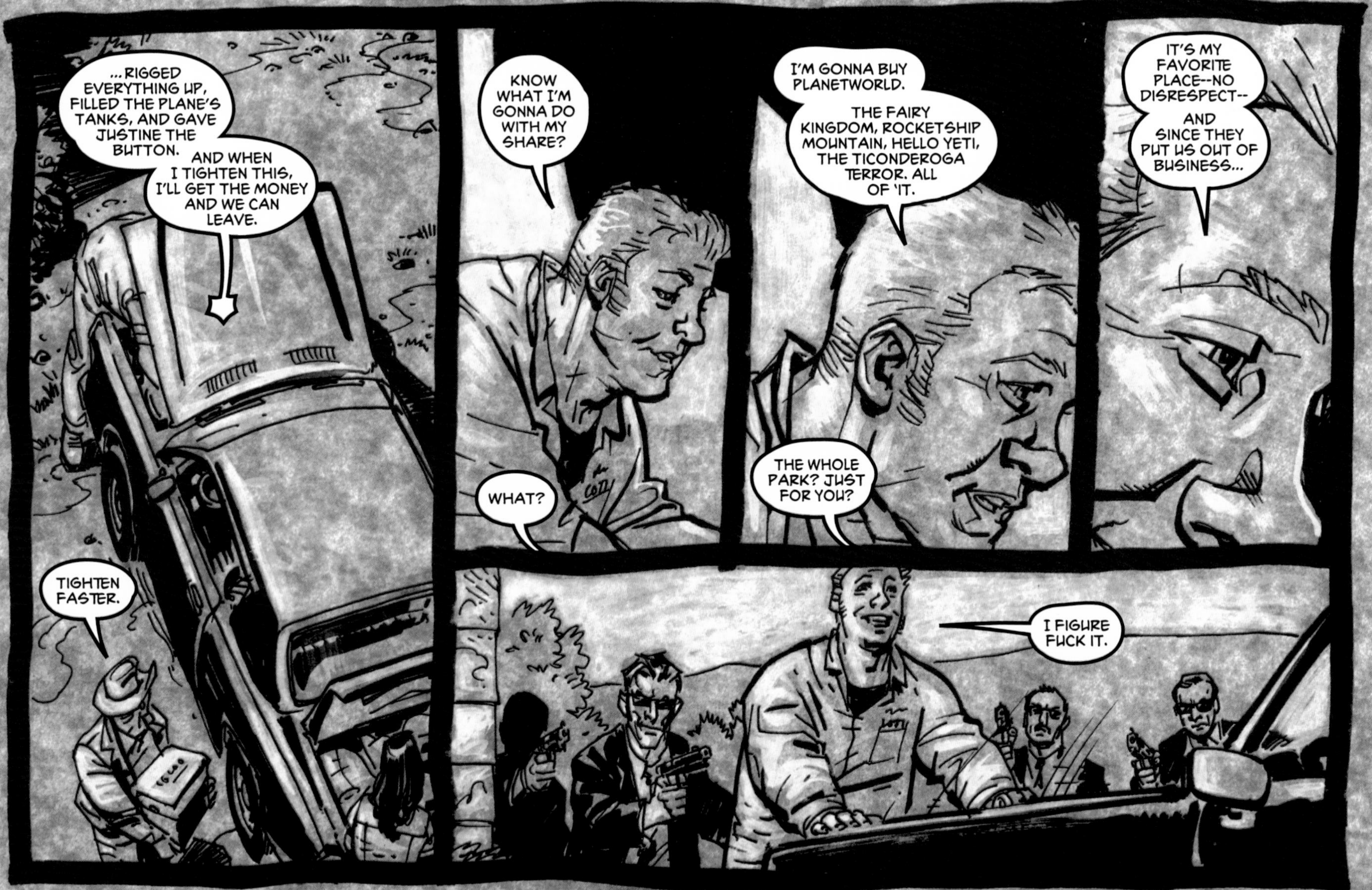
...RIGGED EVERYTHING UP, FILLED THE PLANE'S TANKS, AND GAVE JUSTINE THE BUTTON.
AND WHEN I TIGHTEN THIS, I'LL GET THE MONEY AND WE CAN LEAVE.
TIGHTEN FASTER.
KNOW WHAT I'M GONNA DO WITH MY SHARE?
WHAT?
I'M GONNA BUY PLANETWORLD.
THE FAIRY KINGDOM, ROCKETSHIP MOUNTAIN, HELLO YETI, THE TICONDEROGA TERROR. ALL OF 'IT.
THE WHOLE PARK? JUST FOR YOU?
IT'S MY FAVORITE PLACE--NO DISRESPECT--
AND SINCE THEY PUT US OUT OF BUSINESS...
I FIGURE FUCK IT.

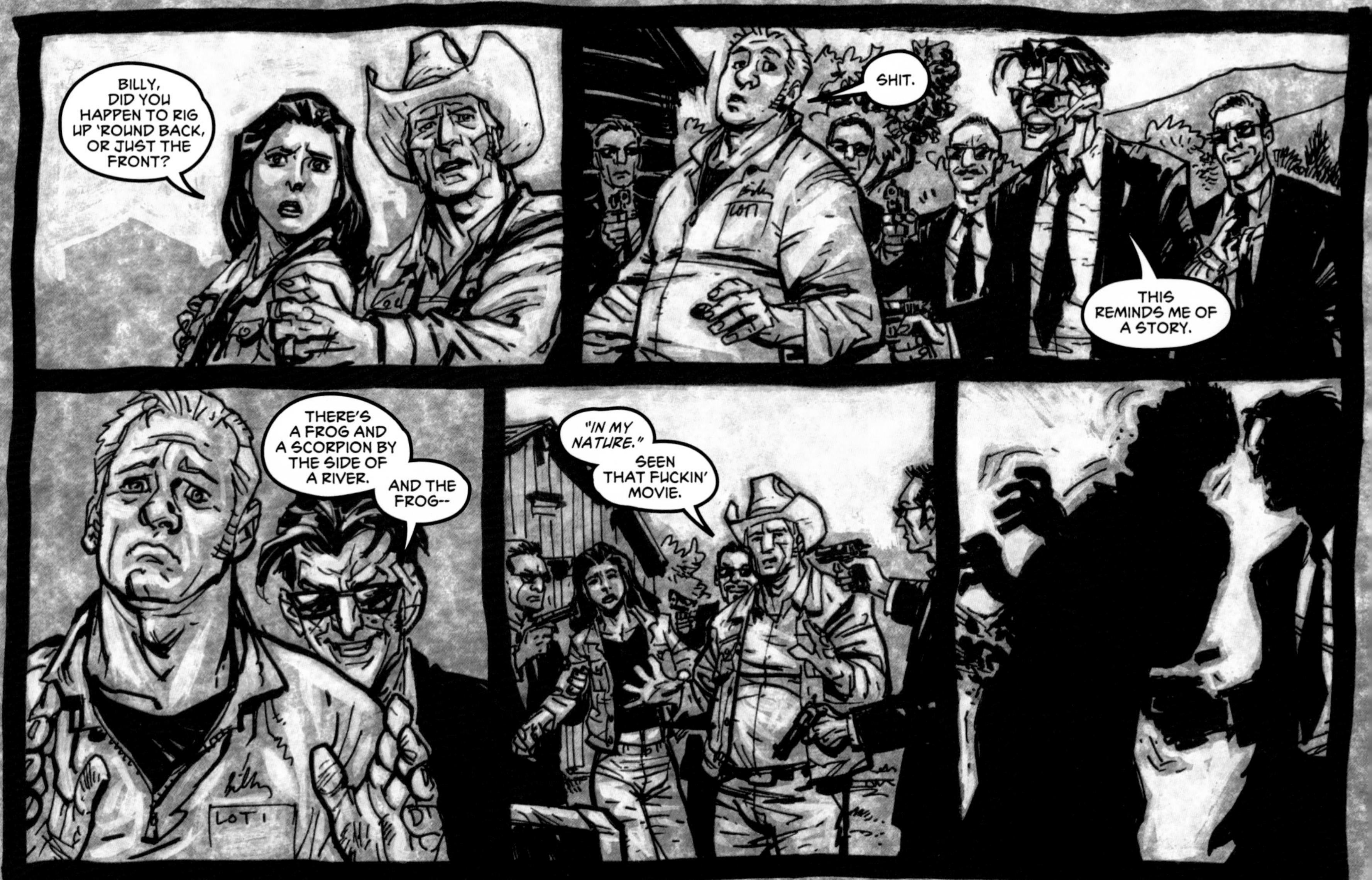
BILLY, DID YOU HAPPEN TO RIG UP 'ROUND BACK, OR JUST THE FRONT?
SHIT.
THIS REMINDS ME OF A STORY.
THERE'S A FROG AND A SCORPION BY THE SIDE OF A RIVER.
AND THE FROG--
"IN MY NATURE." SEEN THAT FUCKIN' MOVIE.
LOT 1

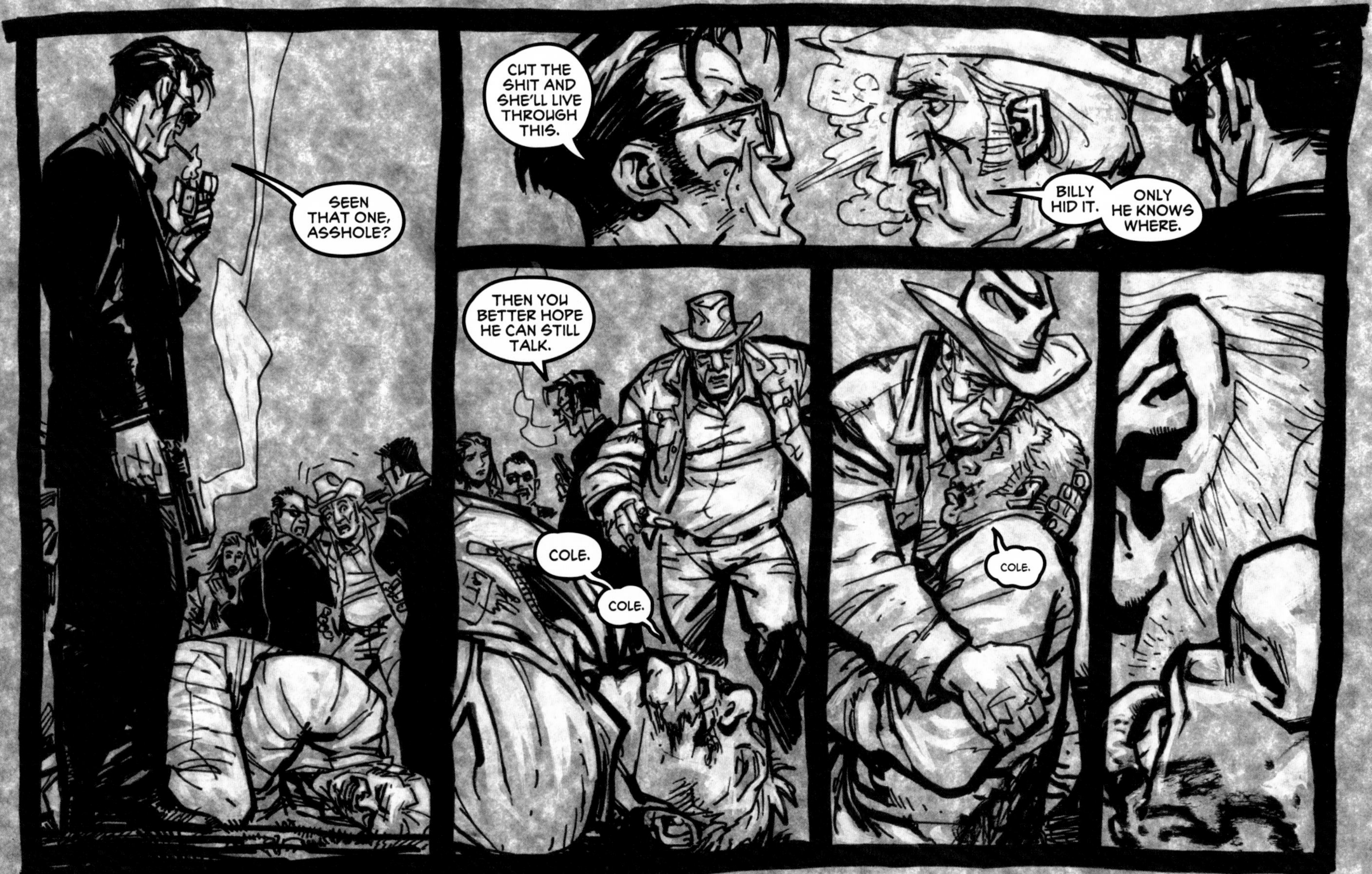
SEEN THAT ONE, ASSHOLE?
CUT THE SHIT AND SHE'LL LIVE THROUGH THIS.
BILLY HID IT.
ONLY HE KNOWS WHERE.
THEN YOU BETTER HOPE HE CAN STILL TALK.
COLE.
COLE.
COLE.

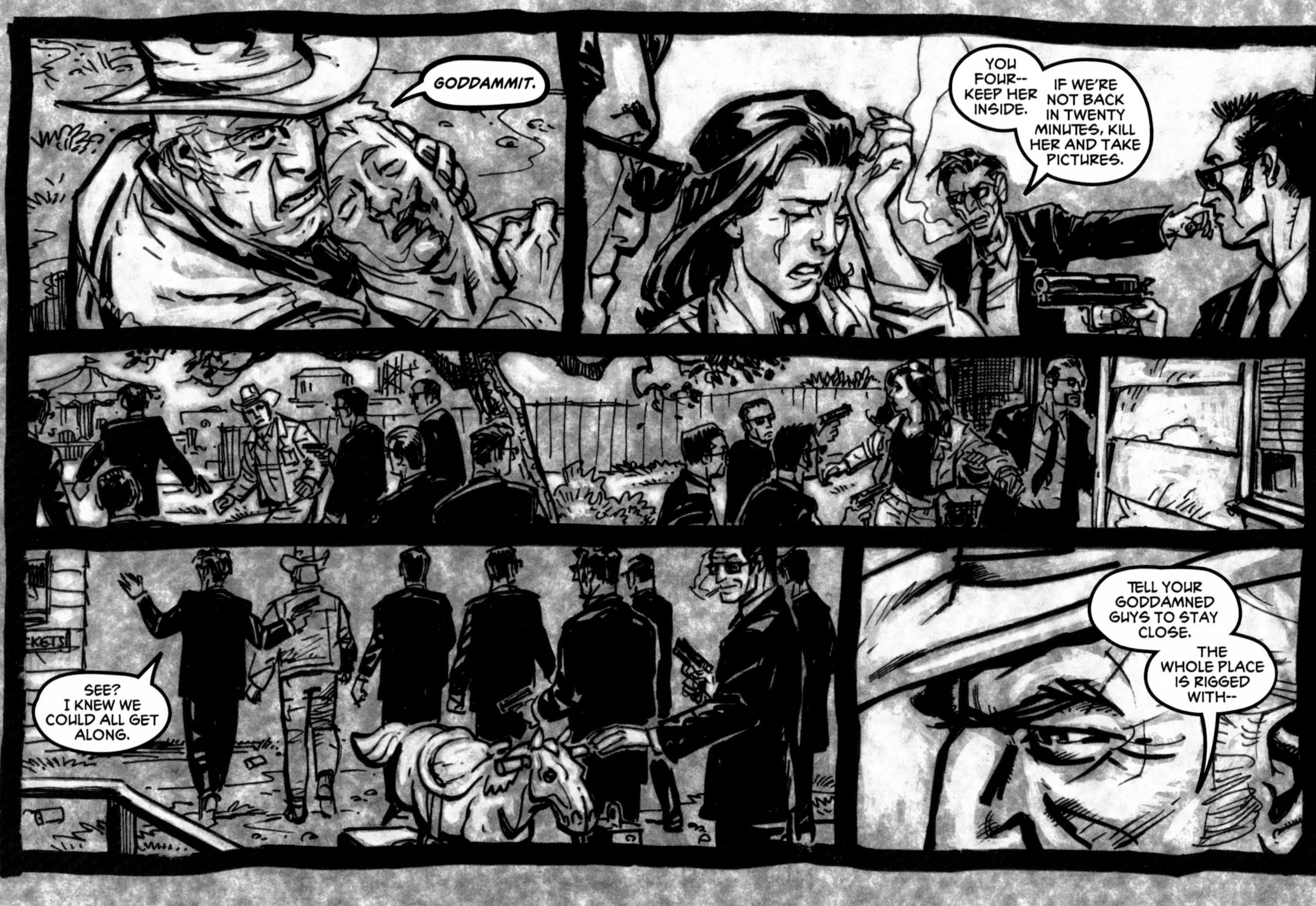
GODDAMMIT.
YOU FOUR-- KEEP HER INSIDE.
IF WE'RE NOT BACK IN TWENTY MINUTES, KILL HER AND TAKE PICTURES.
SEE? I KNEW WE COULD ALL GET ALONG.
TELL YOUR GODDAMNED GUYS TO STAY CLOSE.
THE WHOLE PLACE IS RIGGED WITH--

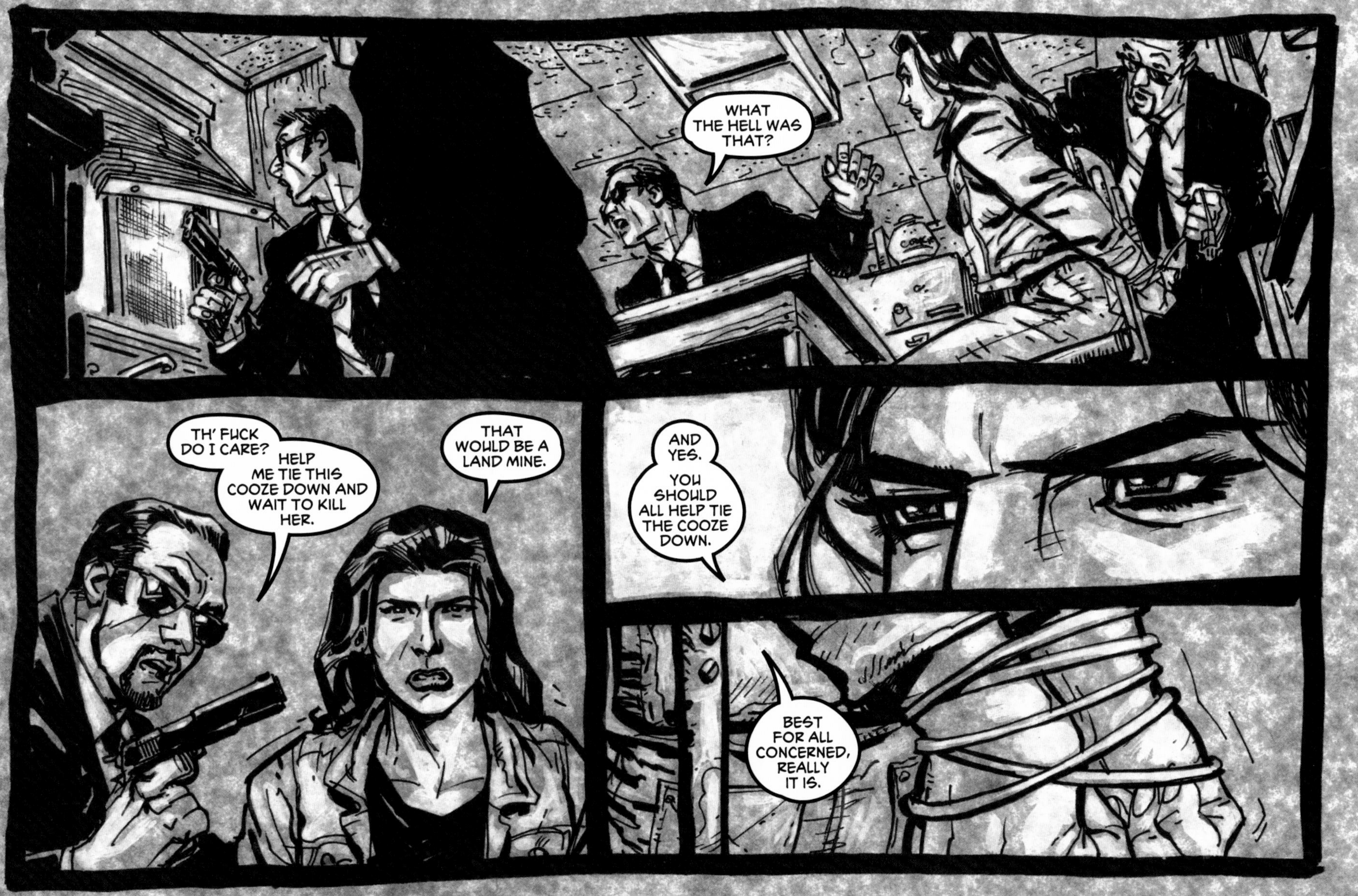
WHAT THE HELL WAS THAT?
TH' FUCK DO I CARE?
HELP ME TIE THIS COOZE DOWN AND WAIT TO KILL HER.
THAT WOULD BE A LAND MINE.
AND YES.
YOU SHOULD ALL HELP TIE THE COOZE DOWN.
BEST FOR ALL CONCERNED, REALLY IT IS.

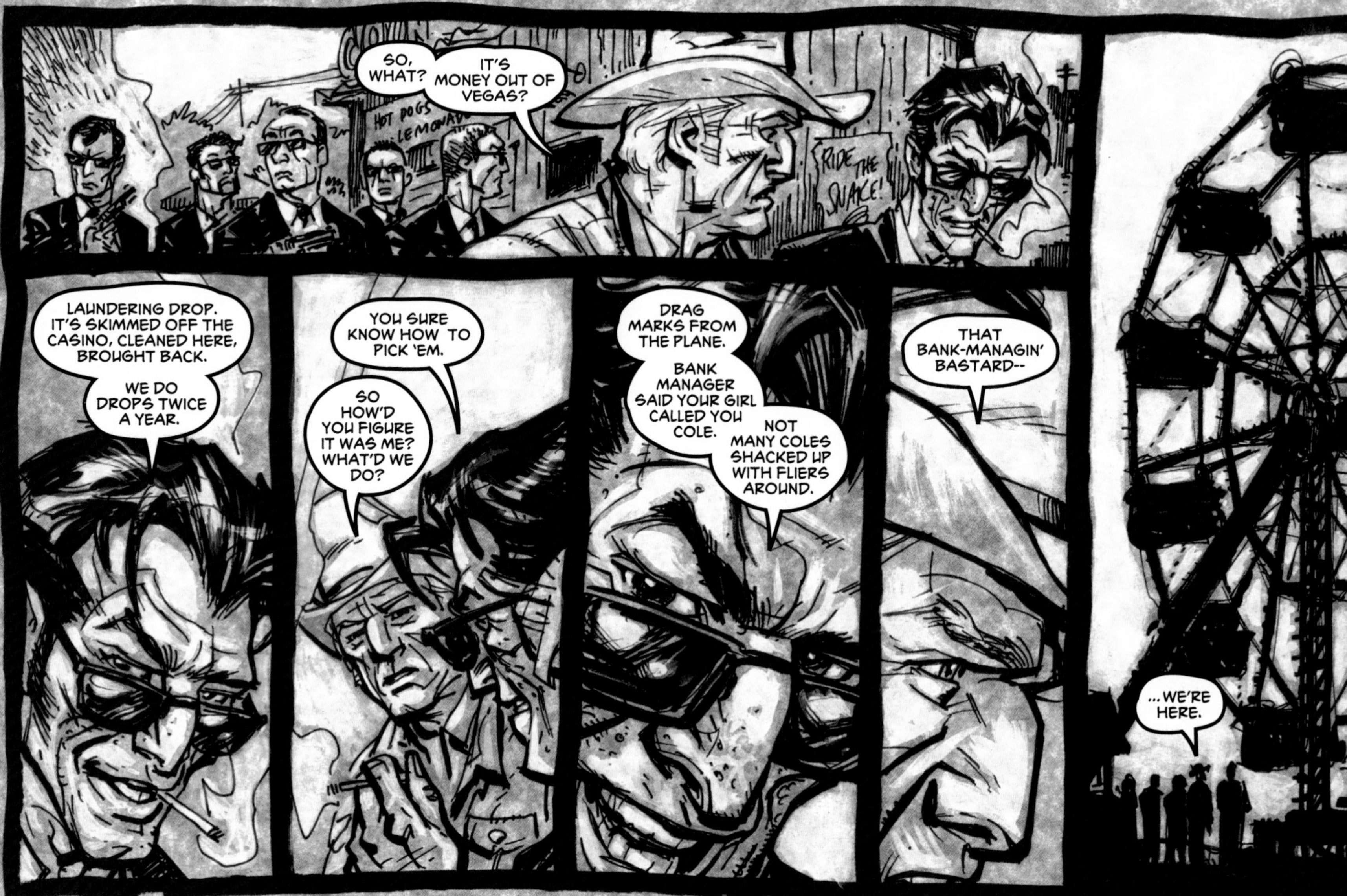

SO, WHAT?
IT'S MONEY OUT OF VEGAS?
LAUNDERING DROP. IT'S SKIMMED OFF THE CASINO, CLEANED HERE, BROUGHT BACK.
WE DO DROPS TWICE A YEAR.
YOU SURE KNOW HOW TO PICK 'EM.
SO HOW'D YOU FIGURE IT WAS ME? WHAT'D WE DO?
DRAG MARKS FROM THE PLANE.
BANK MANAGER SAID YOUR GIRL CALLED YOU COLE.
NOT MANY COLES SHACKED UP WITH FLIERS AROUND.
THAT BANK-MANAGIN' BASTARD--
...WE'RE HERE.

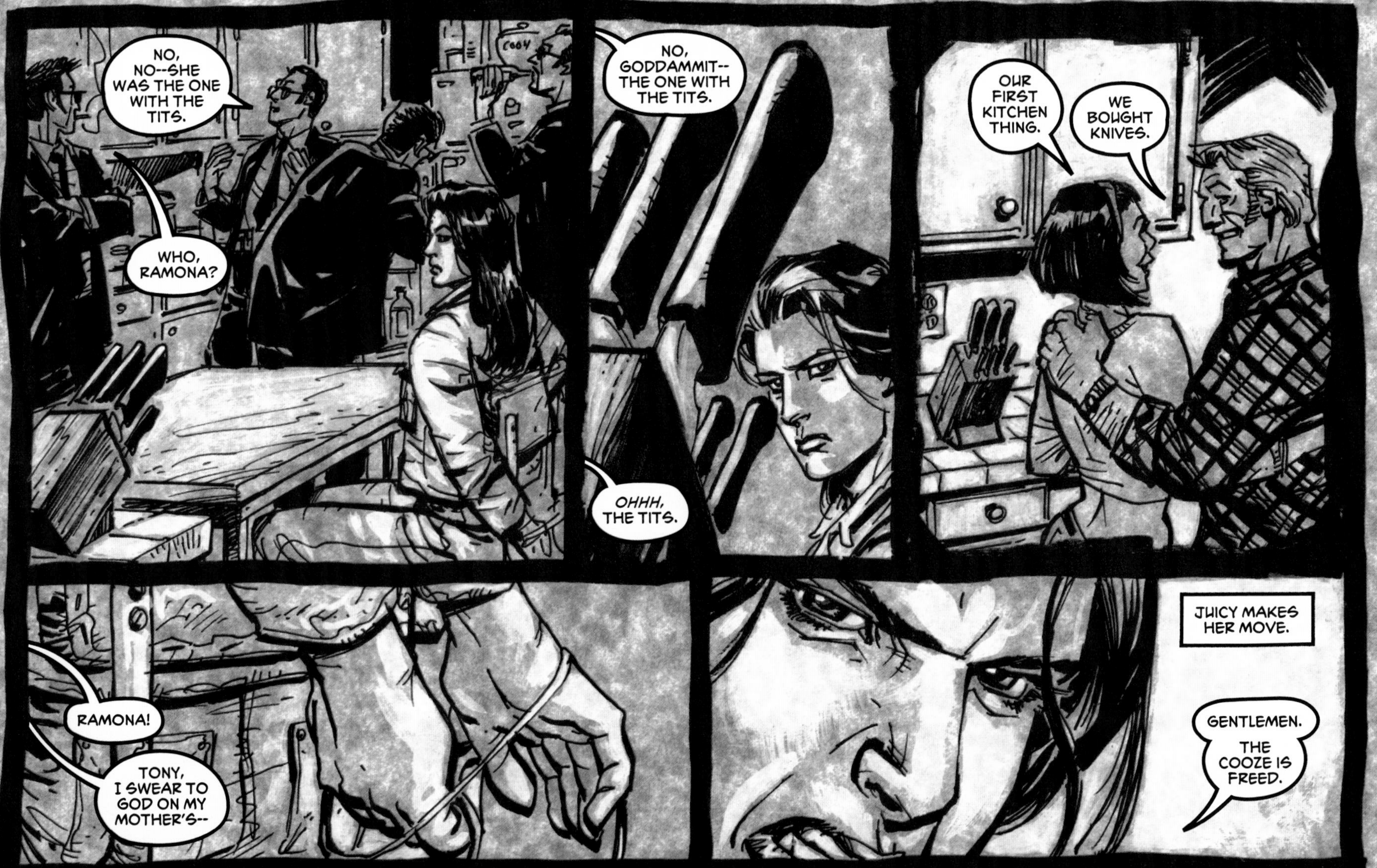
NO, NO--SHE WAS THE ONE WITH THE TITS.
WHO, RAMONA?
NO, GODDAMMIT-- THE ONE WITH THE TITS.
OHHH, THE TITS.
OUR FIRST KITCHEN THING.
WE BOUGHT KNIVES.
RAMONA!
TONY, I SWEAR TO GOD ON MY MOTHER'S--
JUICY MAKES HER MOVE.
GENTLEMEN.
THE COOZE IS FREED.

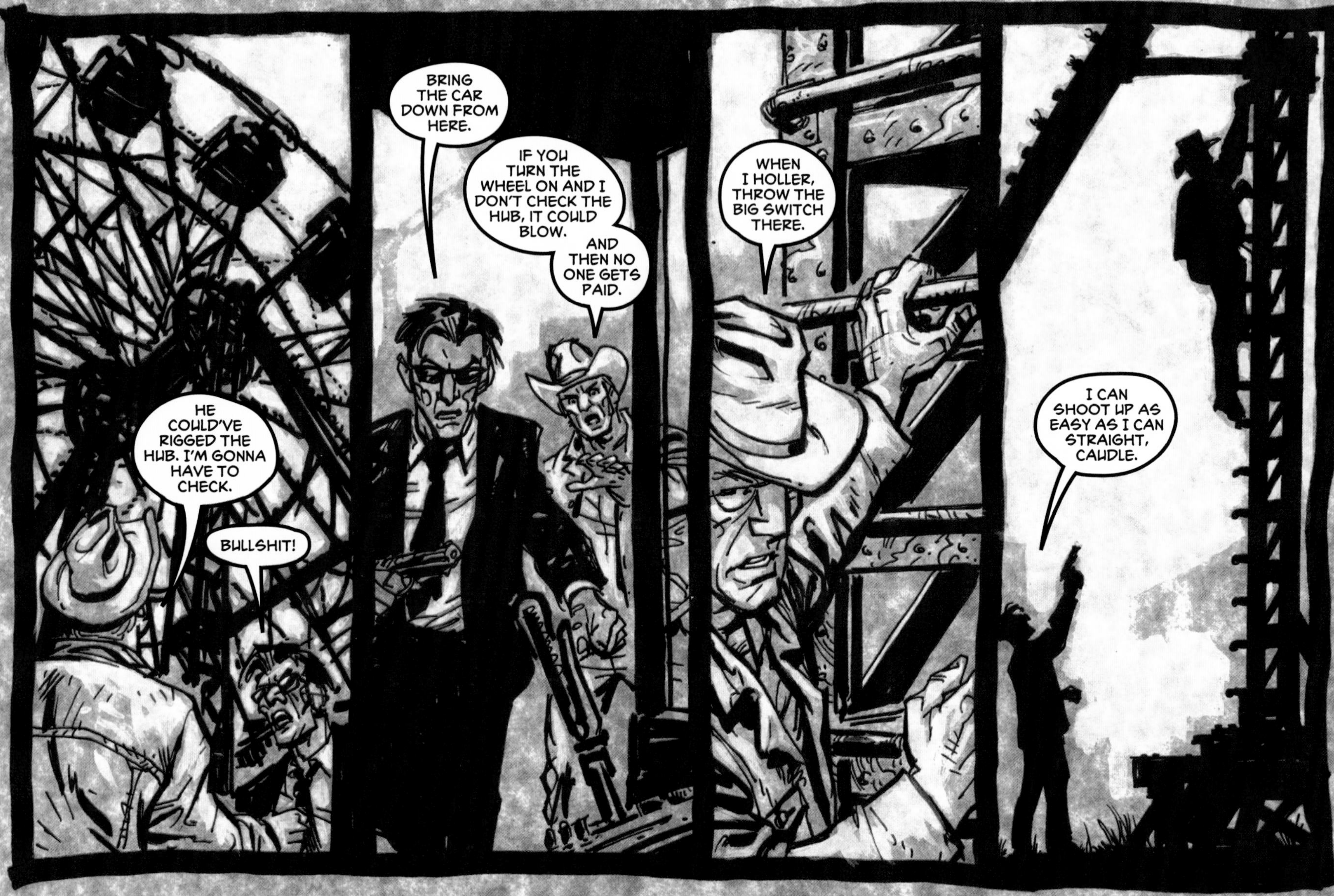
HE COULD'VE RIGGED THE HUB. I'M GONNA HAVE TO CHECK.
BULLSHIT!
BRING THE CAR DOWN FROM HERE.
IF YOU TURN THE WHEEL ON AND I DON'T CHECK THE HUB, IT COULD BLOW.
AND THEN NO ONE GETS PAID.
WHEN I HOLLER, THROW THE BIG SWITCH THERE.
I CAN SHOOT UP AS EASY AS I CAN STRAIGHT, CAUDLE.

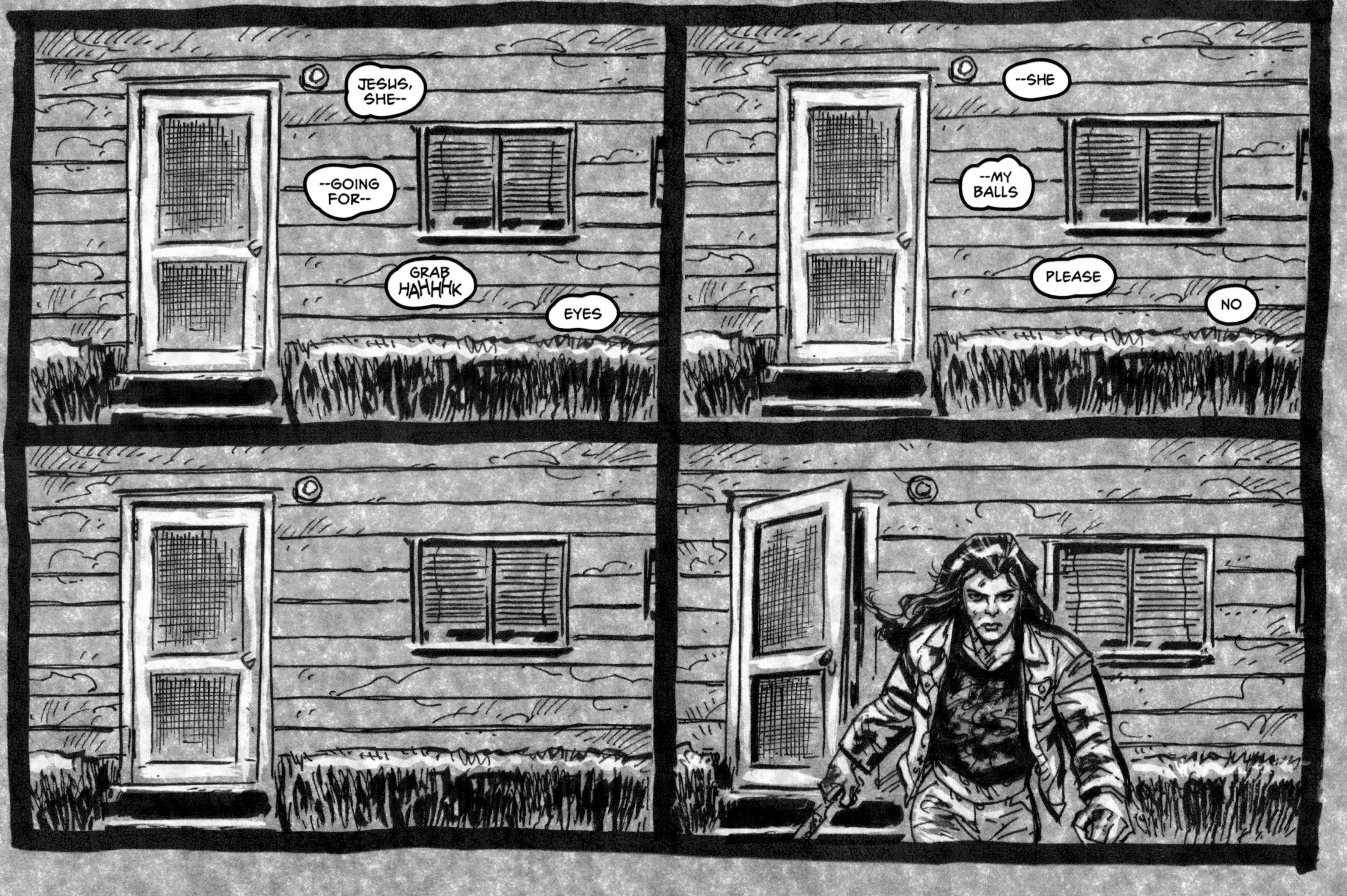
JESUS, SHE--
--GOING FOR--
GRAB
HAHHHK
EYES
--SHE
--MY BALLS
PLEASE
NO

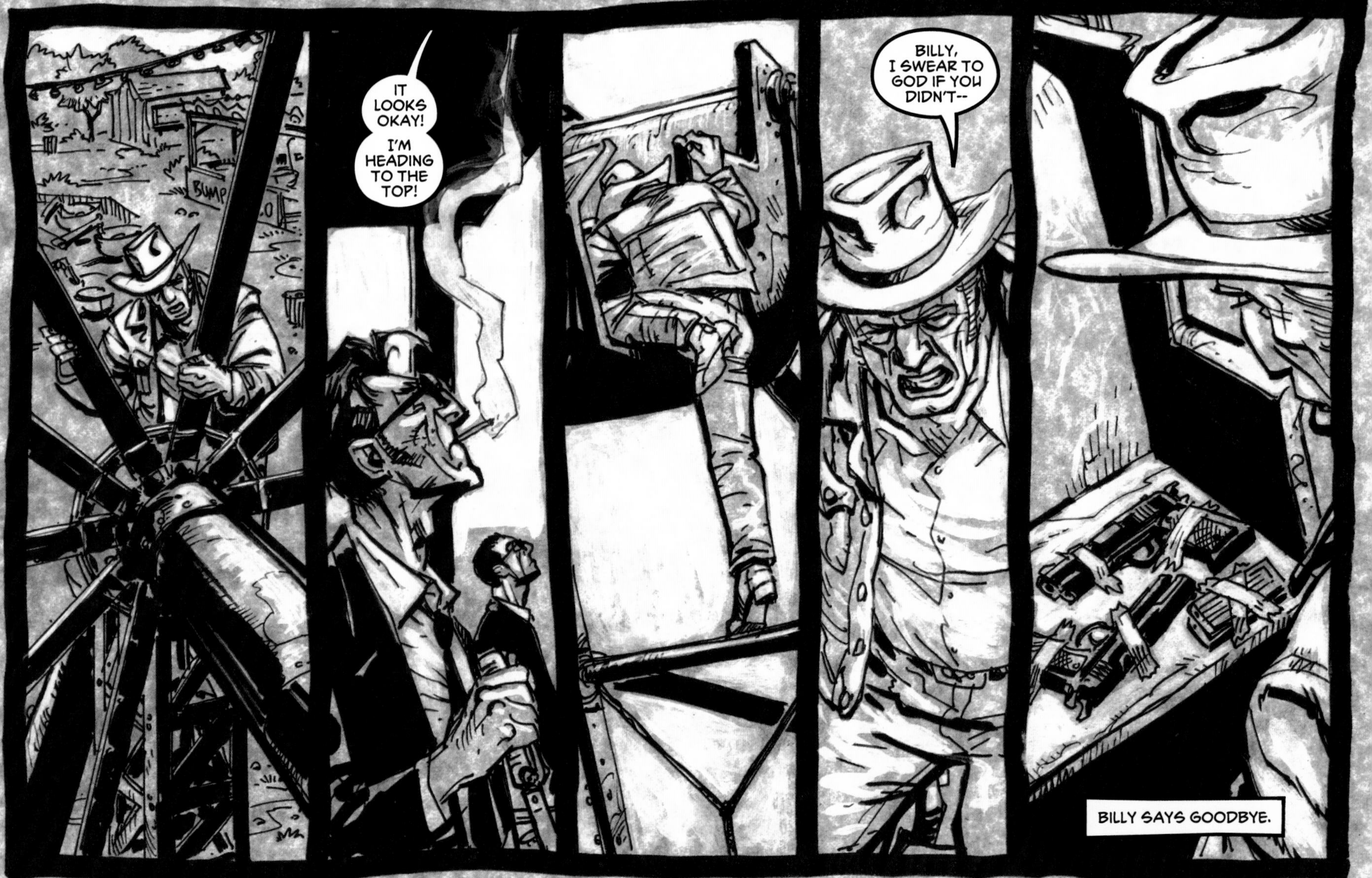

IT LOOKS OKAY!
I'M HEADING TO THE TOP!
BILLY, I SWEAR TO GOD IF YOU DIDN'T--
BILLY SAYS GOODBYE.

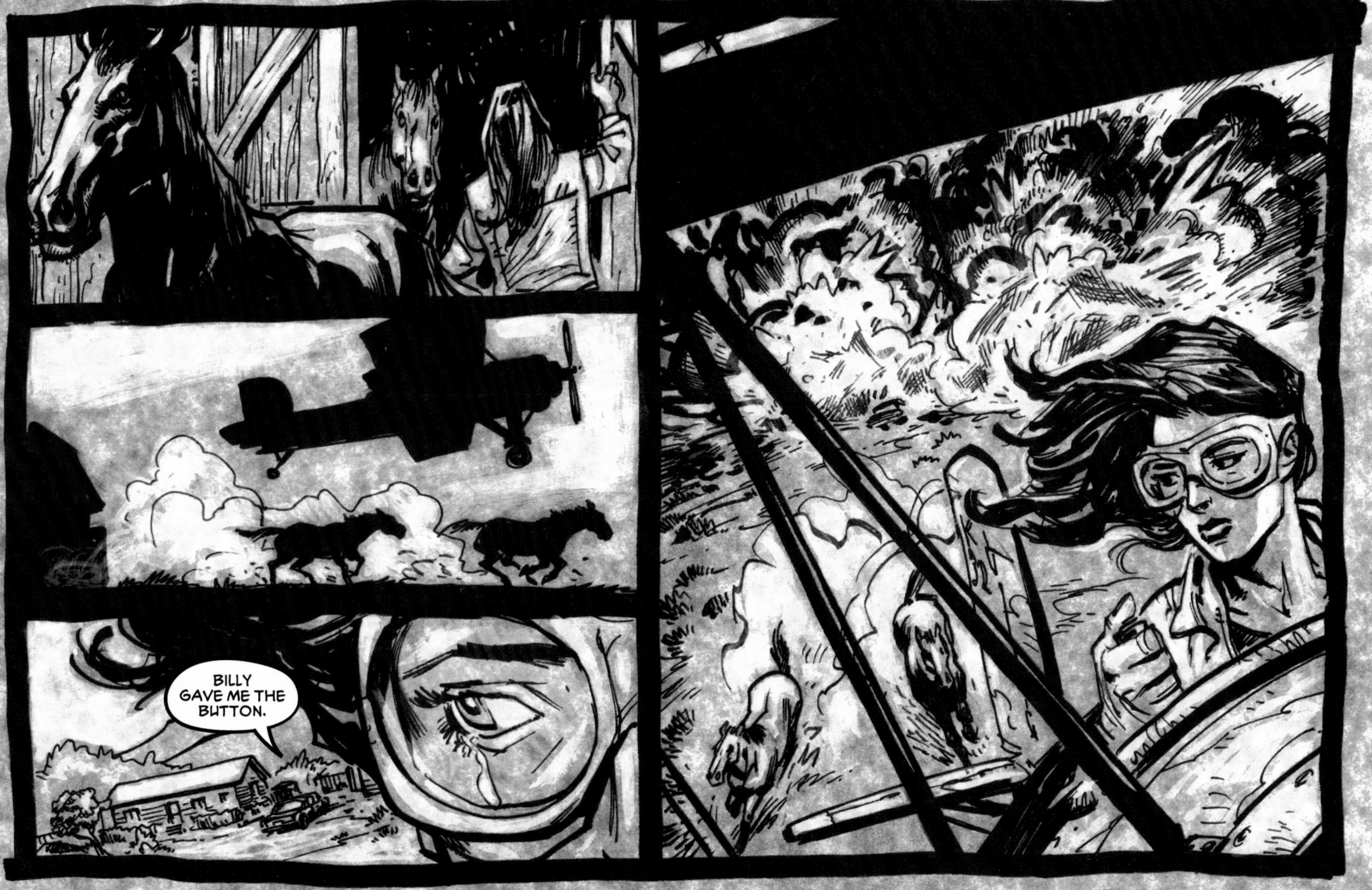
BILLY GAVE ME THE BUTTON.

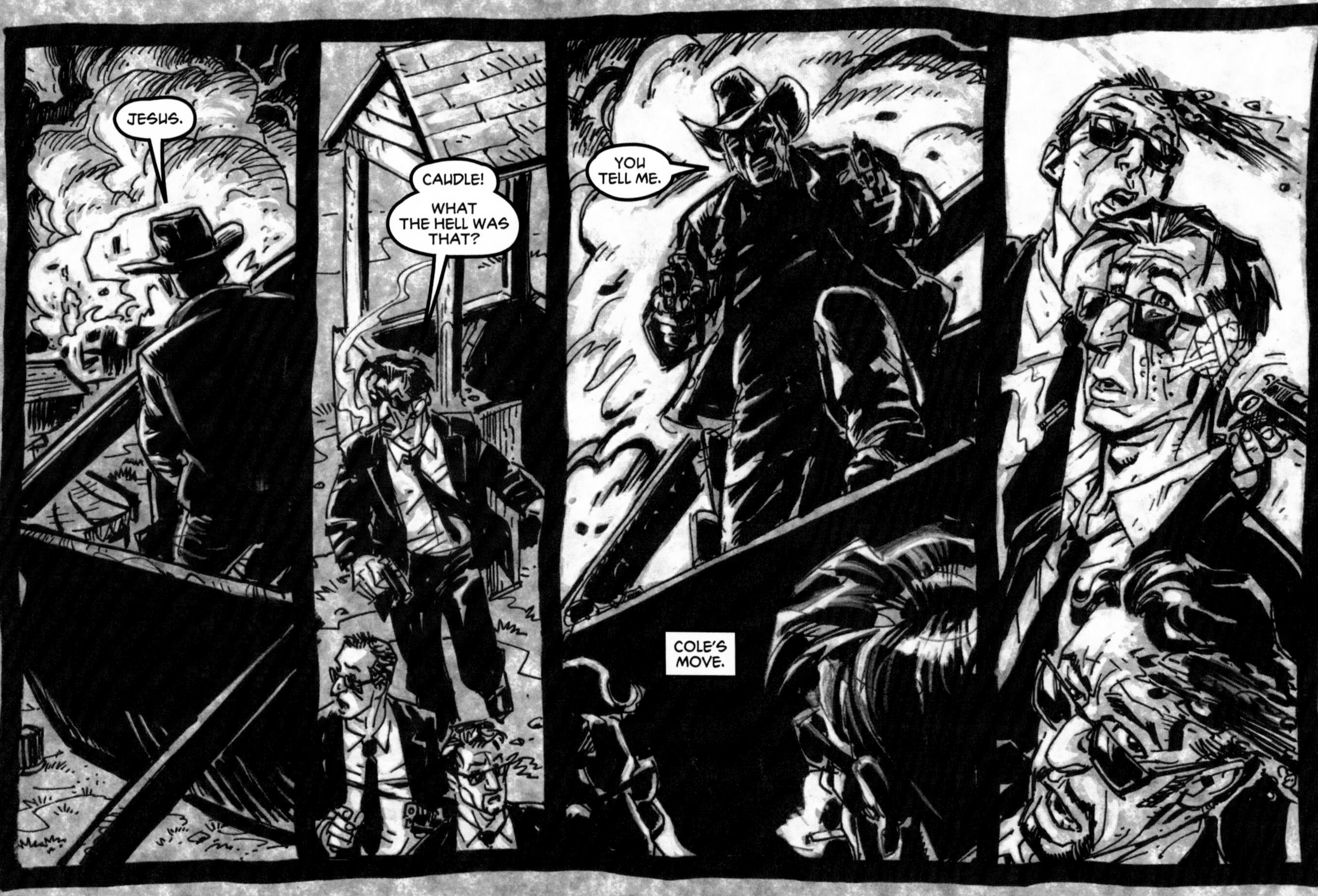

JESUS.
CAWDLE!
WHAT THE HELL WAS THAT?
YOU TELL ME.
COLE'S MOVE.

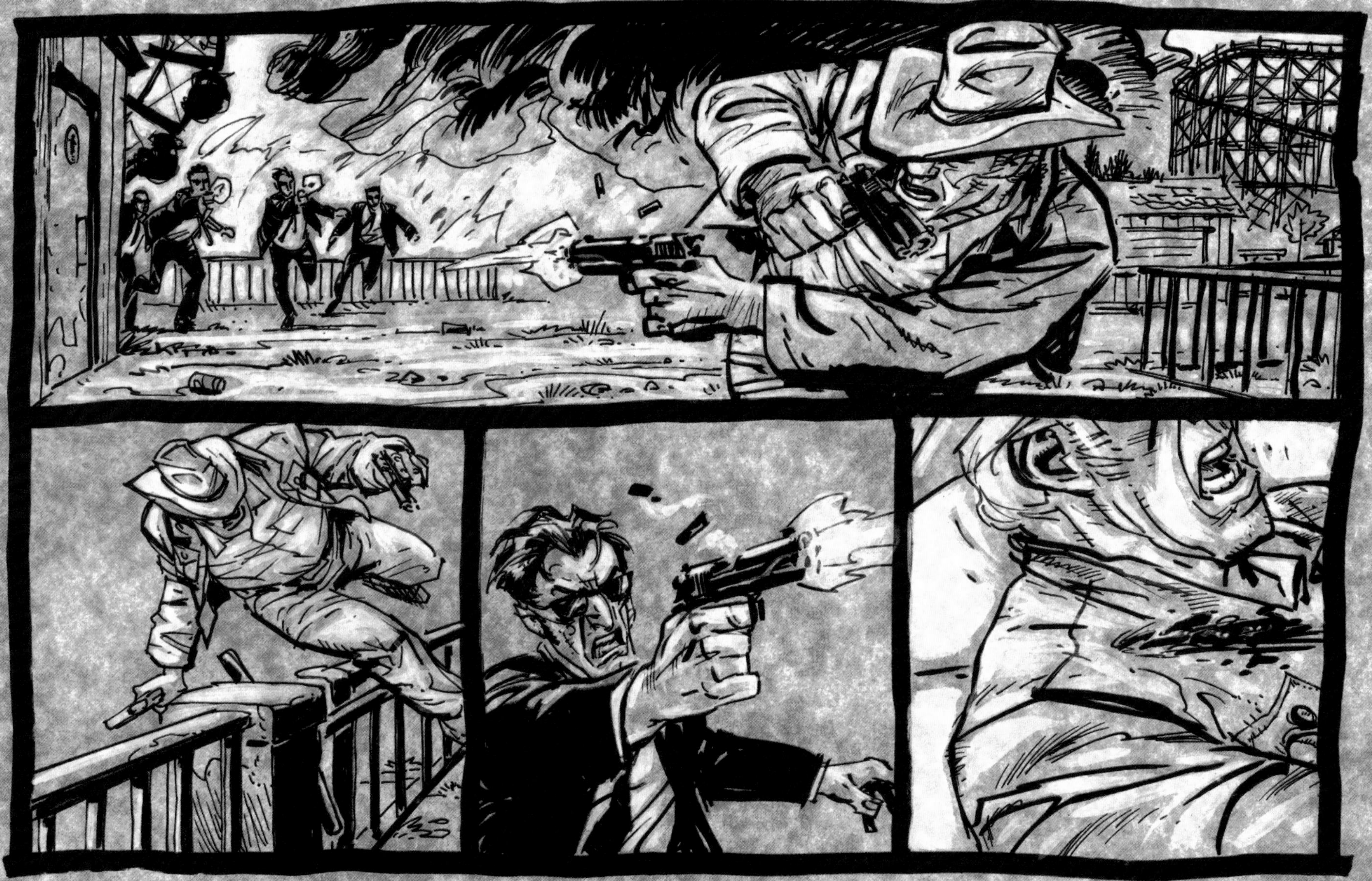

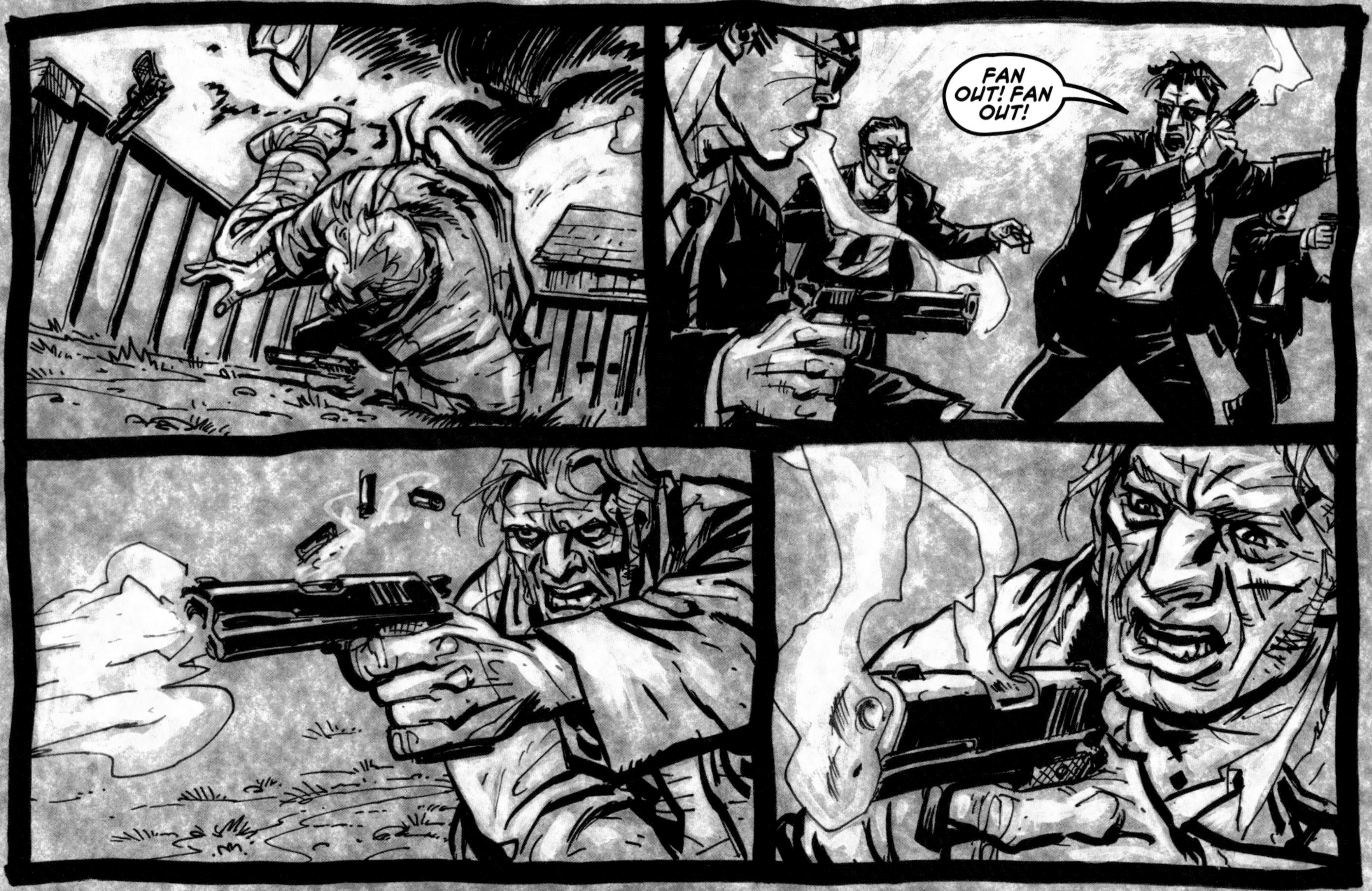
FAN OUT! FAN OUT!

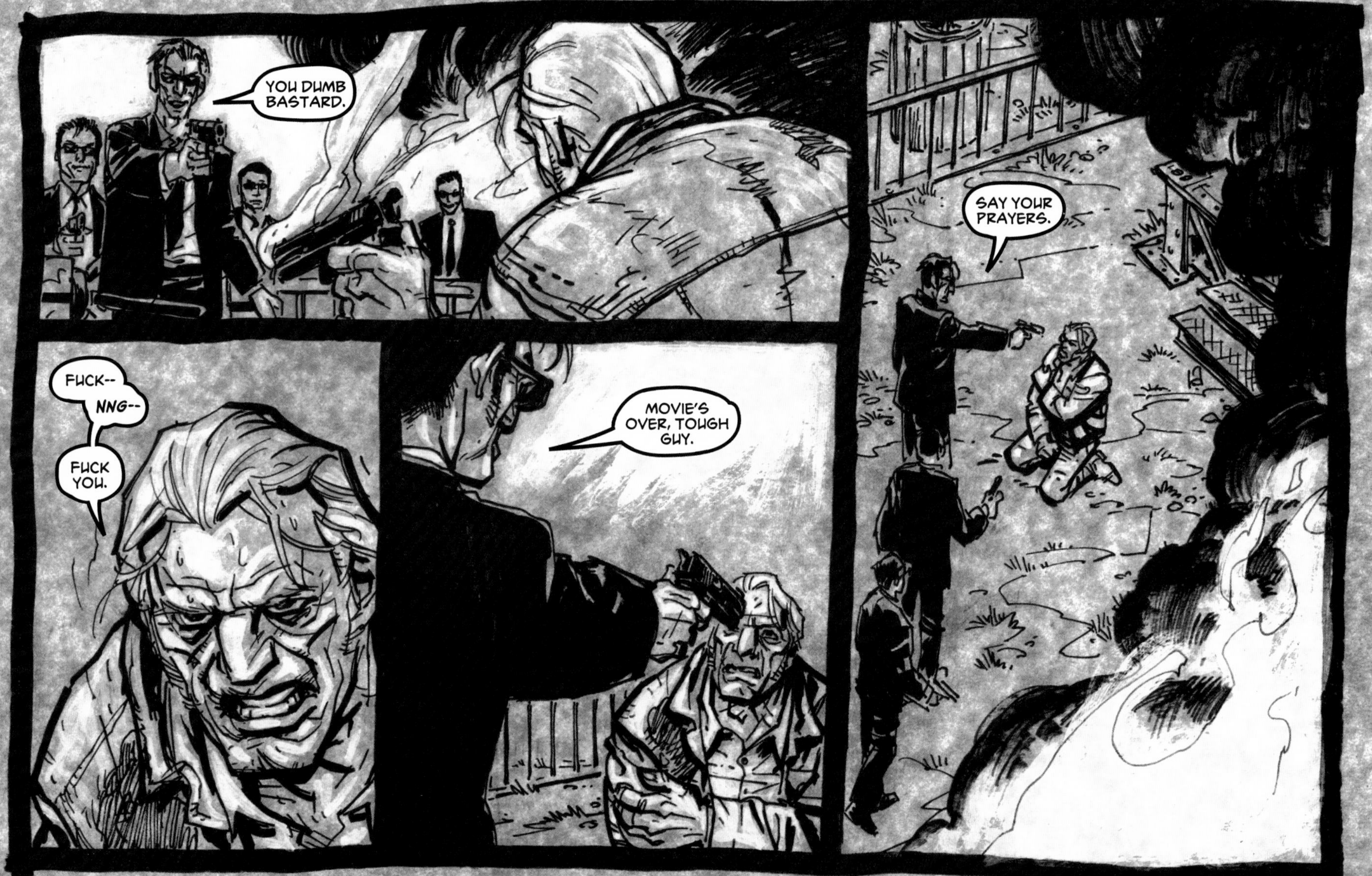
YOU DUMB BASTARD.
FUCK--
NNG--
FUCK YOU.
MOVIE'S OVER, TOUGH GUY.
SAY YOUR PRAYERS.

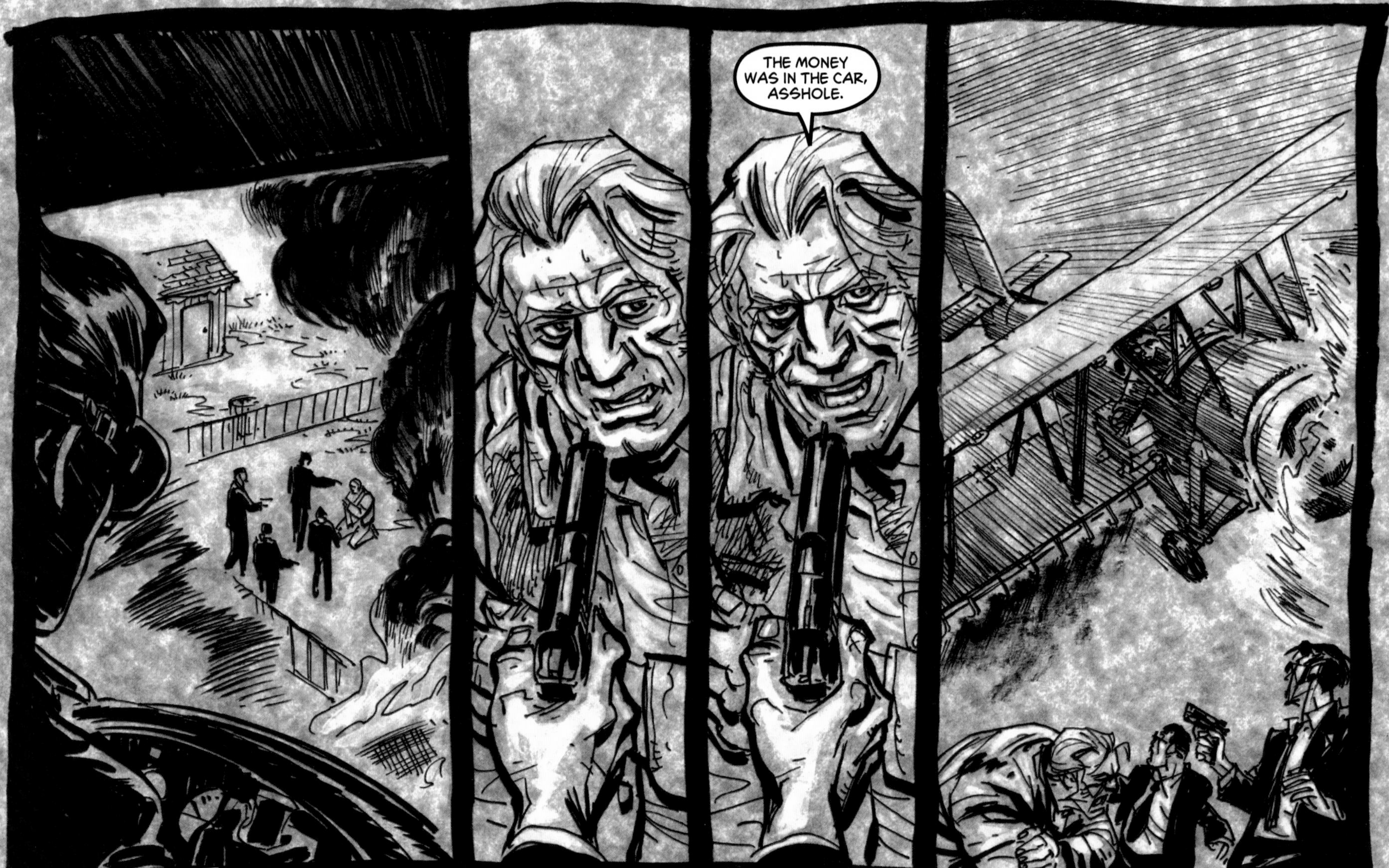
THE MONEY WAS IN THE CAR, ASSHOLE.

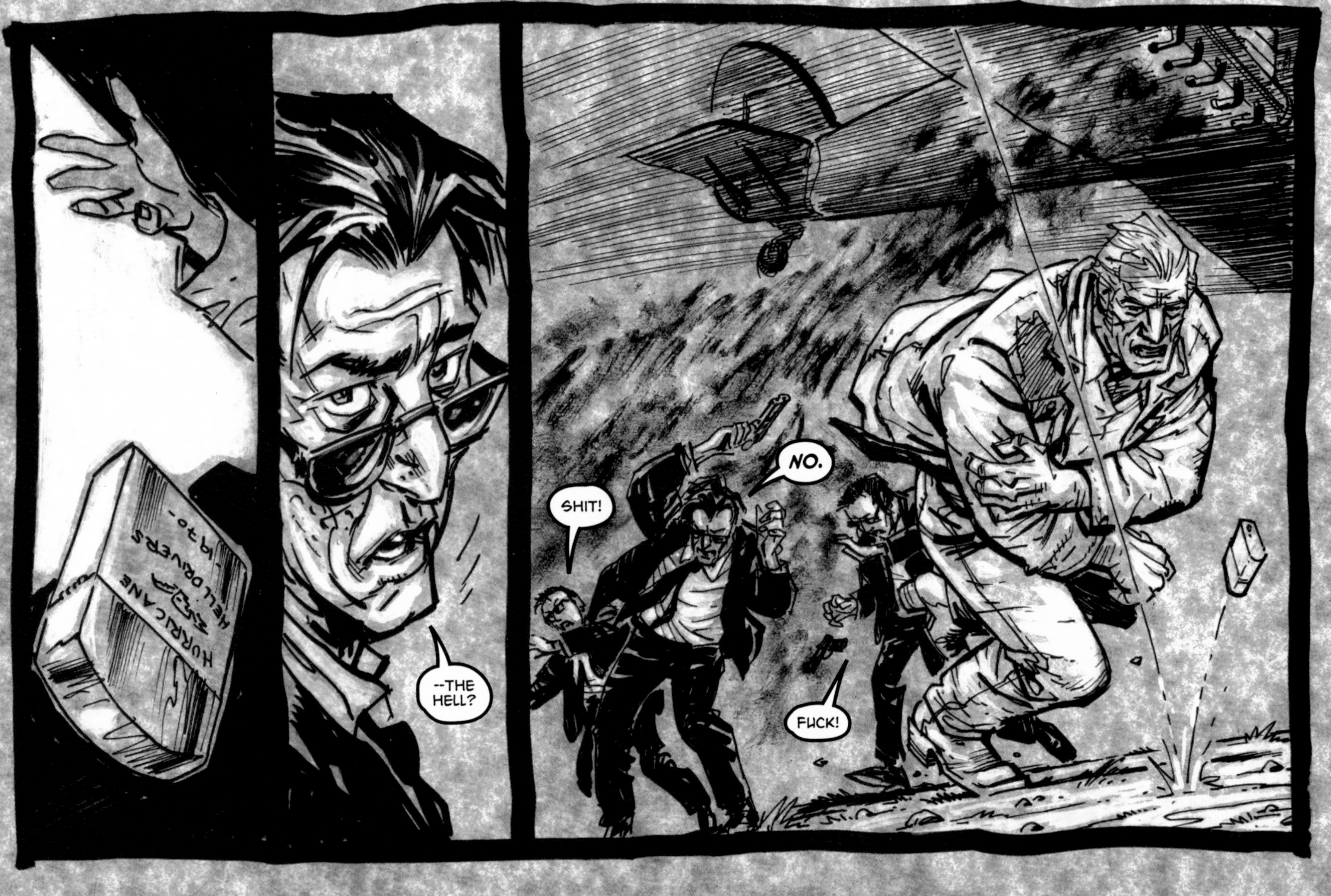

HURRICANE
HELLDRIVERS
1940-
--THE HELL?
SHIT!
NO.
FUCK!

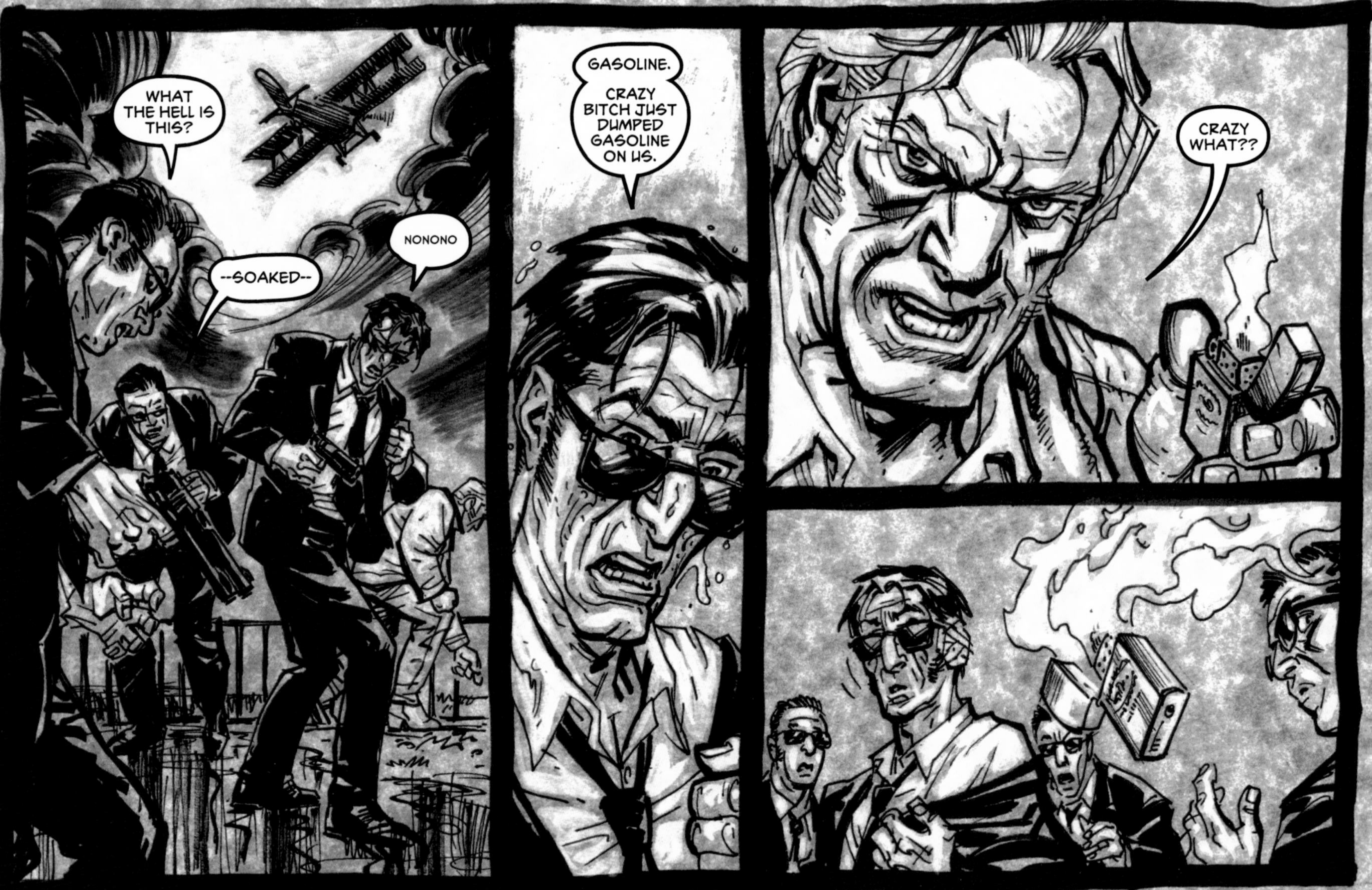
WHAT THE HELL IS THIS?
--SOAKED--
NONONO
GASOLINE.
CRAZY BITCH JUST DUMPED GASOLINE ON US.
CRAZY WHAT??

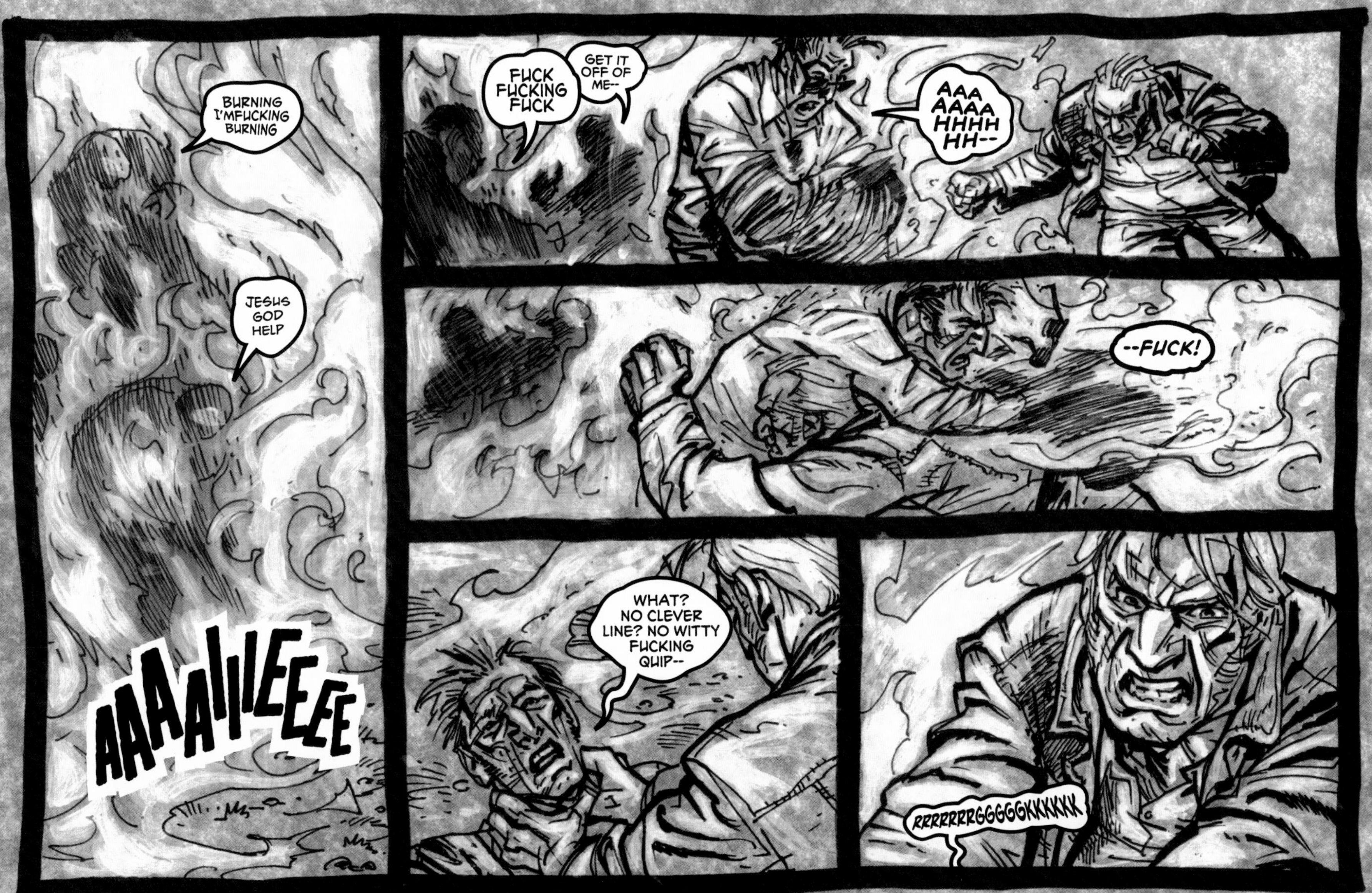
BURNING I'MFUCKING BURNING
JESUS GOD HELP
AAAAIIIEEEEE
FUCK FUCKING FUCK
GET IT OFF OF ME--
AAA AAAA HHHH HH--
--FUCK!
WHAT? NO CLEVER LINE? NO WITTY FUCKING QUIP--
RRRRRRRGGGGGKKKKKK

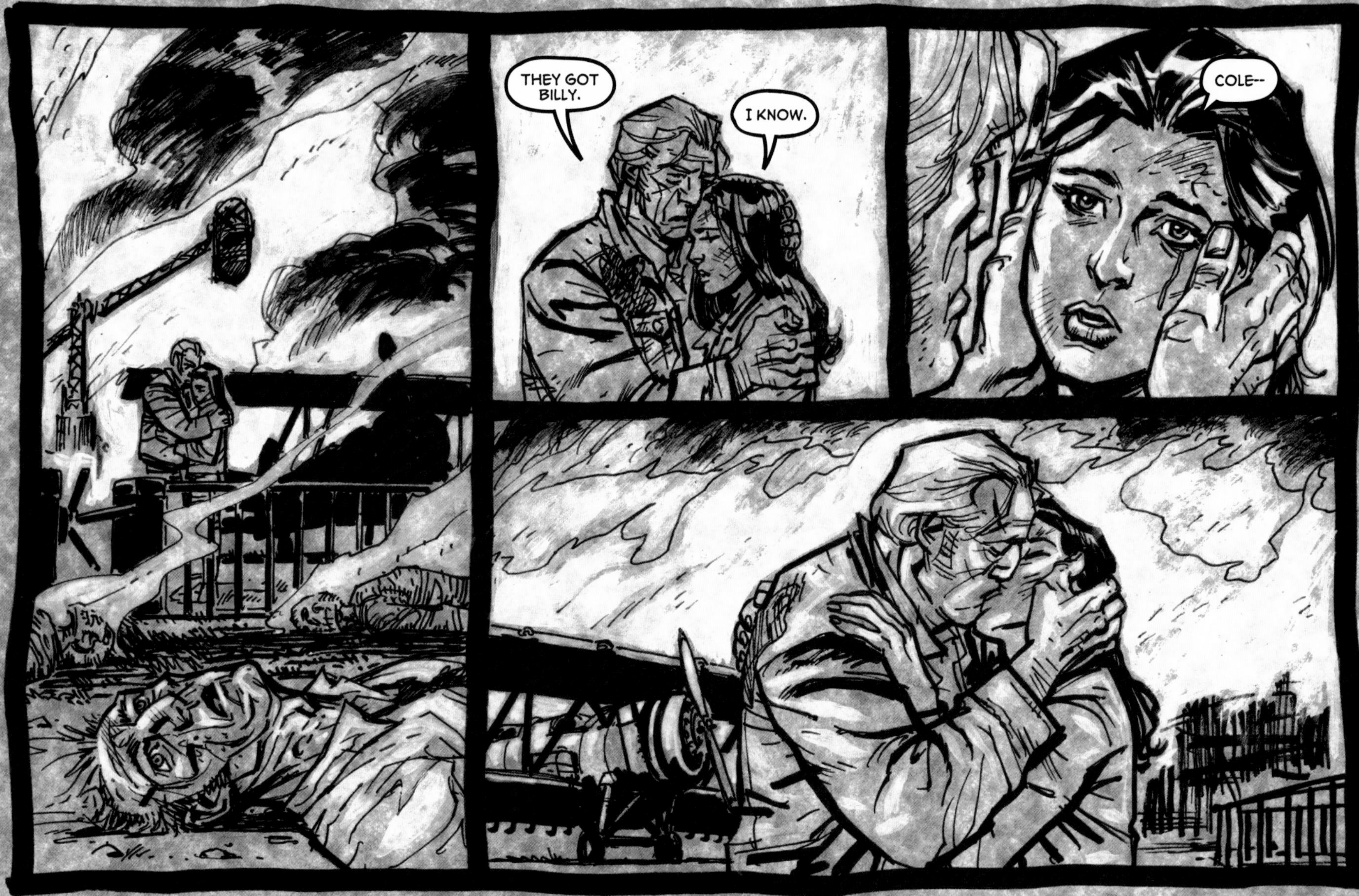
THEY GOT BILLY.
I KNOW.
COLE--

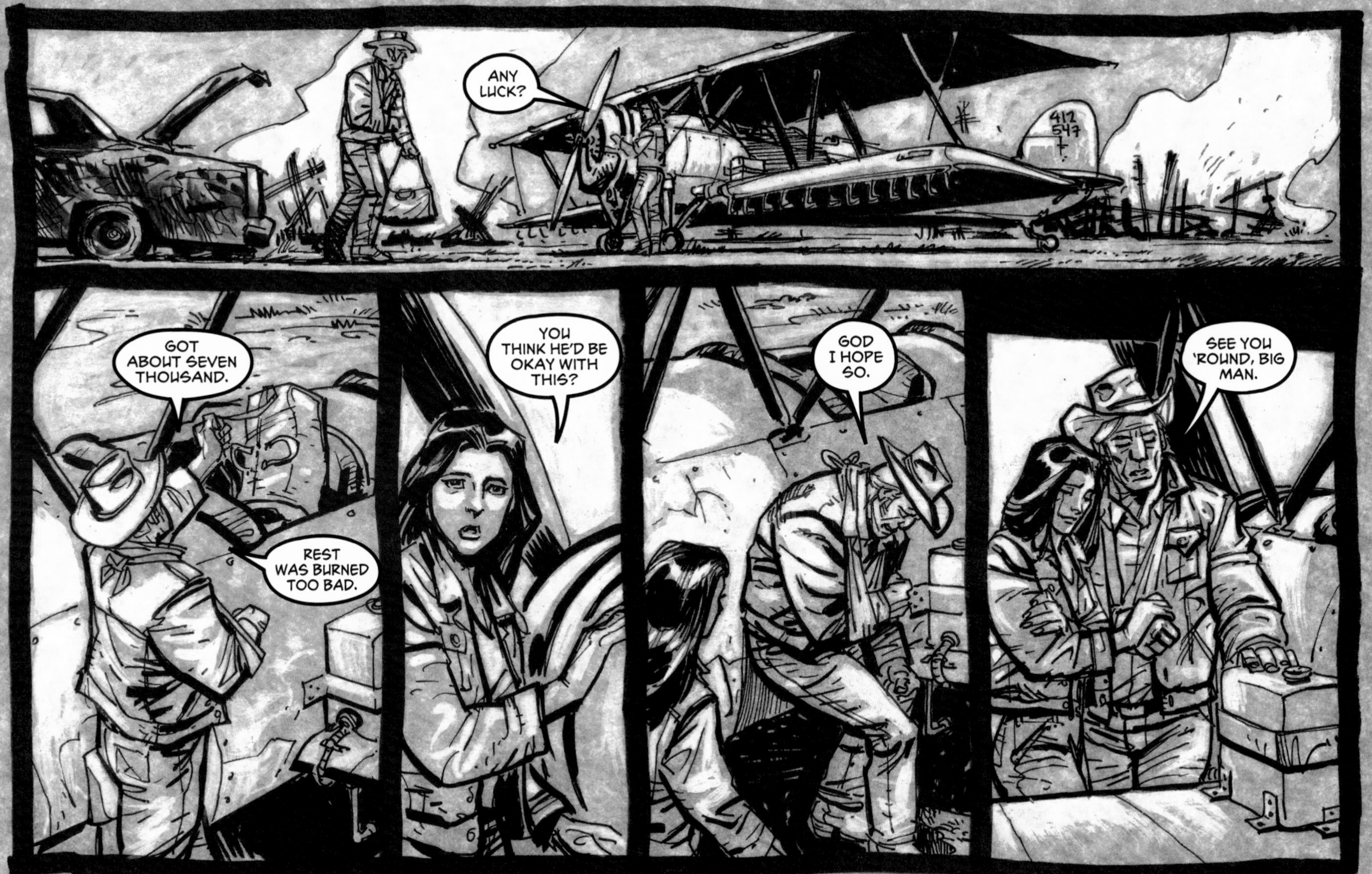
ANY LUCK?
GOT ABOUT SEVEN THOUSAND.
REST WAS BURNED TOO BAD.
YOU THINK HE'D BE OKAY WITH THIS?
GOD I HOPE SO.
SEE YOU 'ROUND, BIG MAN.

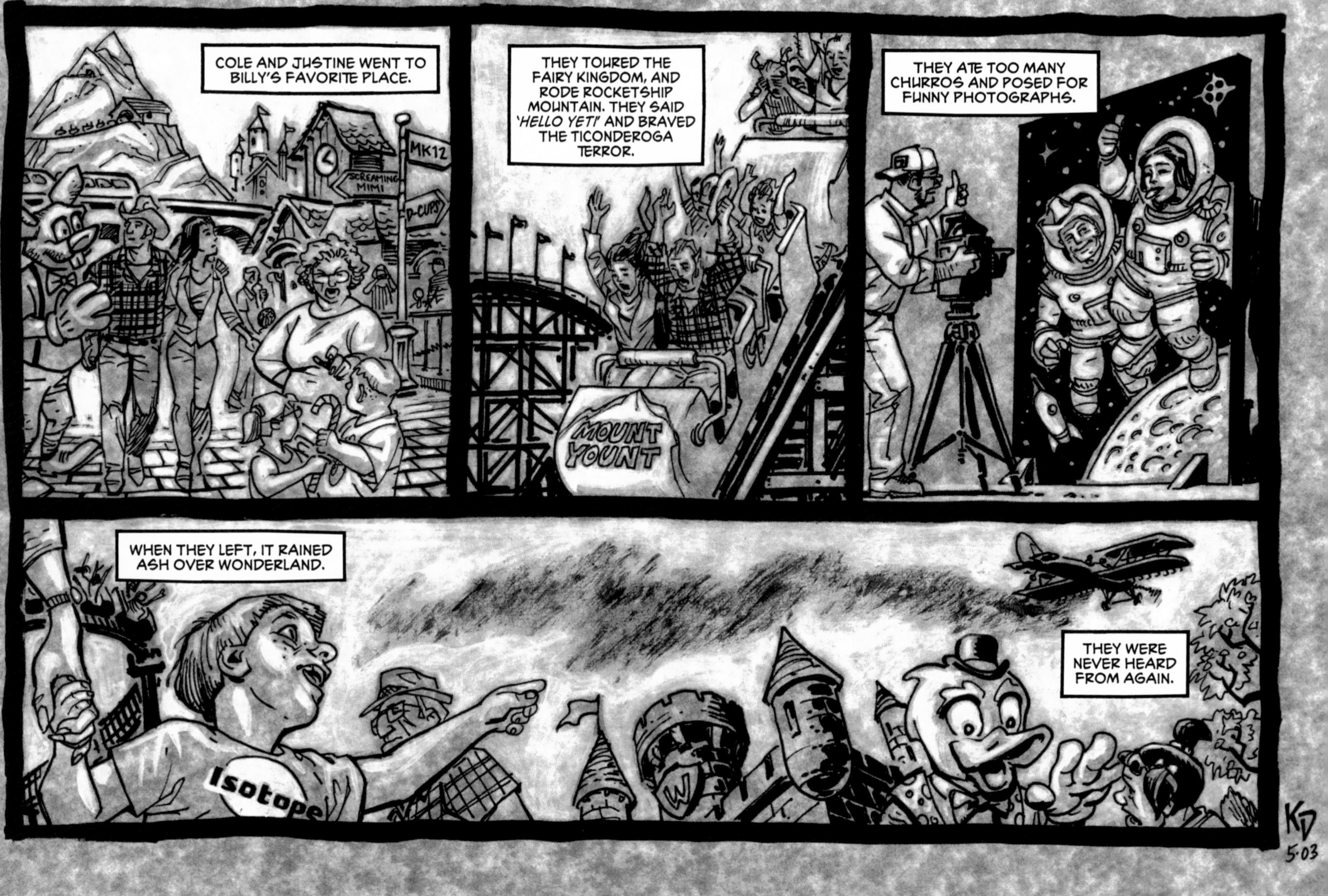

COLE AND JUSTINE WENT TO BILLY'S FAVORITE PLACE.
MK12
SCREAMING MIMI
D-CUPS
THEY TOURED THE FAIRY KINGDOM, AND RODE ROCKETSHIP MOUNTAIN. THEY SAID '*HELLO YETI*' AND BRAVED THE TICONDEROGA TERROR.
MOUNT YOUNT
THEY ATE TOO MANY CHURROS AND POSED FOR FUNNY PHOTOGRAPHS.
WHEN THEY LEFT, IT RAINED ASH OVER WONDERLAND.
THEY WERE NEVER HEARD FROM AGAIN.
Isotope
KD
5·03

POSTSCRIPTS

MATT

I haven't read this since the *last* time I proofread it in 2003.

Everyone that's ever dumped on George Lucas for his inability to leave his work of the past in the past, shut up until you have to go back and proofread the first graphic novel you ever wrote, nineteen years ago (it was written in 2001 and got over a couple years around Kieron's schedule but holy SHIT how has it been nineteen years?), and tell me that YOU would just let it all slide. Because Han, *mah* boogie, let me tell you: *I get it now*.

There's as many things nicked here from sources I loved, liked, or simply knew on a level of *cryptomnesia*. But mostly, like any kid in a garage with a cheap guitar, I stole. (*Paid tribute to! TRIBUTE!*, 25-year-old me insists.) "It's not where you take things from, it's where you take things to," Jean-Luc Goddard says. Let's be kind to the people we were twenty years ago and hope that's true.

Where it came from, then:

I started writing this not long after 9/11, and movies were being pulled from release for content, productions were being shut down, and talking heads were hysterically decrying where and how the *next attack* would come. I have a visceral memory of Chris Matthews screaming on *Hardball* (because it was *Hardball* of course he was screaming) about crop dusters dropping chemical agents over Times Square and why wasn't someone doing something about that. And I knew, a high school chemistry failure, that that wasn't how toxins and shit worked, it'd just diffuse and blow away. But that got me thinking about dropping gasoline or bathtub napalm out of planes (it was this kind of read-a-headline, think-of-ways-to-kill-people-with-it kind of instinct that drove my run on *Invincible Iron Man* a few years later).

And I bucked against the notion of *other people* deciding what was or wasn't appropriate for me to watch and when. I surely didn't feel like watching *Collateral Damage* or whatever—and still don't—but on some base level of obduracy rejected the notion that someone else could make that call for me.

Most of all it came from a love of that weird sub-genre of movies my friend DC Caudle—guess what the middle C stood for, reader? -- dubbed *man movies*. Patton writes about them some in his intro; allow me to further expand on it here and give you a viewing list maybe. These kind of post-Hawksian pulp potboilers had ornery dudes in the middle and over their heads, alongside women as ferocious and sharp as they were. Friendship and loyalty were paramount. Good guys honored their word. Everyone competed with one another all the time. Crime usually was involved. A gun. Drinking. Stewing was for eating. Taking a punch was paramount. Stuff like that. And most of all, the leading men all had to be gnarly, old, and a little seedy and WAY improbably. Preferably they were over-the-hill entirely.

Because for a minute there in the seventies, EVERYONE could be an action star.

These were Howard Hawks, Don Siegel, Hal Needham sorta movies. *Charley Varrick*—where the title of this book and its plot hook come from (or was that *Deadlock*?), with Walter Matthau (!) as the genius bank robber. (Also check out Joseph Sargent's *The Taking Of Pelham One Two Three* for Matthau vs Robert Shaw as poor Martin Balsam hangs in the balance…!). *Rio Bravo* and *El Dorado*—Howard Hawks' man-movie masterworks, so nice he made it twice. "Took ya two." *Hooper*, even. *Get Carter*, *Point Blank*, *The Friends of Eddie Coyle* are close but too mean, too cruel. *The Laughing Policeman*, even with Matthau, is too grim. *Night Moves*. *Rough Cut*? Sure. But not *Prime Cut*. Or *Mr. Majestyk*. Most Marvins, like most Bronsons—maybe *The Dirty Dozen* excluded—are too vicious. Cooler, but too vicious. Nobody was cooler, or more vicious, than Lee Goddamn Marvin. Even Jack Lemmon got in on the action as a skip-tracer in *Alex and the Gypsy*, a movie nobody believes actually exists, but it does. And if you ever wanted to see Jack Lemmon in a mustache with a shoulder holster, this movie has your back. *The Warriors*? Yeah. Carpenter's *Assault On Precinct 13* and *The Thing*, too, you could argue. Which makes sense, as they were either *paying tribute* to or remakes of Howard Hawks films. I could literally do this all day.

The Rockford Files and *Columbo* filled the niche on the TV side, though you can find many others. *Mannix*, sure. *Kojack*? No. *Quincy, Md*? Yeah. *Baretta*? No. *Magnum, P.I.*? No—and I love *Magnum, P.I.*, but no. *McCloud*? Only if *Rockford* wasn't on. *Miami Vice*? Not the show. The movie though, weirdly enough. But not the show. And on and on.

This is a *young work*. I wrote it young, dumb, new, and as on fire as the bastards at the end of the book. I think I wrote it in … four days? Five? Less than a week. I'd consult my records, but I lost my entire digital life back in 2011 or so. I have very little prior to that. The only thing I really cared about were ultrasounds of my kids, and Melanie Brubaker had, bless her heart, kept them. Becca recreated the lettering here from files Kieron had, not me. I was useless in this entire process.

LAST OF THE INDEPENDENTS is of its time as much as I am of mine; in other words, it remains half-baked and, as a thing that is very much *in progress*: flawed and energetic but incomplete and un-considered, with mistakes to correct and a lot of room to grow. I wouldn't write this with the slurs now, even as I can hear 25-year-old me saying "But that's how those guys would *talk*"—no, 25-year-old me, those are how those guys talk in movies and books, and you should *write better characters*; there are strange moments of … almost-punchlines that get deployed with the best of intention but clankiest of executions (I think I still struggle with that urge to deploy those … what, Brechtian asides, the *nouvelle vogue* thing of pointing at the thing you're making while you're making it? What's that about? I don't know but, let me tell you, most superhero readers HATE that in superhero comics); it's mawkish sometimes, but so am I, then AND now; also, as a narrative, there is not a second act here? I am hardly a writer bound by what writing *is* or what stories *must* be but I do know most of 'em have middles and this one has a middle you have to squint and breathe slower to see. So that needs work maybe. There are patterns here I'm still trying to break.

There are things here that surprise me, for what was functionally my first time at the plate. It's far more spacious with words, and that surprises me—that I didn't have the urge to fill every space with *my precious goddamn text*. I think I fight with that now, and consider my rewrite passes these days to be exercises in removing as many words as I can. That I knew and trusted Kieron enough to know I'd never outwrite his hand—that centerpiece horse chase/car chase bit fucking *rips* and I know that was all because I knew instinctively, I needed to *let Kieron be Kieron* and get out of his way. The cutting isn't as baroque and cruel, temporally, as I am now, but still there are chances taken here that impress me for a first-time writer, where the story darts back and forth into the past. Writing gesturally, that's brave for a first timer. Writing those silent pages? I forgot about those, and rereading it not only surprised me (in that I COULD manage to keep quiet) but delighted me in just *how good Kieron is*.

Which is really the best thing about this book for me. Kieron Dwyer was and is a consummate storyteller and professional who took this book written by a loudmouth know-it-all on the internet and not only agreed to do it but added so much of his talent and gifts to the page you'd never know how wet my pants were (because I had wet them because I am a baby, see). His acting, his staging, the way his people all have mass and density, their faces, his control of the page (and his decision to do the book landscape! The marbled paper stock! The not-quite-black, not-quite-brown! That confidence! That was all KD and KD WAS RIGHT!) … I loved Kieron's work going into writing this for him and wanted more than anything to write the best Kieron Dwyer book that I could. Looking back at it now, his work on literally every page is the only thing that gets me to forget about *me* and lose myself in *him*. He's put so much of himself, so much life and energy and cool-fucking-*fun* everywhere. Kieron? In case I haven't said it enough? THANK YOU for this.

The weirdest thing is? I literally just finished a script for a book where one character takes another's face in her hands and says "Everything's going to be okay." I guess some patterns we can never escape.

MF
PDX, OR
2020

KIERON

I'm a child of the '70s, that's the plainest way I can put it. Everything I love came out of that era: films (*Star Wars*, *Jaws*, *The French Connection*, *The Exorcist*), TV shows (*SNL*, *Rockford Files*, *Bob Newhart Show*, *The Six-Million-Dollar Man*), action figures (12" G.I. Joes, Bionic Man, removable cowl Mego Batman), music (classic rock, metal, punk, new wave). And of course, the greatest comicbooks, my personal golden age of *Spider-Man* and *Batman*. Classic badass artists like John Romita Sr, John Buscema, Neal Adams, Jim Aparo, Don Newton. Fucking giants.

There was something purer and simpler about all those things back then, and not just because I was a less knowledgeable, more easily impressed being. Not to say there wasn't plenty of hokey bullshit, too. That's just part of the human condition when it comes to entertainment. But looking back, I think what I appreciate most about that era's pop culture was the fact that everything wasn't spoon fed, market tested, glamorous hokum. Can you imagine a TV detective show in this age built around a fat, mustachioed dude who has to drive his (giant) car after the bad guys because he can barely walk, let alone run (*Cannon*)? Or another one built around your grampa solving mysteries (*Barnaby Jones*)? Heroes and antiheroes alike in film and TV were often very normal looking ones with real character in their faces, people who made mistakes and dressed very badly.

When Larry Young pitched the notion of working on **LAST OF THE INDEPENDENTS** with an unknown, untested writer I'd never met named Matt Fraction, I might have been skeptical if Larry hadn't unknowingly hit on several of my personal touchstones: Don Siegel, Clint Eastwood, James Garner, Gene Hackman. Robert-Fucking-Mitchum (on whom I was modeling Cole from out of the gate). When he mentioned just the basic premise of the book, these were the names that immediately came to mind. A gritty 1970s movie in book form, built around an older anti-hero. When I read the first ten pages of Matt's script, it was a done deal. And to match the notion of a film on paper, I knew the book had to be formatted horizontally, in widescreen. Figuring out the additional aspect of the slipcase so the book could be racked upright like standard books was a design inspiration that I still feel proud about (although moot in this lovely hardcover edition).

The book came together very quickly, and out of necessity, it was something I did in a very short amount of time. There was no money to speak of in doing a small run book at an independent publisher, so I had to portion my time working on it very carefully. I had to find a style that matched the feel of the story and could be done fast. Loose and gestural without being sloppy. I literally set an alarm at each stage of the process to pencil, ink, and paint white on the yellow parchment paper I'd chosen for the book. I couldn't afford to go over the alarm on any single page and didn't. When page 96 was in the can, I celebrated what felt like a major accomplishment to me, even after the many thousands of comic book pages I'd already done in my professional life by that point.

Although it was partly a function of the time constraint, the other reason for the looser feel of the work here was due to my own frustration with how much more energy my sketches usually felt in comparison to my finished work at Marvel, DC, et al. I think most artists can relate to this feeling; there's no pressure when sketching, it's just pure energy, whereas once we move to the polishing stage, we naturally start being aware (even on a subconscious level) that others will see it, so we want it to be *just right*. Which is a silly notion, really. Nothing in the world is ever *just right*. So I approached **LOTI** with the challenge of drawing a book like it was my perfectly imperfect sketchbook version, and honestly, it turned out about as close to *just right* as I think it could have, and it influenced everything I drew from that point on. I learned to trust myself more on this book than any other project before it.

I was, and am, extremely proud of this work, and I truly hope you enjoy it. Thanks for picking it up.

KD
PDX, OR
2020

PROCESS

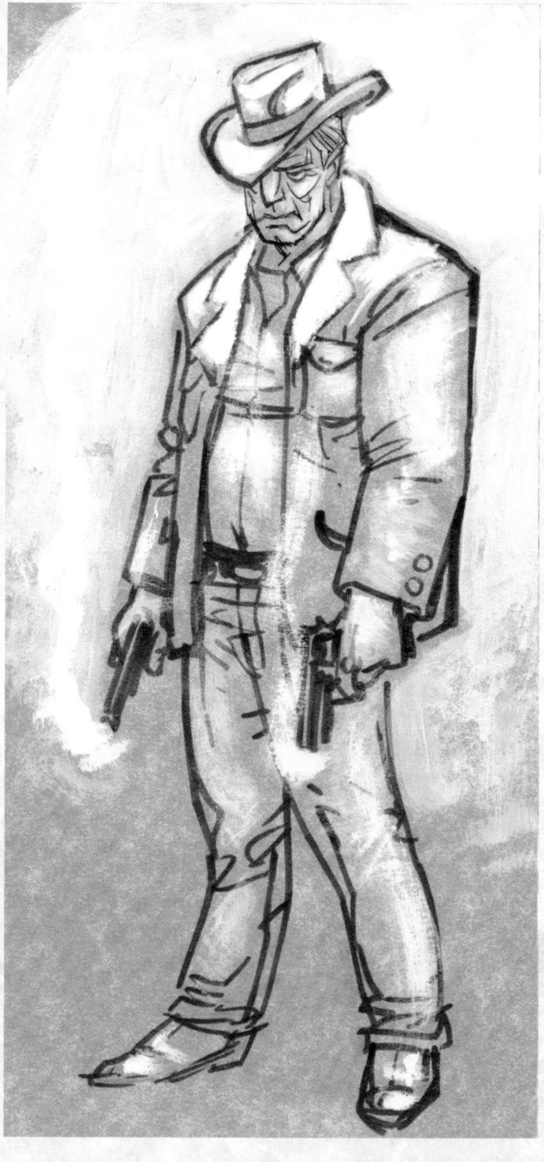

Various studies of Cole, trying to figure out the right process for a one-color treatment.

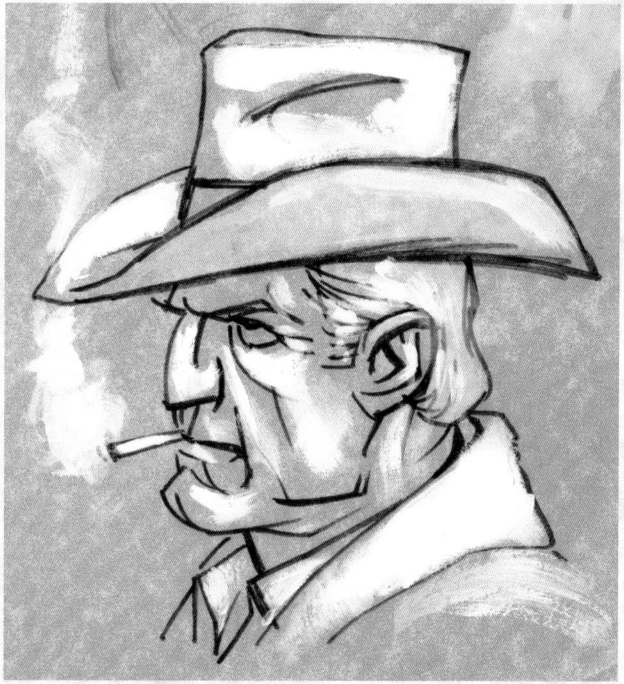

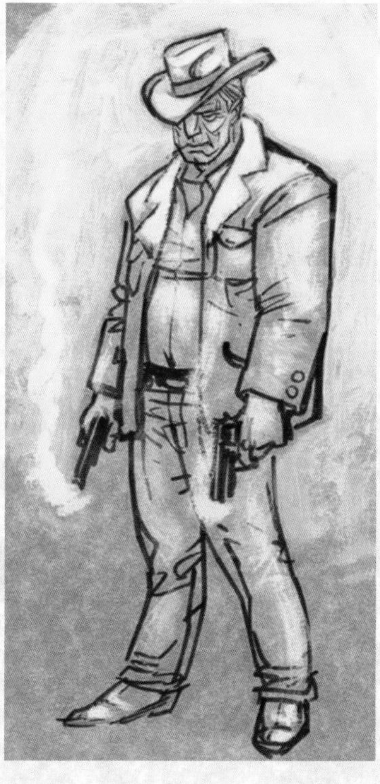

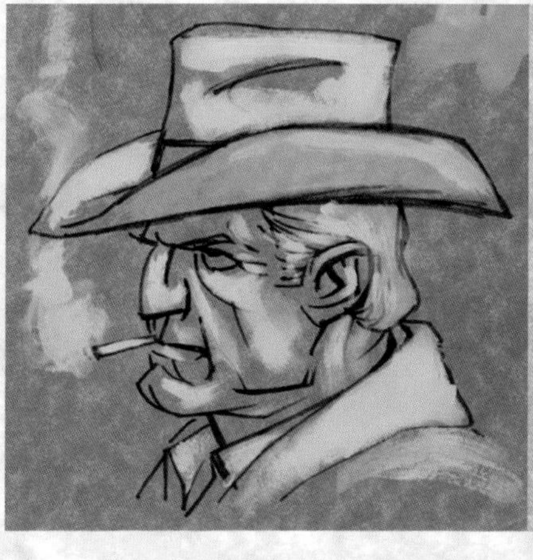

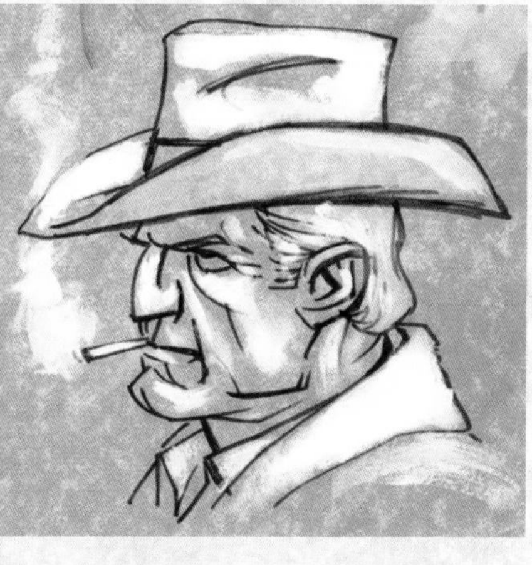

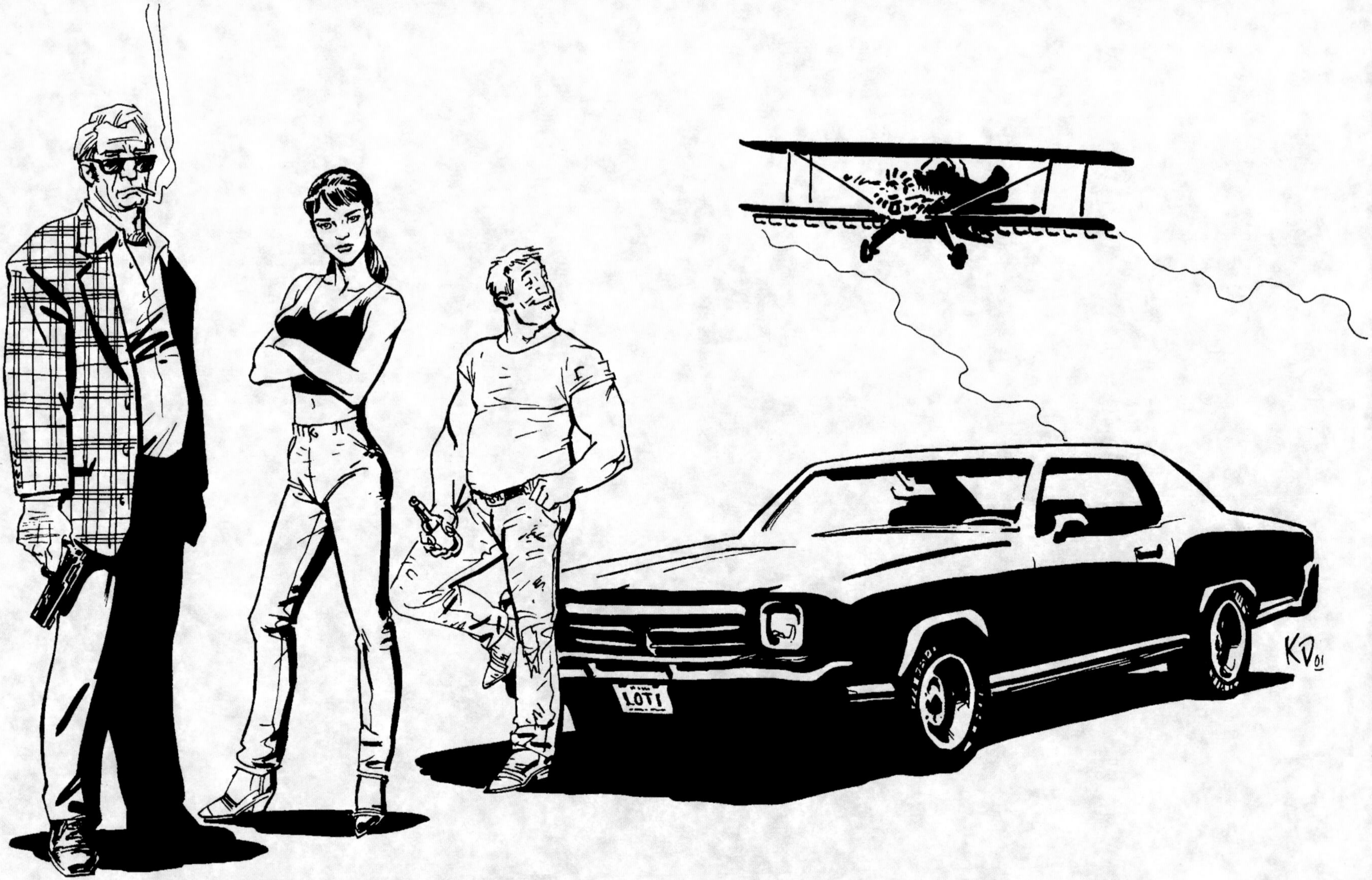

The first drawing of our antiheroes, done as a gift for Matt's birthday, while I was getting myself geared up for working on the book. The Monte Carlo was a car in my neighborhood that I realized was perfect for the book, so I took a ton of photos, and was lucky to find a die-cast scale model of it, too. Still experimenting with different color/style techniques here.

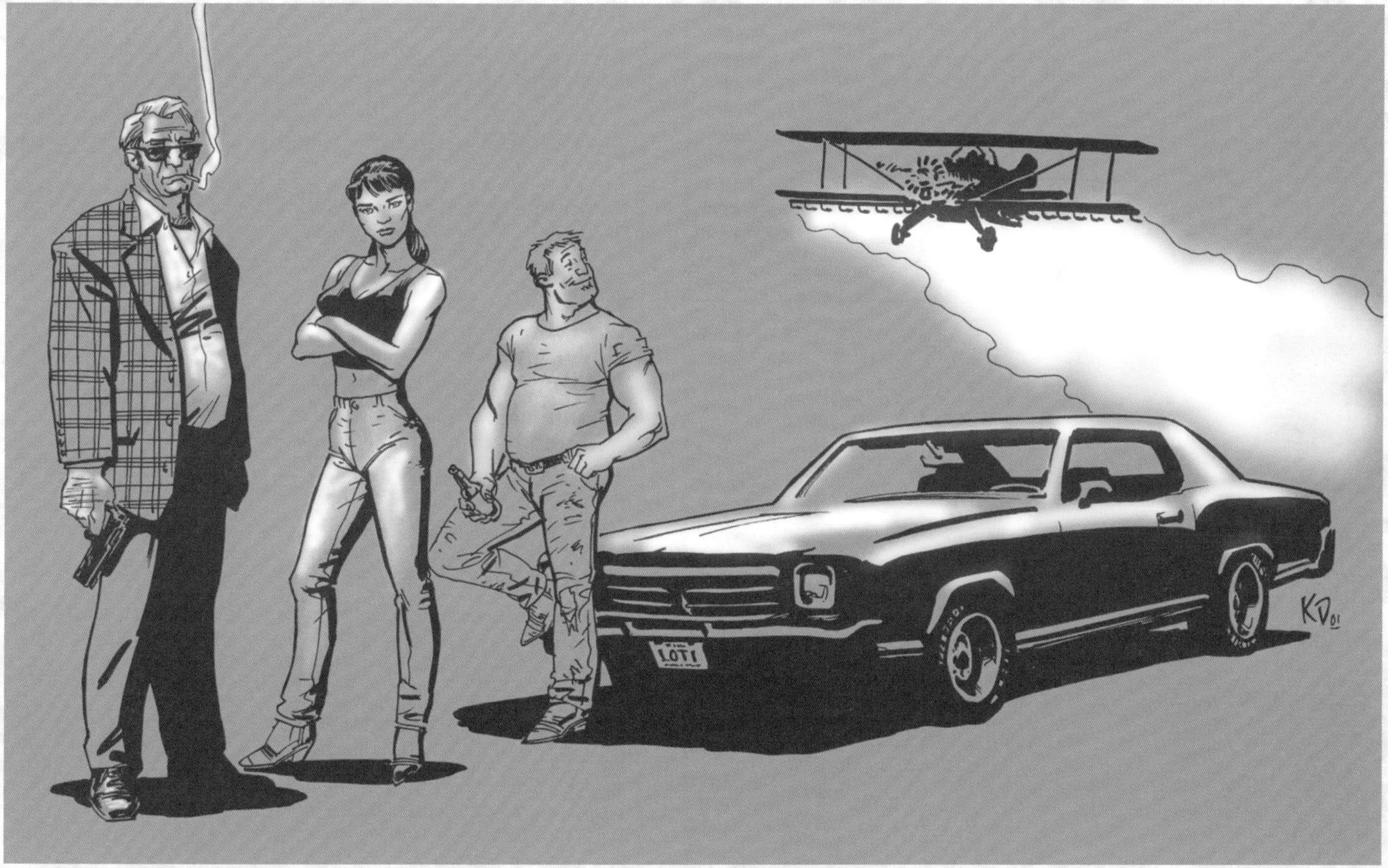

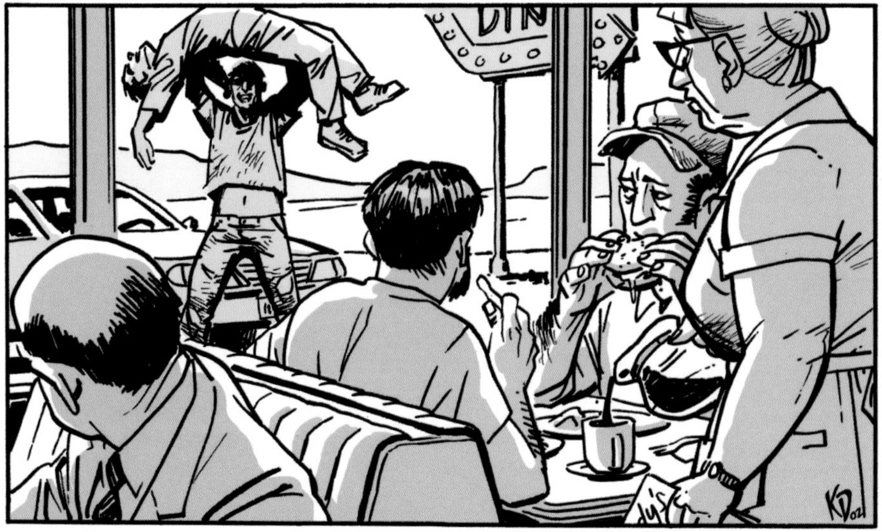

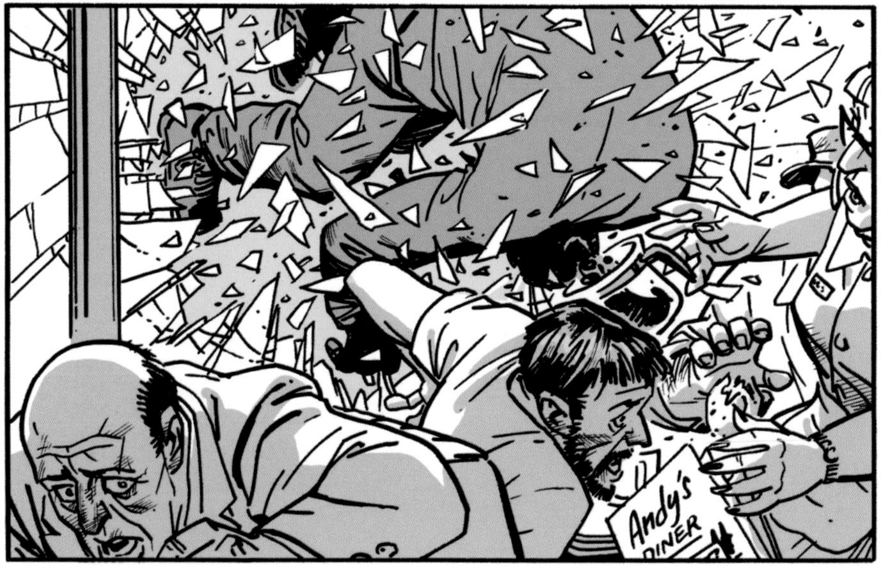
Andy's
DINER

Versions of some interior frames for an art show at Yerba Buena Center for the Arts in San Francisco, CA.

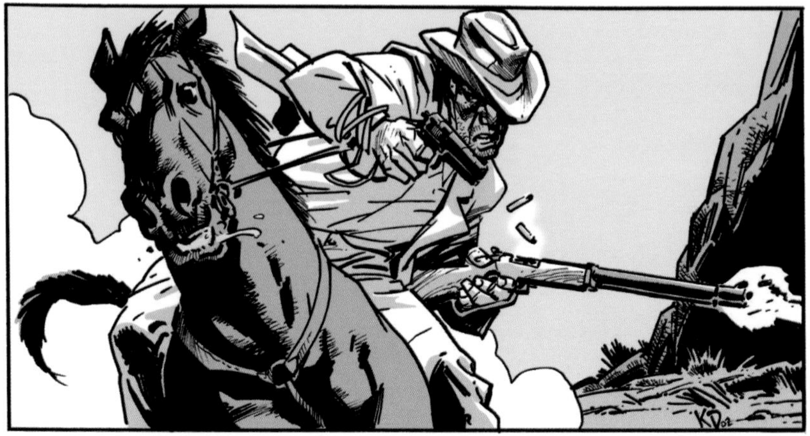

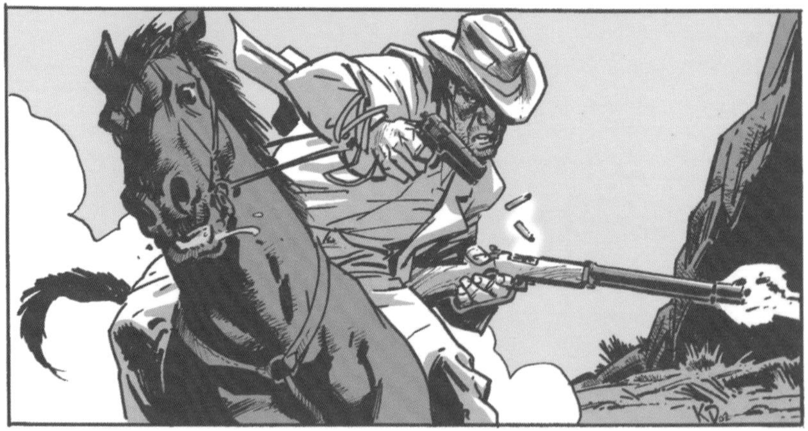